Cathal Kinnery is an arrogant, overeducated jerk, and Damon Eglamore is not afraid to tell him so. But Damon married Cathal's best friend, so they have an uneasy truce. Then she passes away. Now they're stuck together in close quarters, trying to honor her memory without shouting at each other all the time.

At first, they have no idea how to move forward. Damon is a chef, but all his favorite recipes remind him of his late wife. Cathal would love to start tomcatting around town again, except for that annoying promise he made to his best friend about looking after Damon.

Then Damon's son comes to them for help, convinced the only way to win over his first crush is a gender-bending Shakespeare production. After that, Cathal talks Damon into taking up baking as a new way to use his talents. Next thing they know, they've begun a new life working as a team instead of jumping at each other's throats. But can they trust each other long enough to make it last, or will they fall into old bad habits again?

DEATH OF A
BACHELOR

A Cherrywood Grove Novel

M.A. Hinkle

A NineStar Press Publication

Published by NineStar Press
P.O. Box 91792,
Albuquerque, New Mexico, 87199 USA.
www.ninestarpress.com

Death of a Bachelor

Printed in the USA
First Edition
October, 2018

Print ISBN: 978-1-949909-17-3

Also available in eBook, ISBN: 978-1-949909-09-8

Warning: This book contains the off-page death of a side
character.

This one is for Shannon, because you loved them first.

First Prologue: Cathal Crushes Olives and Damon's Dreams.

DECEMBER 31ST, 1997

The man sitting at the end of the bar was older than Damon, maybe twenty-four. He had a thin, foxlike face and long, dark hair that he twirled around a finger as he wrote on a napkin, and he was wearing a Cherrywood College shirt under his suit jacket. A martini sat untouched in front of him, and his eyes were lost in thought. Definitely gay, but he wasn't...intimidating. Unlike every other man who wasn't on the dance floor or making out with someone else.

Damon sat next to him and gestured to the bartender for a beer. He was already a little drunk, but if he wanted to relax, he'd have to get a lot drunk. The other patron continued writing out a math problem. He finished his equation, considered it, and then scribbled the whole thing out, his brow furrowed. Scowling, he drank the martini at one go. Only then did he glance in Damon's direction. "Fuck off," he said, biting the olive from the swizzle stick. "I'm not looking for company tonight. I came here to get drunk."

Damon colored, but he kept the embarrassment from his voice. "Why'd you think I came here for anything different?"

"There's plenty of room, but you sat by me." He looked at Damon, taking him all in, and his eyes narrowed further. The scowl fit his face too well, and Damon didn't appreciate his scrutiny. "And guys like you don't come here for the conversation."

Damon didn't care for the man's tone. But he was the first to admit he didn't know what he was doing—and, anyway, he was drunk enough not to care. "I wasn't aware anyone came here for conversation."

The man snorted. "It's not the fucking sixties anymore. Gays can have meet-cutes as easily as everyone else." He gestured to the bartender for another martini, rubbing his forehead.

Damon didn't know what he meant, and he wanted to ask what kind of guy this man thought he was. But he had a feeling that would piss him off, and he was looking for a good time. Instead, he took another drink of his beer. "I'm Damon," he said, without expecting much.

The man accepted another martini from the bartender and sipped it, looking at Damon over the top. "Cathal."

Damon drummed his fingers on the bar, wondering if he ought to cut his losses and head to a straight bar after all. But he settled for finishing his beer in one long drink.

Cathal watched him. Not friendly watching. At this point, Damon didn't know how to leave, so he signaled for another beer. "What were you working on?"

Cathal glanced at the napkin and made a face. "Bullshit. It doesn't matter."

Damon screwed the cap off his second beer and took a drink. "Who comes to a bar and does their homework?"

Cathal raised his eyebrows. His face was dangerous, but he couldn't be that bad. Too scrawny. "Who comes to a bar already drunk?" He tilted his head to the side and smiled. Not a nice smile. Damon was starting to wonder if he had a nice smile, or if he always looked like someone had pissed in his drink. "Oh. I know. Guys like you."

Damon frowned, feeling the first stirrings of anger. "You said that before. What do you mean?"

Cathal leaned toward Damon. His voice was calm, unhurried, but his eyes were full of fire, the sort that burns unnoticed and then flares up to take a tree down in seconds. "Guys like you. Guys who are maybe straight, maybe not, who come to one of our places for a little fucking fun and then go home to their wife or girlfriend or whatever. Never mind that it's guys like you—guys with enough gay in them to be scared when they see one of us—who cause the goddamn trouble in the first place, because you're not man enough to face down what's inside you." He drank the rest of his martini and bit off the olive again, viciously. "Don't say you play for both teams if you're only going to bat for one side."

Damon blinked. It wasn't only that he was surprised by the onslaught. He was hurt, too. "Are you this much of an asshole to everyone, or just me?" His temper was throbbing now, but he wasn't drunk enough to punch Cathal. Even though he wanted to be, because he could never match him with words.

"Everyone," said Cathal, like he was proud of it. He got up. "If you want a fuckbuddy for the night, that's fine. So do plenty of guys here. But go find someone who doesn't care if you're throwing the rest of us under the bus, because I do." He reached to tuck the napkin into his pocket; Damon grabbed his wrist, even though he had nothing to say. Cathal shot him a look that promised every possible bad thing in the known universe. And some unknown things.

Damon let go of him, scowling. "I'm not like that. I'm not."

Cathal smiled that prim, insipid smile again. "Yes, you fucking are." He walked off without another word.

Damon sat there, stunned. Then he turned around and finished his beer at a go.

Second Prologue: Jane Austen Never Swore, but Cathal Reads Stephen King.

JULY 24TH, 1998

"So are you nervous?" Era asked, sweeping her skirt out beneath her legs as she sat across the booth from Damon.

Damon couldn't make his eyes settle on her face, even though the perfect calm he always found there would have made him calm, too. "Nope. Everything's great."

She seized his wrist before he could bite off a hangnail. "I thought you quit biting your fingernails."

Damon turned his hand so he could hold hers. That helped, a little. Era held his hand like she was ready to catch him if he fell. But she treated everyone that way.

"Your palms are clammy, too," she said, running her thumb over his. "You are nervous. Whatever for?"

Whatever for. She actually talked that way, like she'd strolled out of a Jane Austen movie. Damon studied the wallpaper, even though he'd seen the pattern of stripes and dots a million times. Smithson's was his favorite restaurant. It was supposed to make him comfortable. His voice came out rough. "I'm only meeting your best friend."

Era clucked and squeezed his hand to make him look at her. "I've told you already, he's going to act horrible and not mean a piece of it. He's—guarded." She traced the lines on Damon's palm. "He was only a teenager when he came out, and his family disowned him for it. We're all the other's got, so naturally, he's protective. But he's kind under the surface. Only there's...rather a lot of surface. It's why I haven't talked about him."

Damon looked at their linked hands and wished he could tell her why he was really nervous. Era had somehow convinced herself that Damon was good enough for her, but the moment someone else saw them together, the illusion would shatter, and she'd leave him. She was too good, and he knew it. How she didn't, when she knew so many things, was beyond him, but he wasn't going to question good luck. He lifted her fingers to his lips, and she favored him with a smile.

Then her best friend arrived. Although he was terrible with names, Damon never forgot a face. This one was sharp, and foxlike, and closed off—the man from the bar. You could mistake him and Era for siblings: they had the same glossy black hair and blue eyes, although his eyes were like ice, not the soft forget-me-not blue of Era's. For a minute, Damon wanted to run the other way. Then he remembered, bad meeting or not, this was Era's best friend, and however she laughed it off, she wanted them to get along.

So he got to his feet and held out his hand to shake, hoping he didn't look like he'd been hit in the face with a shovel.

Cathal, for his part, gave no sign he remembered Damon. His eyes were cool and thoughtful and as untouchable as the permafrost in the Arctic Circle. His hair was longer, and he was wearing a nicer suit, but otherwise, he didn't seem to have changed. As Era introduced them, he shook Damon's hand without any hint of a smile.

Era huffed. "I asked you to pretend to be nice. Just this once. Just for a change."

"I'm not insulting him, am I?" He looked Damon up and down, more obviously. Damon stifled the urge to scowl, despite a prickle at the back of his neck. Cathal was good-looking. But also like a king cobra as it reared up to strike.

To Damon's surprise, Cathal's expression softened. "He's—different than your usual man, Era. I'm trying to decide if this is a trick."

"It's not a trick. I like him, and you're going to hush."

A blush crept up the back of Damon's neck at Era's words. He wasn't expecting much more than *like* from her, even though he was already so in love it made his knees weak.

Cathal slid into the booth next to Era. She offered her cheek to kiss, and he did so. He asked polite questions about Damon—college, he was giving it a shot; army, navy, actually, but not long; job, still at the diner where Damon had met Era six months ago. Damon learned a few things about Cathal in return: he was an adjunct physics professor at the local state school, working on a doctorate in astrophysics.

"I'm not sure I'm smart enough to be at this table," said Damon, forcing himself to smile. Era was also working on her doctorate, though hers was in some specialized branch of English literature that Damon still didn't understand.

"Most people aren't," said Cathal. From someone else, it might have been a joke, but Cathal was serious. Damon searched his face, wondering if he did remember. Then Cathal yelped. "Don't kick me! It's the truth. Sheesh, we're not sixteen anymore." So maybe he just said that kind of thing. Probably, if their last meeting was any indication.

When they were finished with dinner but before the check arrived, Era went to the bathroom.

Cathal had maintained a neutral expression, softening only when he spoke to Era. Now, his eyes narrowed. He did remember that night at the bar. "Listen quickly. I need to know something, and now."

Damon bristled at his tone, like he had all that time ago, but he tried to keep his cool. "What?"

"My best friend loves you." Cathal said it like someone else might say *the sky is blue*. Damon drew back, heat coming into his cheeks. Cathal ignored this, his eyes not wavering from Damon's face. "I need to know now—can you love her back? And I don't mean in the emotional way. I mean all the way."

Damon blinked. "I—*what*?"

Cathal spoke as though explaining addition to a child. *Did he ever blink?* "Does the pendulum swing both ways, or are you looking for a beard? I realize I may have given the wrong impression before. I want to make it clear that I was being an asshole because I *am* an asshole and not because I don't think bisexuality exists. But some men marry women because they think they can hide it. Then twenty years later they come out in a loud and messy fashion, breaking their wife's heart. I'd kill you before I let you do that to my best friend."

Damon blinked again, this time at the audacity of the question. His hands were fists under the table; he made himself relax, though his voice was still flat. "I wouldn't date women if I wasn't interested in women. What kind of a person do you think I am?"

"I don't know what kind of person you are. It doesn't change the fact that plenty of my friends messed around with girls so their parents wouldn't find out." Damon opened his mouth, but Cathal waved his objections away. "Never you mind, though. I can tell you're not lying."

Damon's belly was full of fire, and he had no way to let it out. "So—"

"So we're fine," said Cathal, cutting him off. "I don't like you, but don't take it personally. I'm sure Era's already told you I don't like anybody. She's taken hell out of me for chasing her other men off, but that's because they didn't treat her right. You will, and that's all I care about. Never mind I have no idea what she sees in you."

That, at least, they had in common.

Thankfully, Era returned from the bathroom before Damon could calm down enough to say something stupid. She looked from Damon's flushed face to Cathal's cool smile and frowned. "If you were mean—"

"No more than usual, my love." Cathal looked like he'd stepped out to pick daisies, not like they'd almost come to blows. "You know me. I'm good at getting under people's skin."

"That's for damn sure," Damon muttered, trying to rub the blush away.

Era looked him over, still frowning. Then she sat, this time next to Damon so she could put a hand on his knee. He resisted the urge to hide his face in her shoulder. "Perhaps you weren't impolitic after all. I'm impressed."

Cathal just shrugged, expression unreadable.

Third Prologue: Cathal Makes a Promise, not a Joke, for Once in His Miserable Life.

FEBRUARY 20TH, 2016

Cathal made himself march right into the hospital room. If he lingered in the lobby or outside the door, he'd never get the guts to go inside. He'd been to visit Era before, when she first got sick, but this was different. The doctor had been very clear: the options they had would slow things down, but they couldn't stop it, and they all needed to accept that every day was one closer to Era's last.

Accept it. Like you could come to terms with death the way you memorized flashcards.

He managed to keep a smile on, though it was nearly impossible. He'd only been away for a few weeks, getting everything set up for the semester so his graduate students and his replacement teacher wouldn't be left floundering, and he'd spoken every day with her on the phone, but...she'd lost so much weight, even in that short time.

She, of course, saw right through him. Her own smile was tight and quiet, and she patted the space on the bed beside her. They settled next to each other, shoulders and hips touching, like they had twenty years ago when they were teenagers sharing secrets.

"Where's Damon?" Cathal asked because the silence was smothering.

"He's out getting lunch with Felix. I wanted to talk to you for a bit."

Cathal laced his fingers together instead of saying anything. He didn't want to admit it, but talking with Era these days was easier with Damon around to distract them. How exactly was one supposed to say, *You're dying, and it's also killing me*?

"For God's sake, Cathal, I'm not going to drop dead this instant." He flinched, despite himself, and Era sighed. "I'm sorry. But I need to talk to you about it."

"Do we have to?" It came out as a whisper; Cathal closed his eyes, ashamed.

Era picked up his hand, and Cathal squeezed it. "Yes. Just this once, and then we'll go on pretending, all right?"

He nodded but only opened his eyes when he was certain he had himself under control. Damon was already an emotional mess. She didn't need that from Cathal. Not that he had ever been her rock, but he could pretend, for her.

"Good." Era turned her head so they were almost nose to nose, another familiar position. He could pretend they were children, except for the noise of the hospital machines. "So. You've never liked Damon."

Cathal opened his mouth to object. Era just looked at him. Cathal rolled his eyes at the ceiling. "All right, no, not really, but you can't expect me to think anyone is good enough for you. That's my job. And it's not like I have anything in common with him."

"I know, and that's been fine. You've respected my choice, and you've been civil to him, which is all I ask."

"He's been good for you," said Cathal, and that was true. "I know that. But I don't like people."

"I know, and I'm all right with that." Era let out a breath. "I'm not asking you to change. But I need you to promise me something."

"Anything," said Cathal, turning to face her again.

"I need you to look after him for me when I'm gone." Her eyes were solemn. "He's already letting himself go—we're lucky enough he didn't need to keep his job, but I wish he would have, because I have no idea what he's going to do without me, and that thought scares me more than dying."

"He's got Felix," Cathal pointed out. "He's not going to let anything happen to your son."

"There's a difference between not dying and living, Cathal. I don't think Damon will—do anything." Her eyes turned dark, and Cathal saw she had, in fact, wondered about it. "But he won't spring back, either. He'll need help."

Cathal bit his lip. "I'm not really the touchy-feely type, Era, you know that."

"I'm not asking you to be." She ran her thumb along the side of his hand, considering her next words. "I need you to keep an eye on him for a while. Please. Just—try to make sure he doesn't do anything stupid after I'm gone. Stay with them for a while. There's no one else I trust."

That twisted his heart. "You know I will. Although I've no idea if he'll take that from me."

"He won't. I've known you both long enough to think better of ever asking you to be friends. But I'll feel better knowing someone's looking in on him."

"Anything for you," said Cathal, and he meant it.

"It's not only that, you know." She looked him square in the eyes because she knew he couldn't look away from her. Cathal made a career of pressing other people's buttons, but Era knew all of his back to front. "I don't want you to be alone, either."

He tried to smile like it was nothing, but his face betrayed him. "Era, I'm always alone. That's the way I like things."

She looked at him evenly. "I know exactly what you'll do. You'll go home, lock yourself in your room and write up a paper, and when you come out, you'll pretend like you never lost anything. Like you never lost—me."

Something twisted inside him, and he tightened his grip on her hand. "Era, no. You've been everything to me ever since my parents kicked me out—you know that. It's us. Just us." He closed his eyes before the tears could fall.

"That's why I want you to stay with Damon." Her voice brooked no argument. "It's always been just me for you, and it's always been just me for him. You can help each other."

Cathal shook his head. "I don't like him, Era."

"You will," was her reply. For once he knew better than to argue.

One: Cathal Tries to Keep His Promise, even though Who in Their Right Mind Eats Fish Heads; Damon Is Clearly beyond Help.

MARCH 15TH, 2016

"I'm Henry the eighth, I am, Henry the eighth, I am, I am..."

Damon told himself the worst part of all of this was that Cathal couldn't sing.

It wasn't true, but he could pretend.

"Good King Wenceslas looked out, on the feast of Stephen..."

Christmas was three months ago. Damon wanted to tell Cathal so, but that required sitting up, then getting out of bed, then walking over to the door, and then using his voice.

Cathal held the last note. Then silence.

Maybe he was going away. Not likely, but Damon could hope.

Nope. Cathal knocked—lightly, like a hotel maid. "Help me, Damon Eglamore, you're my only hope!"

He did a horrible Carrie Fisher impression. Another thing Damon wanted to say. But, again. Not happening.

Cathal groaned in disgust. Damon knew he was rolling his eyes, too. You could hear it. Somehow.

"For fuck's sake, Damon," said Cathal in his normal voice. If you could call it a normal voice. He sounded like he was about to deliver a lecture. "You can't stay in there forever. Food. It's awesome. So are showers. And kittens. And...I don't know, fucking ducklings or something."

Cathal let out another sigh, but this one was quieter. What Damon heard coming out of his own mouth. There was a quiet thunk, like Cathal had rested his forehead against the door. "I don't even know why I'm doing this."

You and me both.

Cathal moved away—Damon knew because Cathal shuffled his feet like he was going to grab your arm to shock you.

Damon put a hand over his face. Maybe he could go back to sleep.

Except.

The real reason Damon hadn't eaten anything was the same reason he hadn't gone through the photos on his phone or the pile of cards they'd brought home from the hospital and the funeral. His mind was a minefield, triggered by anything even slightly familiar, and cooking was all about familiar. It was his pride at Stephen's—making pancakes that reminded people of their grandmothers, cooking hash browns so crispy other cooks wept to taste them. And everything he cooked, he cooked because Era liked it. Damon had spent the last sixteen years learning whatever could bring even the slightest smile to her lips.

Not to say that he hadn't cooked for himself alone. When Era was gone, at a literature conference or a writing retreat, he missed her, so he made food that reminded him of her. Fettuccini Alfredo, the same recipe she ate between shifts at Stephen's when she still worked with him. Spaghetti carbonara with extra parmesan, since she dumped almost a whole shaker's worth on hers. Minestrone soup with tagliatelle instead of shell pasta, since it didn't lose its bite when you reheated it. Everything the way she liked it.

Maybe he should have kept his job. Going back to work and thinking of different things to make out of leftovers for family meal before service kept him sharp. Here, he didn't have limitations to work with. His pantry and fridge were overflowing with raw ingredients, since all of their mutual friends came from the restaurant business, and they thought Damon was going to cook his way out of this.

Except that cooking wasn't an out for him. It was the only thing he'd ever been any good at.

Still. He could at least clean the fridge. The last thing he needed was mold.

WHEN CATHAL CAME down the stairs later that morning, after an unsuccessful attempt to get Damon to leave his room and an even more unsuccessful attempt to get anything done besides flicking through pictures of Era on his phone, he almost didn't notice that something was different.

The walls had always been covered in pictures, and some of them were still there. Every one of Felix's school portraits, from preschool to sophomore year, were arranged in neat rows leading to the downstairs bathroom. But the rest of the walls were bare. Gone was Damon and Era's wedding portrait. The three pictures of Era walking at graduation for her bachelor's, master's, and PhD. The single picture of Damon and Era together when they were working at Stephen's, a few months after they first met and before they even started dating, when Era still referred to him as "that weird dishwasher who never talks—okay, now he talks, but he's still pretty weird."

Not a single picture of Era, or any of Damon, since he only suffered pictures if she was with him. Just Felix.

Frowning, Cathal looked into the living room. The decorations were the same: the couch was still covered in a hideous Easter egg slipcover, and stuffed rabbits and ducks were scattered about, remnants of the last holiday Era would ever decorate for.

Cathal stepped on that thought immediately. He looked up over the couch, where family portraits had once hung— one for each year of their marriage. But they were gone as well. The only picture that remained featured a line of varicolored bunny butts. Again, for Easter.

Cathal walked back out into the hallway and went upstairs. Here, too, the pictures of Era with different generations of students were gone. Even the last. Now, the only piece of decoration that remained was a truly horrible watercolor of mermaids, hung on the wall between the master bedroom and Felix's room. The whole house looked like a lot for sale decorated by the world's tackiest interior designer. In other words, if Era had ever been allowed to furnish someone else's home.

Swallowing hard, Cathal looked at Damon's bedroom door. It was still closed. So where had all the pictures gone?

Then a loud bang sounded from the kitchen, and Cathal nearly jumped out of his skin. Felix was at school, so apparently Damon was up after all. And he had some shit to answer for.

The kitchen was in total disarray. A pot bubbled on the stove, containing who-knew-what, and the garbage can was full of vegetable peelings. A cutting board with half an onion sat on the table. Damon stood in front of the food processor, frowning around the finger stuck in his mouth.

"Did I come at a bad time?" Cathal glanced around. "Are you having a dinner party I wasn't aware of?" He had meant to be angry, but now he was confused.

"Don't be dramatic. People gave us food. It was about to go bad." He licked the glop off his finger, frowned, and shook salt into the food processor.

"So...this is what you're doing. Two days locked in your room, and now you're...cooking."

Damon's expression didn't change. "You usually bitch about stupid questions. The food was going bad, and you can't cook. So here we are."

Cathal shook his head sharply, putting aside the irrelevant questions. Usually he was better, since science required sorting through the noise to find the signal. But Damon always short-circuited that. "What did you do with all the pictures?"

Damon didn't answer for long enough that Cathal almost repeated the question, this time bubbling over with rage.

Then Damon put his hands on the counter, like that was all that was holding him up. His face was still as emotionless as a mask in a museum. "You've been bitching at me to come out of my room, and I couldn't do that while they were all up there." He might as well have been explaining his decision between one color of wall paint and another. "I can't have her everywhere I look. I can't. So I put them away." He looked over his shoulder at Cathal, and his eyes were as empty as his voice. "It's my house. I can do what I want, and what I want is to spend thirty goddamn seconds thinking about something besides her. Do you have a problem with that?"

He ran the food processor again, drowning any chance for Cathal to point out how stupid that was. Damon sampled the gook and nodded this time.

Cathal wanted to walk out with his hands in the air, but... "All right, what is that crap?"

Damon turned to him, surprised. "It's cashew butter. Like peanut butter, but with cashews."

Cathal stared in horror. "What is *wrong* with you?" But he left before Damon could say anything.

CATHAL PARKED HIMSELF on the couch—he wanted to intercept Felix when the boy got home, since he wasn't sure what kind of mood Damon was really in. If he could, he wanted to shelter Felix from Damon's raw grief.

Felix came through the front door right on time, a frown on his lips and his nose in the air. Cathal slipped out of the living room to block the way to the kitchen. "What's that smell?" Felix asked, his voice suspicious.

Before Cathal could say anything, though, Damon stuck his head out. "I'm making dinner."

Cathal waited for the other shoe to drop.

But Felix just let out a heartfelt sigh. "Oh, thank Mozart. Cathal's not cooking."

Cathal flicked the lobe of Felix's ear and went upstairs. Disaster averted. Maybe.

CATHAL ALLOWED HIMSELF to get lost in research. Before things got so dire with Era, he'd been working on his second book, but first, he had to get his feet wet in academia again. How strange. March already, and he wasn't buried in midterms to grade and research projects to approve.

While reading, he lost all sense of the outside world, and that was the only reason he screamed like a little girl when Damon knocked on the door. Really.

Damon's lips twitched, though he was far from smiling. "That never gets old. There's food, if you want it."

Cathal remembered he'd never gotten anything to eat. His stomach answered for him.

FELIX WAS SEATED at the table. One hand tapped a rhythm on his knee, but Cathal wasn't sure if that was nerves or his usual fidgeting. Felix was never much for sitting still, unless he was reading music. He grinned at Cathal, but it lacked its usual luster.

Cathal was the cool uncle, not the feelings uncle, so he sat across from Felix and asked, "How was the first day back? Catch up with your friends?"

Felix twitched like he'd been goosed and glanced away, his expression turning guilty. Cathal glanced at Damon to see if he'd caught it, but by all accounts, Damon was focused on the food. Oh, well. Cathal could take charge. Especially if it involved making Felix squirm.

Felix's grin returned, albeit forced. "I mean, it was weird. Even my physics teacher was nice to me. But it was good to see my friends again. There's, um, some new kids that everybody's talking about, so that was good. Took the focus off me, I think."

"Are they talking because they're new or because they're interesting?" Damon set three plates on the table, one in front of each of them.

"They're twins, for one thing. And one of them's an insanely talented violinist. Rumor is they got kicked out of their old school, and I guess I believe it, because the other one is a real jerk." He cleared his throat, looking at the far wall instead of at either of them or his plate. "The violinist seems nice, though."

Cathal barely heard Felix. He stared at the food, and the food stared back. It looked like a piece of savory pie, complete with flaky crust and filling that smelled like bacon and eggs. Not that Cathal knew enough about food to be able to tell much by smell.

The only thing that really mattered, though, was the fish head resting against the edge of the crust—empty, dead eyes looking right at Cathal. "Damon. There's a fish in this pie."

Damon didn't bat an eye. "Yes."

"Damon. There is a *fish* in this *pie.*"

"That's because it's stargazy pie. You put the fish heads on top to flavor the eggs. I've always wanted to make it, but I never had any whole sardines before." Damon picked the head off his piece and licked away the filling stuck to it before setting it aside.

Cathal looked at the ceiling because he did not feel like looking into the eyes of the wall ornament that surely awaited you in hell.

"That is kind of weird, Dad." Felix watched with a combination of fascination and disgust.

"Try it," said Damon.

Cathal put one hand up against the side of his face, blocking his view of Damon. He picked the fish off his pie and hid it under a paper napkin. Once the food wasn't judging him for every bad thing he'd ever done—and that was a long list—Cathal decided he was too hungry to leave it uneaten. And the pie itself was rich and luscious, with chunks of fish and bacon throughout. Comfort food, with a side of existential dread

Damon's cooking was about the only thing Cathal couldn't take hell out of him for.

Still. One had to have standards. "Damon, I make allowances for your state of mind, but I draw the line at recreating Dante's *Inferno* with pie crust."

Damon shrugged, which only made Cathal madder because Damon *clearly* knew this was weird. "I couldn't even if I wanted to. I used up all the sardines."

Cathal decided to excuse himself before anything else could happen.

DESPITE HIS LATE night of work, Cathal set an early alarm. He wanted to make sure Felix, never an early riser, made it out the door. He'd expected to find the house quiet, but heard noises in the kitchen and went to investigate, hoping he wouldn't find Felix making breakfast. Despite his father's best efforts, Felix was almost as hopeless as Cathal, absent-minded and apt to let things burn.

But Damon was down there. He'd set up a number of small bowls with toppings and was whisking eggs. "I'm making omelets," he said to Cathal's unspoken question. "See if Felix's awake, won't you? I knocked on his door, but he hasn't come down yet."

Cathal blinked at this. Should he take umbrage at being ordered about? Taking umbrage was fun.

But he decided against it. If Damon was getting better, he could leave without feeling like he was slighting Era.

So he went up and got Felix, who was actually up and cleaning his flute. "Your dad's making breakfast," Cathal said, leaning in the doorway.

Felix looked up, surprised. "Really? He never makes breakfast at home."

This was true, since Damon liked to work during breakfast. He was not a late-night man; he never slept in past seven, another thing that made him abhorrent. Morning people existed only to make the rest of the world feel bad.

"Well, he is now, and if you want to eat, you'd better get your butt downstairs." He left before Felix could reply. He didn't want to give himself a moment to consider how strange this all was—not Damon making breakfast, but talking civilly with him. Then again, they'd never had to work together for the sake of someone else.

His throat tightened, but he made himself swallow.

In the kitchen, Damon swirled a pan, frowning at the eggs coating the bottom like Cathal frowned at student papers. "Perfect timing," he said, setting the pan back on the fire.

"These are normal, right?" Cathal sat at the table to resist the urge to peer at the ingredients in the bowls. "No fish heads?"

"They're omelets, Cathal," said Damon, but absently. "You want cheese in yours and nothing else, right?"

Cathal wondered when, exactly, Damon had learned how Cathal liked his eggs and decided not to question it. He knew how Damon took his coffee, after all—black and tasteless and bitter, like his resting bitch face. Maybe it happened like osmosis. Or dry rot.

Cathal realized he hadn't answered. "Yes."

This was all getting too strange.

Felix came downstairs, still in his pajamas. He peeked over his dad's shoulder as Damon used his spatula to make a perfect trifold. "This is not yours," said Damon without looking at his son.

"Mahhhh," said Felix. "I'm hungry."

"Yours is next. Don't be impatient, or I'll make Cathal another one and make you watch him eat it." But that was teasing. "Give this to him and sit at the table like a civilized boy."

Felix stuck out his tongue, but he took the plate and sat next to Cathal. Cathal seized the omelet before Felix could eat it. He didn't usually eat breakfast, but he'd had a busy night using his brain, and that burned calories.

Damon made Felix an omelet with peppers and ham and cheese, and then he joined them at the table.

"Aren't you going to have one, Dad?" Felix looked up from his already finished omelet. His father didn't respond, just took Felix's plate and got up to make another one. Felix looked at his father's back, perplexed.

"I don't like to eat when I'm cooking."

Felix frowned, but he didn't argue with his father, and, blessedly, they all shut up for the rest of breakfast.

Once Felix left for school, Cathal leaned against the counter. "So instead of starving yourself to death inside your room, you're doing it in the kitchen?" He kept his voice light.

Damon didn't look up from scrubbing the inside of a pot, although his jaw tightened. "I haven't felt like eating."

Cathal frowned. Damon was not taking the bait, and Cathal could only deal with Damon by making him so angry he lashed out. Yet another reason Cathal never should have made that promise.

Cathal kicked his heel against the cabinet. "You could at least pretend. For Felix's sake." It seemed like a reasonable tactic, though Felix was not trouble-prone. The edgiest thing he'd ever done was sneak into a concert without a ticket. And not like a punk concert, where breaking and entering was practically a requirement. Chamber music. Or something.

Damon frowned at the pot. "You know, when you put it that way, it makes more sense why you won't leave me alone." He snorted like a bull scraping his hoof in the dirt before he charged. "Well, you can fuck off, because I'm not going to leave my son by himself. It's just..." He closed his eyes, dropping the pot back into the soapy water.

Cathal looked away. The naked grief on Damon's face was too much like what he saw in the mirror in the middle of the night, when he tried to fall asleep but made the mistake of remembering who had decorated the guest room he slept in, picked out the watercolor of a unicorn that hung over his bed and the duvet set covered in gamboling kittens.

Then Damon started scrubbing with an intensity the remaining crud did not warrant. "Everything I touch feels empty. I don't know what my life is without her. And I know that the answer is supposed to be my son, but Felix is fine. The last thing he needs is my help."

Cathal bit his lip. Desire not to get involved any further warred with love for Felix, who was a good boy and hurting.

Well. Cathal did love telling Damon he was wrong. "He needs you now. You can peck at me for saying it, because what do I know about people, but I know him." He tried to stop there, because anyone would say that, but his mouth kept moving without his input. "Take it from someone who knows. He wants his family."

He pushed off from the counter and walked away before Damon could say anything.

Two: Cathal Discovers Damon Is a Real Person, Only Sixteen Years Late.

TRYING TO OUTLINE another book that night kept Cathal busy, long after the time for dinner had passed. He was hungry, but it was too late to go out for food, and he didn't dare look in the refrigerator to see what crime against nature lived there now. But when he opened the door to his room, he almost stepped on a covered bowl sitting in a tray of ice. A note in Damon's broad handwriting was taped to the top: *This is vichyssoise. It's supposed to be eaten cold.*

Wrinkling his nose, Cathal lifted the cover off the bowl. It was full of a light green soup, garnished with parsley. He frowned at it—in case it did something weird, and also to make sure he projected the correct demeanor if Damon should be watching around the corner of his door. Then he took it in his room.

Cathal liked it, but he still flipped the note over and wrote on the back: *It's not soup if you eat it cold, you filthy heathen.* He taped that to Damon's door.

WHEN CATHAL WENT downstairs to dispose of the bowl and ice, he found Felix with his hand in the box of Lucky Charms. Felix blinked. Then he shoved the box back in the cabinet.

Cathal shook his head. "I know high school is a zoo, but sometimes you remind me of those night vision videos of raccoons digging in garbage."

Felix made a face but didn't reply immediately since he was chewing. At least he had some manners. "It's not as good when you eat them from a bowl."

"Why, because you look less like a monkey?"

Felix perched on the table instead of answering. "You actually ate the stuff Dad left for you?"

Cathal glanced at the dishes. "I was hungry. And it wasn't that bad. But if you tell him I said that, I'll skin you and feed you to the piranhas in the aquatics department."

"There are no piranhas at Cherrywood College."

Cathal raised an eyebrow, daring Felix to challenge his judgment further. Sadly, Felix was too old to squeak and stammer like he had when he was five. And also Cathal suspected Era had shown Felix that Cathal's school was fish-free. She had no appreciation for good jokes.

Cathal put that thought away, then set his dishes in the machine and reached under the sink for the soap. Judging by the drying rack, Damon had done most of the dishes by hand again, but there was enough in the dishwasher to justify a load.

"Hey, Cathal?" Felix's voice was quieter and weirdly nervous.

Cathal wanted to turn to study the boy's expression. The last time Felix had sounded like that, he'd had questions about some explicit Harry Potter/Draco Malfoy fan fiction, and Cathal wasn't sure he wanted to revisit that discussion. But he didn't turn, in case Felix spooked. Instead, he focused on making his scoop of dishwasher soap perfectly even. "Yes?"

"If somebody doesn't answer if you talk to them, are they being mean or do you think they're shy?" The words came out in a rush.

Cathal didn't turn right away. High school problems seemed charming and simple with the benefit of age, but to Felix, they were the end of the world and needed to be treated as such. When he was sure he could hold a grave expression, he faced Felix, putting his hands on his hips. "I'd say it depends on the circumstances. When and how did you try to talk to this person?"

Felix blushed brighter. "In study hall. I ended up sitting with those twins I was talking about yesterday. I tried talking to them, but Gareth is, like, really intimidating and swears a lot, and Morgan just...sat there, staring at his papers."

"Hmm. I know you like to befriend every possible person, but it sounds like those two were giving off pretty strong signals that they didn't want anything to do with you. You can't win 'em all, kiddo."

"I know." Felix traced a design on the counter, his eyes thoughtful—a rarity. Felix wasn't foolish, but he let his feet get away from him when he was excited, and he was *always* excited. "But—" Felix rubbed the back of his neck. "Well, I keep thinking about the triplets minus one. You know, they're minus one because their brother doesn't talk to them for whatever weird reason. And I don't blame *them* for when he's mean or whatever. They can't do anything about him, and they're not like him. So I wonder if Morgan is the same way." Felix dropped his eyes to his feet.

Cathal frowned. "Felix, not that I mind, but why are you coming to me about this instead of your dad? You and I both know that I have the social skills of an elephant seal during mating season. Not that your father's much better, but at least he keeps his mouth shut most of the time."

Felix blushed, still avoiding Cathal's eyes. "I didn't really want to bother Dad. Don't want to jinx it, you know? At least he's cooking again. He hasn't done that in a long time."

Cathal raised his eyebrows.

"Okay, *okay*. I wanted to talk to you because—" The next few words came out so quickly they were not so much words as a blur. "I think I might have a crush on Morgan."

Cathal's eyebrows went higher, this time from surprise. Felix had never talked about liking anyone before. "Now I understand why you think I have a more relevant opinion."

Felix nodded, still blushing.

"So is this the first...?"

Felix nodded again. "I think I like guys and girls. But it's never been like—*whoa*, you know what I mean? Where I get why everybody acts so stupid." He rubbed his palm against his cheeks. "I mean, I could barely even talk to this guy. I looked like an idiot."

"It's hard when you're young, I won't lie to you about that. But talk to him. You're probably not making as much of a fool of yourself as you think you are." Cathal turned his chin down, doing his best imitation of Era's parenting face. Not that it ever worked, but still. "So am I allowed to tell your father about this, or..."

"I don't think I want to do anything about it. I just—had to tell somebody, and my friends would just think it was funny." Felix glanced away, twisting his fingers together. "Anyway, I don't think I want Dad to know. Not like he'd care or anything, but... I don't want him to think I'm not thinking about Mom, because I totally am." A shadow passed over his face.

Cathal put his hand on Felix's knee. "Don't make yourself feel guilty for feeling good. That's the last thing your mother would want. Or anyone who loves you, for that matter. I'm sure Damon'd be very happy to hear you've found somebody you like." He paused. "Actually, I'm not sure of anything after learning that people put whole fish in pie, but your father baffles me."

Felix looked up at him. "I never got that, you know. Mom would never tell me why you guys don't like each other."

"Damon and I are nails and a chalkboard, respectively." Cathal patted Felix's knee. "So. Back to the matter at hand. Felix, as happy as I am that you've found someone you like, I don't like the sound of this other boy. He's rude to you. There's no reason for you to put up with that. And as for the triplets minus one—Alex and Zach stand up for you when their brother is mean. If this boy was good for you, wouldn't he do the same?"

Felix bit his lip. "I've thought about that too. But—well, people think that you're a jerk, and you're not, really. You make it hard to get to know you, but that's so people don't waste your time, right?"

Cathal stifled a scowl. Era had used this trick all the time, but he'd never expected it from Felix, who had as much guile as a basset hound puppy, flopping around and stumbling over his ears. "Well, yes, but—"

Felix went on before Cathal could stop him. "And you're only mean because you've been through a lot of bad things, so maybe he's the same way, and that's why Morgan isn't doing anything. Because they're both hurting, and they need help. That could be it, couldn't it?"

"Felix—" Cathal sighed. "Yes, I'm mean, but not to people I like, and especially not to people I want to date. I adjust my behavior when I'm ready to let someone in, but I don't meet very many people I want to let in."

"But then who would ever get to know you?" Felix asked.

Cathal wanted to snap, but he pushed it down. The question was innocent, and Felix needed reassurance, not a lecture on romantic clichés. "I want you to listen to me." He turned to look Felix in the eye. "Your job in a relationship is never fixing someone else, do you understand? Maybe knowing you will make them want to be better, but they have to come to that decision on their own."

Felix stared back, face open and wide and vulnerable. Then he sighed and pressed his forehead into Cathal's shoulder. Cathal took the cue and hugged him. "This stuff is complicated. I want to go back to not liking people."

Cathal rubbed his back. "It's not easy. It's never easy. But it's this or be alone."

Felix glanced up. "But you're alone."

"I'm mean, like you said." And he managed to stay glib even though something inside him twisted at the familiar words. He let go and stepped back. "Now, it's much too late for this. Go to bed. You've got school in the morning."

Felix fidgeted. Then he said, "I want more Lucky Charms first."

Cathal threw up his hands in fake exasperation. "This is what I get for trying to pretend I am a responsible person. Eat your horribly unhealthy food. I've got work to do."

"Hey, Cathal?"

Cathal turned, raising his eyebrows.

"Thanks. I mean it."

Cathal waved that away. Anything he said would have been sappy.

He tried to go back to work but kept imagining how it would have been to have someone to talk to when he was struggling. Not that he'd have listened. But he'd been alone then, and he was alone now. Was that a problem or not?

CATHAL JERKED AWAKE. At least he didn't scream this time, if only because his mouth was full of sleep fuzz. He peeled the paper off his face and looked at the clock on the table—three in the morning. Hopefully it wasn't Felix at the door. He'd be contractually obligated to tell Felix to go to bed, even though teenagers had a different sleep cycle than adults and it didn't hurt them, and he hadn't liked their previous topic of discussion. Too serious. Too close to home.

But it was Damon.

Cathal stared at him, wondering if maybe he was still asleep.

Damon studied Cathal, as though Cathal were a picture that wouldn't hang straight no matter how Damon adjusted it. Cathal did not care for this, but saying so would have required him to use words. English words. In a sentence.

Finally, Damon said, "I don't understand you," the way a contractor might say, "Your foundation is shot."

Cathal blinked. "It's three in the morning." Anything more complex was beyond him. He was a night person, but that meant he slept hard.

"It is," Damon agreed.

Cathal stared at Damon's feet. "Is there a reason you're talking to me, about me, at three in the morning?" He wanted to be snarky, but he was still having a hard enough time making words, much less making those words cutting. This was why he didn't talk to people before he'd had his coffee. Especially people like Damon.

"Yes." He looked like a bouncer. The awful kind that you couldn't talk out of the entry fee and who would not let you in if you were drunk, even though you were awesome when you were drunk.

Cathal waited what felt like an appropriate amount of time before asking, "Are you going to tell me what that reason is?"

Damon shifted. "I don't understand why you're hanging around. And acting like you care what I do. You're not that way. So what's the deal?"

Cathal would have liked to respond with a smart remark, but when he tried to think of one, he could only picture the spinning wheel of death he got whenever he tried to use a Mac. Therefore, he had to tell the truth, which was a bad idea, but bad ideas always looked like good ideas at three in the morning.

Also, he never would have talked about it when he was awake, because it made him remember Era, weak and drawn in her bed, and he was doing his best to put those memories away where he could never find them. "Era asked me to keep an eye on you."

Damon took a step back, as if Cathal had hit him. "She...she what?"

Cathal let out a breath, wondering if he'd made a mistake. Probably. Other things he did at three in the morning were mistakes, although those things were along the line of "write down a brilliant idea for a book that is, in fact, complete sleep gibberish" or "take home the guy who's been winking at you all night but automatically isn't up to your standards because he's *winking*."

Well, as usual when he made a mistake, he could only forge ahead. "She asked me to keep an eye on you because she was worried you would fall apart. Like you did. I told her I was a terrible candidate for the job, but she told me I was her BFF and therefore obligated. Not in so many words, but that was the gist."

Damon pressed one hand to his forehead. Then he tipped his head back. Cathal wondered if he was about to cry and, if so, how terrible of a person he'd be if he shut the door in Damon's face.

Pretty terrible. So he didn't shut the door. *Damage control, damage control.* "I mean, it's not like she thought you were stupid or anything. She just knew—"

"That I'd be lost without her." Damon had closed his eyes, his hand still pressed to his forehead.

"Yes." Cathal wondered if he should have disagreed. But it was the truth, and he erred on the side of truth-telling. Even if the truth put the cat among the pigeons. *Especially* if the truth put the cat among the pigeons.

Damon brushed his hand over his eyes and turned away. "You know, the worst part is she was right."

Was Damon still talking to him? Probably not. Could he shut the door now?

Still no. And, anyway, he was nosy, and he wanted to know what kind of three a.m. revelation Damon was having. Probably better than *everything is or isn't ring-tailed lemurs, discuss.*

"I was good at being a husband. I knew what to·do with that. Now I'm a widower. I have no idea how to go forward. And the only person I have to talk about this with is you, and you hate me."

Ah. Damon *was* still talking to him. Sort of. Cathal leaned against the doorframe, suppressing a yawn. "Yes, well, at the moment, I'm a captive audience, so please feel free to continue unloading. It's not like either of us have somewhere to be in the morning." He gave up and yawned. "Also, I won't remember, so you're safe there."

"You will remember. You can never find your keys, but you can rattle off every conversation you've ever had, word for word." That was offhand, not an insult. Damon put his hands over his face again, and his next words came out in a mumble. "God, even my own wife knew I was bad at being a person."

Cathal was socially obligated to disagree. But that would have been nice, and Cathal was never nice.

However. He was telling the truth. "It wasn't like that."

Damon frowned, giving Cathal that crooked picture look again, and Cathal let out a disgusted sigh. He'd tried to make things simpler and instead had made them more complicated, so he would have to do more talking. "It wasn't like that. Era knew I was going to hang around anyway to get my head on straight. She wanted me to multitask." He squinted at the floor. "I mean, fuck's sake, Damon, your wife just died. Nobody expects you to be A-okay and whistling *Dixie* or whatever it is happy people do. There's nothing wrong with you." He wrinkled his nose. "Besides the fish thing. Because what the fuck."

Damon crossed his arms over his chest again. Now he looked like a bouncer again, this time with a severe migraine. Possibly an as-yet unnoticed aneurysm. "You're not at all like I thought you were."

Cathal squinted harder. Maybe if he looked at things hard enough, the kaleidoscope would stop spinning and he would wake up in a world that made sense. "You're repeating yourself."

"No, I'm not. I don't understand you, and you're not like I thought you were." Damon paused. "I should explain why I'm talking to you about all of this."

Cathal blinked. He was maybe, *maybe* starting to wake up. At least, he didn't feel like gremlins were sitting on his face pulling his eyes shut anymore, which usually only happened after his third cup of coffee. This was momentous. "No, that's about the only thing about you that makes sense. We don't like each other, and I won't leave you alone. Hence." He groped for a big word, but his vocabulary failed him, so he settled for gesturing at the space between them. "Hence."

Damon shook his head. "That's not why. I...I heard you talking to Felix. In the kitchen."

Cathal shut his eyes tight and then opened them in an attempt to wake up more. Felix had come to him in confidence, so this was important. "He talked to me because he's got a thing for a boy, and he knows I'm gay as a picnic basket, Damon. Don't read too much into it. 'S not like you've ever told him you like dick on the side."

Damon ignored that, though his mouth tightened. All in all, he was being very diplomatic—for Damon. And the hour of the night. Trying to have a civil conversation after midnight was like having cat and dog lovers work out their differences while grooming their animals: something might get accomplished, but it wouldn't be good, because everyone was too emotional to think straight. And then you ended up with an ugly Labradoodle or Egyptian Mau or whatever.

Cathal glanced over his shoulder, wishing he could reach his sticky notes to write that down.

"That's not what I meant," Damon said, snapping Cathal out of his thoughts. "You..." He glanced away. "I didn't think you could be that...nice. You never talked to Era like that."

When had the serious conversation started? "That's because Era didn't need me to talk to her like that. Era didn't need anybody." It ached, to speak of her in the past tense.

He thought of Labradoodles instead. That was a ridiculous word.

Damon closed his eyes and nodded. "She didn't." He let out a breath and looked at Cathal again.

His eyes were clearer than they'd been in days. Cathal found himself staring. Damon wasn't that old, but the lines on his face stood out sharply because he'd lost so much weight since Era's diagnosis. He still looked like he belonged in the navy, just...not as much. And his eyes...

Era had eyes the exact color of a forget-me-not, but Damon's were more like that one crayon in the box Cathal could never pronounce. Cerulean.

They were nice eyes. If you liked that sort of thing.

Cathal shook himself. If he was thinking about Damon's appearance, he was too tired for anything, much less a heart-to-heart.

"Can we put a pin in this for now?" Cathal bit back another yawn. "Felix thought everything he told me was a secret. I don't want him finding out that you know."

Damon paused as though he had not considered that last. "I feel like I should be upset that he came to you and not to me, but you're right. He doesn't know about—that side of me."

"You're bisexual. Say it like a fucking man." That, at least, sounded like himself. Probably because it was the oldest bone of contention between them, familiar and worn-out like tennis shoes you wore every day.

Damon ignored that, again because it was familiar and worn-out. He bit his thumbnail. "You're right. I don't know what I was thinking. Maybe that you wouldn't talk to me during the day."

Cathal rubbed his forehead. "Yes, well, it seems like I'm going to be stuck talking to you during the day, so we'll pick it up later." He blinked. That had almost sounded like...a compromise.

He shook his head. It was definitely too late. *Now* he shut the door in Damon's face.

WHEN HE WOKE up, he found several Post-it notes about Labradoodles and was very confused.

CATHAL DIDN'T WANT to get out of bed the next morning, partly because he felt like a zombie from lack of sleep and partly because the next step was talking to Damon, and that thought was as pleasant as the neighbor downstairs flushing the toilet while you were showering.

But. Better to get the unpleasant things out of the way first.

Except... It hadn't been unpleasant. Weird, and yet they hadn't shouted at each other. Swore, yes, but Cathal couldn't go two sentences without swearing unless he was in a lecture hall. Era had refused to let him visit for a week after Felix started yelling *fuck*.

Still feeling bleary, Cathal headed downstairs. His only thought was coffee, and there was coffee. But there was also a plate with a slice of something yellow on it.

Damon was doing the dishes by hand again. He glanced at Cathal when he walked in but looked away before they could make eye contact.

Cathal got himself coffee and then looked at the yellow thing.

"I saved you some frittata," said Damon, like that was a sentence. "It's good at room temperature, so you don't even need to heat it up."

Cathal sat, slowly, and stared at the yellow thing. "What's in it?" he asked when his mouth started feeling like something that could form words instead of a place where something had crawled in and died.

"Egg, Gruyère, shitakes, arugula, and cherry tomatoes."

Cathal closed his eyes, hoping that would make him feel like he'd gotten more sleep so he could decipher this conversation. He'd always wondered what it felt like to be Alan Turing cracking Nazi codes. Now he knew, and it sounded like Damon talking about food. "None of those are words. Except 'egg.' And 'and.'"

"You know, if somebody gave you a million dollars, you'd find a way to complain about it." But Damon's tone was almost...cheerful. Or at least not sad. Damon had never been sunshine and rainbows.

"Yes. Because who just gives you a million dollars?"

Damon rolled his eyes. "Eat it or don't. I mean, you were picking at me for not eating, but you barely get anything down. And it's not like you can afford to lose weight."

"I'm *lithe*. It's a legitimate body type."

"No, you're gaunt. Like you're auditioning to be a vampire or something." Damon frowned, then set down the dish and the drying rag. He pressed one hand to his forehead. "This is what always happens when I talk to you, you know that?"

Cathal shrugged. "Yeah, we argue. We don't like each other. I know the drill."

"No—I mean, yes, we argue, but that's because you say things that are weird, and I can't tell if you're fucking with me or if you're honestly like that, and it pisses me off." He strangled the air, a gesture Cathal was used to at this point.

Cathal looked at him flatly. "I'm fucking with you. Because you make it easy." This was true. Although, to his credit, Cathal didn't always intend to fuck with Damon. It just happened, like buying things off Amazon after midnight when he'd had too many shots. Only fucking with Damon didn't get him awesome surprise presents a few days later.

Damon considered this and then shook his head. "That's not my point. And I told myself that for once I would not let you drag me away from the point."

Cathal decided to keep his mouth shut, although he wished he'd brought his notes downstairs so he could write down what he wanted to say about dragging and points. Never mind that it looked less funny when he wrote it down.

"My point is, we were talking last night like people. You can do that, but you choose not to." Damon broke off again, waving his hands and flinging soap bubbles everywhere. "No, that is *not* what I'm trying to say, but you piss me off so much I can't think." He pressed his hands against his forehead with an irritated noise.

"You sound like a goat in heat," said Cathal.

Damon parted his fingers. "How—no, never mind, I don't want to know how you know that."

"It's called the internet, Damon. I'd say you should join the twentieth century, but that would mean kicking your horse into a gallop, and then your buggy would bounce around, and you'd probably break something."

"That doesn't answer my question, but whatever. Shut up for thirty seconds. Please."

The *please* made Cathal listen. Much as he didn't want to. He'd finished his coffee, so he set the cup down and arched an eyebrow at Damon.

Damon put his hands at his side, clenching and unclenching them like he wanted to punch something. Or whatever manly men like Damon did to let out their feelings instead of drinking and watching cute kitten videos. "I didn't want to talk to you like this. The point I was trying to make is that it's—" He scowled. "It's driving me up the wall that I'm only learning now that you can talk to people and be nice. I mean, I guess I knew you were nice to Era, but I thought she just liked you picking fights all the time."

"She did." The comment was supposed to be flippant, but it came out maudlin. Era was Cathal's favorite person to argue with. She understood that shouting at someone meant you had a good point, not that you didn't like them.

Damon's eyes moved over Cathal's face; Cathal avoided his gaze, tapping one finger on the table. He wished he hadn't come down here, but he'd said that he would, and he wanted to pretend he was a man of his word.

"I don't like to think of myself that way," said Damon at last, and Cathal narrowed his eyes, not in frustration but confusion. "I don't like to think I wouldn't see how good you are underneath it all—but I guess you were right. I don't know what kind of person I am either. I knew how to be a husband, but now..."

Cathal wrinkled his nose—not because he faulted Damon for feeling adrift after losing his partner, because that was what happened to people who wanted partners. The only way to win was not to play.

No, he had a choice to make.

Instead of going with the option that involved less human interaction, his usual strategy, he asked himself what Era would have told him to do. Only he didn't have to ask, because she'd already told him.

Cathal massaged his forehead. He couldn't even swear at her when she was right anymore.

"You know, if this whole thing is about learning how to be a single person instead of a husband." But Cathal could not finish the sentence. He couldn't abide people who left their thoughts unfinished, and yet there he was. Blatantly not-thought-finishing.

Damon frowned. "I guess it is," he said cautiously, as though waiting for Cathal to talk over him. "I have no idea how to do that. I never—I never thought of myself as anything much before I met Era. She was always trying to break me of that, but..." He shook his head. "I knew it wasn't true."

Cathal was surprised to hear that. He'd been quick to inform Damon that he was not smart enough for Era, but he hadn't thought Damon believed him.

Well, damn, now he was feeling guilty.

Oh, get over yourself, said Era's voice in the back of his head, as she often did, and that settled it.

To make it easier, he didn't look at Damon. "You know," he told the glass of smiling rainbow daisies in the kitchen window, "I happen to be an expert in the art of being single. And in liking myself." He said it casually, though it didn't feel casual enough. He didn't want Damon to take him up on this offer; he wanted to go back to his own apartment and never talk to anyone again.

But he didn't want Felix to have to deal with his crush on his own, and...he didn't want to forget Era. Not yet. And if he wasn't ready to be done, he'd have to find some way to get along with Damon but still save face.

This was the problem with being perceived as a selfish bastard. You could never live up to the image. Then people would think they'd gotten the jump on you when, really, you weren't sure how you ended up with that reputation in the first place but decided to stick with it because people left you alone.

Damon had his eyes narrowed, like he expected Cathal to shed his human skin at any moment. "Are you offering to help me, or are you looking for another excuse to make fun of me?"

"I'm always looking for an excuse to make fun of you. But I'm that way with everyone. You need to stop taking it so personally." Cathal should have felt guilty, but Damon needed to loosen up. He approached everything with the gravity of a baby struggling to pick up a Cheerio.

"That doesn't answer my question, but I have no idea why I'm surprised."

Cathal shrugged. "I don't understand why you do anything, so there we're square." Damon frowned again, and Cathal made himself look at Damon.

He didn't want to look at Damon, because it was okay to look at Damon when he was Era's husband and therefore not a person.

Now...

Well, Damon was a person. A person with nice eyes and an honest face and biceps like Captain America. Cathal was noticing, and he didn't care for that shit.

"I guess I am offering to help you." Cathal's voice was as revolted as his sigh, although at this point, he wasn't sure who he was revolted with. Maybe the part of him that listened to Era when she said she believed in him.

"Why." It wasn't a question; Damon's eyes were narrowed.

Cathal growled. "Why is it that the one time I don't want to tell you why, you're actually asking me?"

Damon didn't answer, just kept staring at Cathal. Damon didn't blink much. He could stare for hours without his eyes watering, but maybe that was Cathal having to blink himself and thus missing Damon's blinking.

Whatever. Damon didn't blink, and he was a freak, but that didn't mean Cathal could wiggle out of giving an explanation, if only for consistency's sake. When you were consistently a jerk, you didn't have to listen to people calling you a jerk, because you could point to all the things you'd done and say it wasn't supposed to be a surprise.

"Okay, fine. Because—" Cathal's voice faltered, and he stopped, making sure it wouldn't happen again. "Because. I'm as lost as you are. Without Era, I mean." Cathal looked at his hands. Now the words wouldn't stop, and that was awful, too. "I wanted to go home and do nothing, except that's not enough anymore, because there's this hole where she used to be, and I thought I was used to holes where people used to be, but I guess that doesn't apply to Era because she helped me fill them, and now I have no idea how to do that myself, which is goddamn pathetic but there we are."

Damon kept squinting. "Was that all one sentence?"

Cathal wanted to throw something at him, but there wasn't anything in the kitchen that wouldn't either break or cause serious injury, and the insurance companies might get suspicious if Cathal took Damon to the emergency room so soon after his wife's death.

Instead, he pulled the plate of frittata closer, since he didn't want to talk anymore. And also he was hungry.

And. It was delicious. He still had no idea what most of those things Damon had listed off were, but they were goddamn tasty.

Three: Bread Pudding Is Dramatic. And Delicious.

WHEN CATHAL WENT back upstairs, Damon sat and tried to think. He'd made the dough, and now it needed time to proof.

But he'd forgotten how much he sucked at sitting and thinking. Bad enough before, when he'd been busy. Now there was a giant sucking abyss at the center of his world, and he had to keep running or he'd be pulled in.

So he made lasagna. Era hadn't liked it—too heavy— and the thought of what Cathal would do when he discovered the ingredients...well, it didn't make Damon smile, exactly, because nothing made him smile anymore. If he touched his mouth, sometimes his lips were turned up at the corners, but that had nothing to do with his feelings. Inside he was dirt tamped down after a burial.

But irritating Cathal was funny, and maybe someday he'd laugh and actually mean it.

HE THOUGHT HE'D have to call Cathal down for dinner— not that he cared if Cathal ate or not, but because he wanted to see the other man's face. But Cathal came into the kitchen a few minutes before Felix was due home. He always looked like he'd bitten into a lemon. Not the most irritating thing about him, but high on the list.

Before Damon could think of a way to try to annoy him, the front door slammed. "So good to know he's still crashing around like he's about to start a musical number," said Cathal, resting his cheek on his hand.

Nope. There was Cathal's most irritating trait: he always knew how to describe things. No matter how pissed he was, Damon could never ignore him, because some part of him was nodding along even as he moved to strangle the other man.

Felix skidded into the kitchen, sliding up next to Damon to peer at the pan on the stove. "Ooh, what's that? It smells good."

"It's lasagna. We're waiting on the garlic bread."

Cathal coughed suggestively, and both Felix and Damon turned to look at him. But Cathal didn't say anything. He just raised his eyebrows, waiting for the other shoe to drop.

Since Cathal didn't launch into another unwelcome, uncomfortable lecture, Damon hoped maybe he'd keep quiet. But that would have been too easy. "You've got a look on your face. What is it?"

"Of course I have a look on my face," said Cathal. "That's the point of a face."

Damon glared at him. As usual, Cathal smiled like a poker player with a winning hand, but then he turned his gaze to Felix, his eyebrows still raised. Damon followed him, confused. He'd meant what he said about his son.

"What? Why is everyone staring at me?" Felix's voice was plaintive. He always cracked after thirty seconds of silence and told you every bad thing he'd done that day, even though his only sin was finishing the milk and putting the carton back in the fridge.

Cathal let out a delicate sigh. He must have gone to some kind of gay academy to learn those; he had a sigh for every occasion. "The plot has thickened, nephew mine. Like a fart in a crowded room, you cannot hide the truth forever. Out with it."

Felix clapped his hands over his face. "I...I don't know what you're talking about." His voice cracked, and he peered at them through the gaps in his fingers.

Damon looked from his son to Cathal. "This is really what you want to talk about now?"

Cathal shrugged. "This is the logical next step." Damon opened his mouth. "And if you argue with my logic, I swear to God I will punch you in the dick. No more secrets. We're all on this goddamn feelings boat together." He turned his attention back to Felix. "Therefore. Fess up, kiddo. The cat is not only out of the bag, but he's also gone and fathered a litter of adorable kittens in the time you've spent dancing around the point. I keep telling you this is real life, not cabaret."

Felix wrinkled his nose. "I don't know what that means."

Cathal covered his face. "Oh, how I have failed you as the token gay man in your life."

"Enough." Damon stepped between them. "There's no need for this." He crossed his arms over his chest. "Felix, I'm sorry, but I eavesdropped on you last night. I know about your crush."

Felix dropped his hands, his eyes wide. "Seriously?"

Cathal spread his fingers so Damon could see his skeptical look. "You know, I was trying to let you off the hook here, Damon."

Damon looked back without blinking. "In this house, Cathal, we tell the truth."

Cathal looked confused. "I wasn't saying lie to him, but you didn't need to tell him the embarrassing part. It's called saving face."

"He's my son. I've got five million ways to blackmail him. I don't need to worry if he's got something to guilt me over."

Cathal raised a finger and then lowered it. "That was surprisingly ruthless. Objection rescinded. The court may proceed."

Damon wanted to point out how weird he was, but then they'd never get Felix pinned down.

And, as it turned out, Felix was scooting out of the kitchen, though he froze when Damon looked at him. "Okay, okay!" Felix hung his head. "I like the new guy, okay? He's really cute and really talented and he's got eyes like—like eyes that are really great eyes."

Cathal made a stifled noise. Damon shot him a look, but Cathal had already recovered, his fist up against his mouth like he was stifling a cough.

Again. Distraction. "Why didn't you tell me, son?" Damon only realized as he said the words that he was...hurt. He was such a complete fuckup that his own son had gone to his tone-deaf uncle first.

Goddammit.

Felix didn't answer. Damon let out a breath, pushing those feelings away. They weren't important. What was important was his son.

Trust me. He needs his family.

Damon shook his head to banish Cathal's words. "Did you think I'd have a problem with you liking a boy?"

But Felix shook his head. "No, I know you wouldn't care." His eyes slid away and grew grave. "Just...after everything that's happened..."

"You thought I wouldn't want to hear about it." Felix nodded, his expression miserable. Damon closed the distance between them and put a hand on Felix's shoulder. Felix hugged him. Not like he was upset—Felix hugged anything that would stand still long enough, and even things that didn't.

Damon patted his back, staring out the small window over the kitchen sink. "I've got no one to blame but myself for that. I'm sorry, Felix. I'm glad you like someone. It's part of being your age. For most people, anyway." He took a step back to look down into Felix's eyes. "And it doesn't matter who this person is or what they look like as long as they treat you well."

Felix blinked rapidly, then pressed his face into Damon's chest again. "It's not an after-school special, Dad. You don't have to tell me it's okay to be gay. Or bi. Or whatever I am. I've got Cathal for that."

Damon couldn't help glancing over his shoulder at Cathal, who was watching with an unreadable expression. A frown touched Damon's lips, but he was confused, not upset. "I suppose you do," he said at last.

Cathal cleared his throat, but he choked on something and doubled over, coughing.

Felix lifted his head. "You okay, Cathal?" he asked, standing on tiptoe so he could peer over Damon's shoulder.

Cathal rubbed his throat, narrowing his eyes. "I happened to notice there's a lavender elephant in the room. You understand."

Damon got the hint. He rolled his eyes and stepped sideways to let Cathal into the conversation. "Okay, okay."

Cathal smirked. Felix wiped his face clean of tears with no shame and then looked between the two of them, confused.

Damon hadn't explained as much to Cathal, but he'd only never told Felix about his sexuality because he didn't know how. Cathal had always had boyfriends, and they were treated as normal parts of life, so much so that Felix wasn't even surprised when gay marriage was legalized. If Felix had ever talked about it with anyone, it was with his mother or Cathal.

Probably Cathal. Era was straight, as far as she'd ever told Damon.

But he didn't want to think about that. He pushed his hand through his hair and grasped at the first thing that came to mind. "Did I ever tell you how I met Cathal?"

"It's kind of implied, Dad." His eyes narrowed, and he glanced at Cathal. "Unless you're like some secret spy person and not actually Mom's best friend."

Cathal snorted. "I was disowned, Felix, not imported. And don't interrupt your father, or he'll weasel out of this. I'm the one who's bad at getting to points, remember?"

Felix considered this, then nodded and looked back at Damon.

Damon hooked his thumbs in his pockets and leaned against the counter. "I met him first, actually. In a gay bar. I like women and men."

Felix's brows snapped together in horror. "Not—"

"We didn't do anything!" Damon and Cathal said at the same time. Damon felt better that Cathal also looked shocked.

"Please, Felix. I have standards." Cathal shuddered. "I threw him out on his ass, and we've never got on since. So there is the grand story of our ancient grudge. Minus the star-crossed lovers crap. And also all the murder."

Felix looked between the two of them, his face still scrunched up. "Actually, that makes a lot of sense."

Cathal opened his mouth to reply, as though that were a normal thing to say.

"No." Damon pointed at him. "No. We are not going to encourage him. We are going to eat lasagna."

Cathal blinked. Then he nodded. "That's the first sensible thing you've ever said."

Damon took the garlic bread out of the oven—luckily he'd turned the broiler off before Felix came home and just had the oven on to keep it warm—and set it on the stove beside the lasagna pan. Felix reached for a piece, trying to be sneaky, but Damon smacked his fingers with the oven mitt. "Don't even think about it. You'll burn yourself like you do every time."

Felix let out a dramatic sigh, but he sat down and let Damon put everything on plates and bring it to the table. Felix reached again and then promptly pulled his hand back so he could suck on his burned fingers. Damon did not say *I told you so*, because he was a good dad. Instead, he served the lasagna.

Cathal squinted at it. "So what's weird?"

"It's lasagna. Don't be paranoid." Damon turned his attention to Felix to avoid giving away the surprise. "So tell me about him."

Felix hunched in on himself, but not enough that he couldn't also eat lasagna between descriptions of Morgan. Who could apparently do everything and also was the cutest guy in existence.

Cathal made a frustrated noise. "Okay, what is in this? It's not right." He'd already eaten half his piece and was now picking apart the layers with his fork, glaring at his plate.

Damon finally, finally allowed himself to smile. "I used slices of eggplant and zucchini instead of noodles. It's better for you that way."

Cathal looked at his plate, then at Damon, and then back at his plate. "You are a vile human being." Then he stuffed another forkful in his mouth.

DAMON DIDN'T KNOW what to do with himself after dinner. For once, he didn't want to go up to his room and go to bed. Things...things had happened today, and he needed to think about them, and he wouldn't if he turned his brain off.

Even though turning his brain off was the only thing that helped.

Well, there were other ways to turn off his brain.

The TV in the living room had sat untouched since Era got sick, since only Damon used it on a regular basis. Felix preferred watching things on his laptop or phone, and Era only liked it for background noise as she graded papers. They'd spent plenty of time on the couch together—Damon with his arm stretched along the back, Era curled into herself, her tongue between her teeth so she wouldn't curse as she worked. Her hand resting on his knee. His fingers carding through her hair as she read a particularly bad passage to him.

Needless to say, nobody'd been using the living room. Damon walked in slowly, waiting for his mind to stop working, for his breath to catch, for his legs to give out underneath him.

There, after all, was the stain on the corner of the coffee table when Era had laughed so hard she'd knocked over a bottle of champagne after their wedding. The wall over the couch had once held pictures of their milestones as a family: their vow renewal, Felix's first birthday, Felix's first day at Cherrywood Elementary and then at high school. Now there were only blank spaces.

It hurt. But it was like stepping on something sharp instead of drowning. Bright and gone, not deadening. Endless.

Damon stood in the doorway, letting himself breathe. Then he sat down. After a moment, he got back up, but only to go to the fridge.

He had just gotten settled on the couch and picked one of his recordings from several months ago—how long ago he did not think about—when Cathal passed by with a sleeve of Oreos. Damon stared straight ahead, but Cathal still came into the living room and perched on the edge of the couch. He drew an Oreo out and twisted it apart, though he didn't eat it. Instead, he stared at the screen as though the opening text of Damon's food show was written in Swahili.

Damon wanted to turn the TV off and run.

Had he thought Cathal was annoying because of his expressions?

No, no. The really annoying thing was that he was as good at silence as he was at talking. He could always make you screw yourself.

Either way, Damon couldn't stand the quiet anymore. "I figured I'd catch up. You're the one who's always saying how backward I am."

Cathal did not rise to the bait. Rather, he nodded at the six-pack sitting on the edge of the table. "With a beer."

His voice was...neutral. Damon hadn't thought that was possible. Cathal cast judgment on everything, from candy flavors to dog breeds. And he enjoyed it.

Damon squared his shoulders. "Yeah, with a beer." He waited for Cathal's next comment. But Cathal kept staring at the beer, his eyes narrowed. It was almost the way he stared at food he didn't like, but not quite. Then his upper lip curled in unconscious disgust, like with the soup. No, now...

Damon frowned. "Wait, are you worried about me?"

Cathal jerked upright and nearly fell off the arm of the couch. Damon knew he was right, even though Cathal said, "Absolutely not." Cathal steadied himself and crossed his arms over his chest. "I thought you were trying to keep alcohol out of the house, so I was respecting that by not drinking. But now you've got some, and I want one."

Damon thought about raising a stink. But he wasn't as good at raising a stink as Cathal, and he didn't feel like being humiliated.

And they had...come to an agreement. Sort of. So he broke one of the beers off the plastic ring and passed it to Cathal.

Cathal took it, but he settled it against the back of the couch instead of drinking it. He licked the cream center out of his Oreo, his eyes still narrowed. Damon watched Cathal's tongue. He hadn't thought anyone could look grumpy eating a cookie.

Damon realized he was staring at Cathal's mouth and turned his attention to the TV. He unpaused it and listened to the announcer explain the show even though it was the same every time. But the repetition helped clear his head. "Fine. You weren't worried." He took in another breath. "And you don't need to be. I'm only having one. That's...that's not the way to handle this."

Cathal ate the rest of his Oreo. "Well. None of that is relevant, because I wasn't interested in your drinking. I didn't want to get crumbs in my room, and I was curious what you were watching. I don't have a TV." A minor irritating thing about Cathal was that his voice was always crisp and clear like a radio announcer's. Sometimes Damon half expected him to launch into a weather report.

"Of course you don't."

Cathal straightened his back. Another thing—he had perfect posture. And you knew he was judging you for slouching. That wasn't top of the list, though, since the reminder to sit up straight was helpful. Unlike everything else about Cathal. "So. What are we watching?"

Instead of answering, Damon rewound the recording back to the host's explanation. He expected Cathal to make fun, but instead, Cathal watched with an intense expression—the kind he saved for scribbling nonsense on Post-it notes. And it was nonsense. Damon had cleaned up enough notes that said things like "If Jimmy cracks corn and no one cares, and we don't know where Cotton Eye Joe came from or where he went, we have an epidemic on our hands" or "Is there a number one pencil? Research."

Cathal's expression brightened when they introduced the contestants, since the first one was a feminine gay man with an adorable husband. "Ooh, a token sassy queen. I love this crap."

Damon decided not to say anything. Maybe if he kept quiet, Cathal would lose interest.

Or...maybe Cathal would enjoy himself. Damon expected him to get up and leave after finishing his Oreos, but he cracked his beer and...didn't say anything.

It had to be a trick.

Well. Whatever. Damon loved this show, so he was going to enjoy himself. And he did, for the first forty minutes. Then they got to the dessert round, and Cathal spoke up again. "Okay, what the fuck is bread pudding and why are they all acting like it's the worst idea ever?"

Damon frowned and glanced at Cathal. But Cathal, to all appearances, was invested. His eyes were narrowed, and he was leaning toward the TV like that would get him closer to the action.

Actually, it reminded Damon of Felix. He did the same thing when they were listening to music. Only with giggling.

"You mean you want my opinion?" Damon couldn't help the distrust in his voice. He'd never been smart, and he knew it. Worse, Cathal knew it.

But, to his surprise, Cathal glanced at him, and his expression was actually... Well. Not kind, because before yesterday with Felix, Damon would have insisted Cathal was incapable of kindness.

Not threatening, maybe. Cathal normally looked like he'd poisoned your coffee and was waiting for the cramps to hit. But...not now.

"Yes," said Cathal. "You're the subject matter expert. I don't know anything about cooking, and I want to know why everybody thinks cute gay boy won't win."

Damon tucked his hands in his armpits. "Why can't you be an asshole all the time?"

He hadn't meant to say it out loud, but Cathal laughed. Real laughter, not scornful. "I am many things, Damon, but I am never predictable. Now. Bread pudding."

Damon stared at him. Cathal never said his name. It was weird. "Okay, fine. Bread pudding is stale bread mixed with a custard." Cathal frowned as if Damon had switched to French. "Which is eggs and milk and sugar. But it takes a long time for the bread to soak up the custard, and it takes a long time for the custard to set in the oven. If he waits too long to bake it, he ends up with raw eggs. If he doesn't let it sit long enough, he gets flavorless bread cubes."

Cathal squinted, but it wasn't the type of squint where he said something asshole-ish. That one involved his brow furrowing and his lips pursing until they almost disappeared. Instead, he wrinkled his nose. "Is this what passes for drama in the food world?"

Damon rolled his eyes, turning his attention back to the TV. "If you don't like it, you can leave."

"Just for that, I'm staying."

Four: Potato Pancakes Disappoint Everyone.

NOW THAT DAMON had gotten back into cooking, he felt... Not better. Less bad.

Other people said they liked cooking because it helped them think, but nothing helped Damon think. His brain was one of those marble labyrinths where you had to tilt and twist the box to make the ball bearing drop out the bottom. No matter how hard he tried, he could never be as fast on his feet as Era or Cathal or even his son.

But cooking was nice. Something to reach for on days like today, when he woke up and the bed was empty and cold but he'd still curled into the corner to leave space for another person. Era was a bed and blanket hog. Damon was still adjusting to waking each morning covered.

Downstairs, they had russet potatoes on the verge of sprouting eyes, so he got out a grater and a bowl. Cathal came into the kitchen right when Damon got a good rhythm going. He looked so tired as to be deranged, but that wasn't anything new.

What was new was the legal pad tucked under one elbow.

"I'm making potato pancakes." Maybe that would delay the legal pad.

Cathal set it on the table.

Well. One more tactic. "Is that for whatever you're working on up there?" Not that Damon was interested in Cathal's new project. Good that he was working, but it would go straight over Damon's head.

"No." Cathal frowned at his pad. "It's about this. What we're trying to do."

Damon looked at his potatoes. Then he sighed and set down the grater so he could look at Cathal's writing. What he saw was not heartening, and not because Cathal's spiky, tight handwriting was illegible even to people without dyslexia. "This is highlighted."

"Yes," said Cathal, missing the disgust in Damon's tone. Or ignoring it. It was hard to tell.

"And there are sticky notes."

"Yes." Cathal nodded firmly.

Damon scrubbed his hands down his face. "I was going to try and concentrate on what you were saying, but this will be unbearable, and I need something to do with my hands." He sat back down and picked his grater up. With this to do, he wouldn't feel like strangling Cathal. Hopefully.

And now he was thinking about the way Cathal had looked at him last night. Like he was being sincere.

No, no, that was the really annoying thing about him. One second, everything was fine, and he was saying you weren't worth the air you breathed, and then he'd turn on a dime and say something so nice you wanted to push him out of a window, *Game of Thrones*–style, so he couldn't do it again.

Case in point. "You think better with your hands busy anyway," Cathal said. "Era always said that." Damon's head snapped up, and his eyes narrowed, waiting for the punch line. But it wasn't there.

Not touching that with a ten-foot pole. Or a twenty-foot pole. Or any kind of pole. Damon didn't understand that expression.

Cathal tapped his lips. Then he pulled one of the Post-it notes off his paper, flipped it over so the sticky side was facing up, and wrote a single word on the back.

Despite himself, Damon peered across the table. "Obdurate? What the hell does that mean?"

"Stubborn, intransigent, obstinate," said Cathal, like those were simpler words.

Damon's first instinct was to ask if Cathal had eaten the dictionary, and, if so, how soon they'd have to take him to the hospital. But there was a more important question. "What does that have to do with anything?"

Cathal blinked, and his eyes came back into focus. "Nothing, really. But it's a good word." He said that like it was a sane sentence.

"So you wrote it down."

"So I wrote it down," said Cathal without changing his tone. "What I had there wasn't useful anyway. I need to stop making plans at three in the morning, but someone disrupted my sleep patterns."

Damon kept staring at him. "You were up at three a.m. doing this?"

Cathal glared at him. "Yes, I made a plan, because that's how I think. The idea of teaching someone else how to be a human being is a foreign language to me, because I have been told on several occasions that I'm not human. Therefore, I had to make sure my thoughts were in order, or we'd never get anywhere."

Damon couldn't suppress a snort.

Cathal leaned toward him, his voice a barely veiled threat. "You said you wanted to make progress. Hence.

Sticky notes. Highlighters. Synonyms. This is my process. It's gotten me my doctorate and tenure, and therefore, it's going to get you a fucking life."

Damon, as usual, was at a loss for words.

Cathal smiled brightly. "So. Shall we get started?"

"Yes." Cathal put on his lecture face, and Damon added, "But if this gets too weird, I'm pulling the plug. I don't know how much of this I can take."

"Limits are important. If I feel too much like beating my head against the table, I'm also pulling the plug." Cathal's mouth twitched, and then he grabbed another sticky note.

Damon glanced at it, saw the word "butt," and rolled his eyes. He reached for his next potato, realized he'd finished them, and scraped the hash browns off his cutting board into a bowl of cold water. Only when he finished did he notice Cathal was staring at him like his fly was unzipped. (He was wearing sweatpants, so he didn't have to look on reflex.) "What?"

"Are the potatoes dehydrated or something?" Cathal asked.

"They'll get brown if you leave them out in the air." Damon wasn't even defensive. He was too confused.

Cathal scrunched up his nose, looking almost upset at this information. "I didn't realize potatoes were so needy."

Damon looked at him for a long moment; Cathal's expression did not change. "I can never tell when you're serious and when you're fucking with me."

"We've already had this conversation. But I was serious." Cathal clucked. "Anyway. Not hardly the point. The main thing I came up with is where we need to start. Here, as I understand it, is your main problem. You and Era didn't do things together." Damon opened his mouth, but Cathal glared him down. "Let me clarify. Era did things. You tagged along."

Damon stopped spreading apples out on the table and frowned at them. "That's not true." He hated the uncertainty in his voice.

Cathal's face flattened. "Name one time in recent memory where you participated in a social event that wasn't a work function or initiated by Era. Or one of Felix's school things."

Damon didn't have to think very long about the question, since nothing came to mind.

"Precisely." At least Cathal didn't sound happy about it. Damon wasn't sure he *could* sound happy. Smug. Confident. Satisfied. But never simply...happy. Relaxed.

Damon shook that thought away. "Okay, fine, you're right. I didn't want to admit it."

"If it makes it any better, I only put it that way because Era always complained about it."

Damon closed his eyes tightly, though the sound of her name was only a pinch, not a stab. "You don't have to tell me that part. We fought about it—and don't say she didn't tell you about every single one of our fights, because I know she did. You were the only one she trusted with that stuff."

Cathal didn't say anything. Damon didn't want to see his expression. He knew this was hurting Cathal just as much, but he didn't want confirmation. Then Cathal said, "So what are the apples for?"

Damon glanced at the table. "Applesauce. It goes with the pancakes instead of syrup." He realized he was staring blankly at the apples and shook his head, though it didn't help. His head was always nothing but noise. "Stop changing the subject."

Cathal made an irritated noise. "I can't help it. I don't know anything about food, and everything you've been making is really weird, so it's distracting. I can't stand not having the answer to a question once I've thought of it."

Damon scowled. "Get to the point."

Cathal cleared his throat. From someone else, it might have been nervous, but in addition to happy, Cathal was never nervous. "Okay, fine. You need to figure out what you did before you met Era. You cooked, but there's got to be more to it than that."

Damon realized he had nothing to say.

He set the apple down slowly, so he wouldn't bruise it, and pressed the heel of his hand to his forehead. He wanted to turn around so he couldn't feel Cathal's eyes moving over his face, judging his every gesture, but his body was as frozen as his brain.

When he could speak, his voice shook, but he couldn't stop it. "That's the thing. Food makes me feel like myself instead of some—useless idiot. But I can't make anything—*anything*—without it reminding me of her."

He closed his eyes and breathed through his nose, trying not to cry. Crying was okay. It made him feel better most of the time—as better as he could feel. But he was not crying in front of Cathal. Not ever.

Then Cathal said, "You never made dessert."

Damon's eyes snapped open, and he reached for something awful to say.

Then he rewound what Cathal said. "I—what?"

Cathal pursed his lips, as always when someone asked him to repeat himself. "You never made dessert." At least he didn't say it slowly to rub it in. "You always bought it or someone else made it."

Damon stared helplessly at the apples. Then he laughed. It was hoarse and weak, but it was still a laugh. When was the last time he'd laughed?

He pushed his hand against his forehead again. Maybe if he hit himself hard enough, he'd snap out of his coma and he'd wake up in a world that made sense, where Era wasn't dead and Cathal wasn't spouting words of wisdom.

"The fuck of it is, you're right," he said, still staring at the apples. "They make you pick in culinary school, and I already knew how to cook, so I did that instead of pastry." He swallowed hard and waited for the urge to cry to overwhelm him again, but it didn't.

Damon took in a breath. "I hate it when you're right."

He hadn't meant to say it out loud, but Cathal didn't seem to mind.

He flicked his ponytail over his shoulder, as he did when someone complimented him and he couldn't be too smug. "You just hate admitting I'm always right."

Damon did hate it, but he wasn't upset. He'd glimpsed the edge and almost tipped over, and Cathal had pulled him back. Damon would have bet on him putting spikes at the bottom of the cliff, not yanking on his shirt to save him.

Fuck, maybe he was living in the wrong universe.

But none of that was relevant. Cathal was right.

Damon ran a hand over his hair. "I don't know where to start learning, though. I guess I could ask the pastry chef at Stephen's and see if she'd let me sit in or something..."

Cathal rolled his eyes. "YouTube is a thing, Damon. You can learn everything on there these days. I learned how to arm knit."

Damon put that aside, because whatever arm knitting was, it was not part of their conversation. This, at least, Cathal would understand. "I don't want to use the computer. Or my phone. They're...they're covered in things that remind me of Era, and I need to make sure I stay out of that hole. You're right. Era wouldn't want me to wallow in it. She'd want me to have a life."

"I can back everything up on her computer and wipe the drive for you, if you want." The offer was almost hesitant, and Damon looked over at Cathal to make sure he wasn't hearing wrong. But Cathal was avoiding his eyes, with a frown tugging at the side of his lips. He wasn't making fun, and he wasn't comfortable either.

Damon sighed. "Fine, do whatever you want. Telling you no only makes you do it more."

"See, we understand each other." Cathal jumped off the table.

"Hang on, you don't even know her password."

Cathal shot him a pitying look. "Bitch, I knew everything about that woman. Everything." And he left the room before Damon could demand to know what he was implying. Even though he had a pretty good guess.

CATHAL RETURNED A while later, his face studiously neutral in that way Damon was beginning to understand meant he was thinking about Era. He missed her, but he was shitty at admitting it. Not that Damon could blame him. Why go around telling everyone you had an open wound?

Damon sprinkled cinnamon on the apples, which were now boiling down in a large pot. Maybe if he pretended to be busy, Cathal would leave the computer alone, and Damon could noodle around with it in peace. He had to spend the first few minutes finding the right font and zoom that would make the characters stop moving around.

But, of course, Cathal set the netbook down and started it up. "Leave that be so I can show you."

Damon stabbed one of the apples that hadn't burst yet. "You do realize I'm younger than you, right? I know how to use a computer, but I don't like spending all my time looking at cats."

"That, more than anything else, is proof of your deep-rooted problems. And also more fuel for my hypothesis that you might be a time traveler from the 1940s. I'll find the cryogenic chamber eventually."

Damon pinched the bridge of his nose. "You're not going to leave me alone."

"Think of me like your AA sponsor. You need someone to hold you accountable, or you won't make positive change. In other words, if I don't watch you like a hawk, you won't do it."

Damon glared at him, but Cathal just swung his legs and smiled a disarmingly handsome smile.

No, no, that was the most annoying thing about Cathal. He was so goddamn good-looking sometimes. You couldn't bring yourself to smash his face against the table because his cheekbones were too perfect.

His eyes weren't bad either, for all they looked like liquid nitrogen.

Damon turned his attention to the computer. As Cathal had promised, everything was blank, and the only program still installed was Chrome. He opened YouTube and hesitated. "What should I search for?"

"Baking lessons?"

Damon tried it, ignoring the way Cathal snorted at his typing. Yes, he had to look at his hands, but that was because the letters on the screen never looked right. The ones on his keyboard didn't shift around.

Cathal glanced at what Damon had typed and made a face. "Oh, damn, hang on." He took the laptop before Damon could protest and looked something up. Then he passed it back.

Damon half expected Cathal to have pulled up porn. Or maybe a Rickroll. But he'd changed the font, and suddenly

Damon could read the text. Damon couldn't help but frown. "Is this a trick?"

Cathal let out a sigh, though it wasn't as annoyed as usual. Maybe he knew it was justified. "It's a Chrome extension to make it dyslexia-friendly. Felix's got the same thing. I promise, the laptop is not a bomb, and it will not explode."

Damon thought about glaring some more, but what was the point? Cathal had done something nice. This time, he found a series of videos featuring a pleasant blonde woman talking about baking techniques.

Cathal clapped him on the shoulder. "There you are. Go nuts." He walked out of the kitchen.

Damon glared at the blonde woman, but it was a front. He shut his eyes. "Cathal?"

"You rang, Jeeves?" Cathal paused in the door of the kitchen.

Damon didn't throw his laptop at Cathal, though it would have been satisfying. "Thanks."

Cathal stared at him, his brow furrowing as though he didn't know what to make of it either. "Sure. But don't go hacking alien technology or whatever the kids are doing these days. You know, since you're a whole two years younger than me."

"You'll be forty before me!" Damon yelled after him.

"I'm going to burn your house down!" Cathal yelled back.

Damon returned his attention to the laptop and realized he was smiling. When had that happened?

FELIX SEEMED DISTRACTED when he came home from school, but that just meant he wasn't singing. He wasn't upset. Or at least, he perked up when he saw Damon starting the first round of potato pancakes. "Ooh, brinner!"

"That's not a word." Damon frowned at the pancakes. Not that he was paying attention to them. The most important rule of pancakes: the first batch always came out like crap. Too bad they didn't have a dog.

Felix sat backward on one of the chairs. "It's on Urban Dictionary."

"How many times have I told you not to tell your father about things you learned on Urban Dictionary?" said Cathal. Damon looked up, unsure when Cathal had come in. "You'll confuse his poor dear heart."

Damon rolled his eyes, moving the pancakes off the heat to a plate. "I'm ignoring that, but only because I'm in the middle of something. Felix, get plates for us, then take this stack to the table."

Felix bounced over, though he frowned at the pancakes. "Oh, they've got potatoes in them."

"You say that like it's a disease." Damon bumped Felix with his elbow.

Felix blew a raspberry. Damon ignored him, so Felix did as he was told and went to the table. He picked four pancakes off the stack with his fingers.

Cathal made a disgusted noise. "Good God, I thought they sent you to a private school for a reason."

Felix blew another raspberry. "I have to act all formal and fancy at school. I don't want to do it at home."

"You are a trial."

"For once, I have to agree with him, son," said Damon, suppressing a smile. Again, he had no idea where it came from. "Bring that plate back. I need it."

Felix did, but then he tried to prop his head on Damon's shoulder, which didn't work—first, because Damon was six inches taller, and second, because Damon was using that shoulder.

Damon nudged him again. "You know how to make pancakes. Sit down and eat."

"Mahhhh," said Felix, but he went back to the table.

"Why so fidgety, Felix?" said Cathal, his voice innocent. "It's almost like you've got something you want to distract us from."

Felix narrowed his eyes, which was not intimidating, unless you thought kittens and other cute things were intimidating.

Damon rolled his eyes. "Yes, keep making fun of him. It's worked so well."

Cathal set his cheek on his hand. "Look at you, trying to be sarcastic. It's adorable. Like goats wearing pajamas."

Felix stared at the massive pile of applesauce on his pancakes and sighed. "Okay, okay. He still won't talk to me."

"Your ears are all red," said Cathal, his voice fond.

Felix hunched up his shoulders. "Cathal, you're mean."

"Dearest boy, I never pretended to be anything else. But I merely draw attention to your blush because it suggests to me that you're holding something back." Cathal gestured for Felix to continue. "To use the vernacular, spill."

"Well, he didn't look like he was going to die of embarrassment when I sat by him. That's good, right?"

Cathal rubbed his face, hiding a smile. "All successful romances do require that you don't kill your partner."

Damon shot him a look, warning him to back off, but Cathal deliberately did not acknowledge it. "Well, what did you talk to him about?"

"Not anything bad." Felix cut his pancakes into smaller and smaller pieces. "I told him about my classes and stuff. He's in a bunch of advanced things, so maybe he thought it was boring and didn't know how to say so."

"You could ask him to tutor you," Cathal suggested. "You've got study hall together, and heaven knows you need help with math."

Damon and Felix both turned to stare at him.

Cathal did not notice. He'd divided his pancake into threes. One part was already covered in applesauce, and he was spreading sour cream on the other. The third he left blank.

Damon told himself he didn't want to ask why.

Then Cathal looked up. Apparently, he'd been truly unaware they were watching him, not pretending for effect. "What?"

Felix wrinkled his nose. "Yeah, that's romantic. I've heard so many songs about how math is the language of love."

"First of all, math and science are sexy. Second, tutoring is a time-tested strategy. It worked for me, and it's part of how your mom and dad got together, isn't it?" Cathal gestured at Damon with his fork. Damon raised his eyebrows, daring Cathal to continue.

Felix looked at Damon, scrunching his face up even further. "But you didn't go to normal person school, Dad. You've got a culinary degree."

Damon made a face that was probably similar to Felix's. He'd never told Felix that story for a reason. And also, he'd assumed Era had talked to him about it. She was fond of turning her experiences into teachable moments. "I tried college for a semester. I didn't know what else to do with myself, so I thought it'd be a good idea. But I sucked. I only passed English 101 because Era helped me."

He had to close his eyes, but that wasn't bad. She'd looked so good in college. Her hair was cut short then so she wouldn't have to pull it back for waitressing. Funny what stuck.

Damon could feel Cathal staring at him, and he didn't like it. Felix, for his part, looked curious. Unlike most kids, he liked hearing stories about his parents. "She helped me fix up my essays. She pretended I was doing a good job, but I could tell they made her want to puke."

"To be fair, it wasn't entirely your fault," said Cathal, which was not the comment Damon had expected. But Cathal always remembered he was dyslexic, even though before Era got sick, they'd go weeks without seeing him. Maybe because Felix had inherited it.

"It wasn't that. I'm a terrible writer, even without the brain fog, and don't pretend like I'm not. But she helped me anyway. I couldn't believe it when I got a B-plus on the final even though I'd already decided I wasn't coming back to school." He frowned at the table. He'd nearly forgotten that part of it. Or had suppressed it. At the time, he thought it was the closest he'd ever come to losing the best part of his life. "She was pissed at me. Said I needed an education. She put us on a break, but then she didn't dump me. I never found out why."

"Because I told her it was a stupid idea." He sounded like he was stating gravity made things fall, the same way he'd told Damon that Era loved him.

"You spoke up for me?" said Damon, his lips numb.

"You didn't know that?" Damon shook his head without feeling it, and Cathal scowled. "For once, I wasn't trying to throw a wrench in the works." He flicked hair out of his eyes. "She was all incensed, but I told her it was stupid. Academics were distracting you from food. She just didn't know how to tell her dad she wasn't dating a student, and I told her that was a dumb reason to dump the best guy she'd ever met."

Damon stared at Cathal, feeling like he'd never seen him before. Cathal ignored him, digging into the sour cream triangle of his pancake and eating as thoughtfully as a man studying a language handbook in a foreign country.

"Huh," said Felix, and Damon startled. He'd forgotten his son was the only reason they were discussing this at all. He still couldn't wrap his head around the idea that Cathal had saved his relationship. *Cathal*, who wouldn't piss on him if he were on fire.

Except...that wasn't true anymore.

"I wish you would've told me that, Dad," said Felix. "I like stories."

Damon tried to focus on the present moment. Emphasis on *tried*. Part of him was back on the lawn in front of the student center, his fingers running through Era's pixie cut as she looked over his work, but most of him was still reeling at the idea that Cathal had ever done anything to help him. "It was embarrassing. Yeah, I went to culinary school, but that was a couple years later. At the time, it felt like a failure."

"It was a judicious decision based on your strengths and weaknesses." Cathal had taken another pancake and was spreading applesauce on this one. Apparently that was the winner. "Some people require a broad base of knowledge to draw on in order to ascertain their true passion. Others know from the start and don't need a bunch of bullshit cluttering the way. I see too many kids who should be going to technical school wasting their time with a four-year degree because that's what society expects, not what's good for them."

Damon wanted to think this night couldn't get weirder. But Cathal could start tap dancing on the table or something.

Felix stroked his chin, digesting all of this with a thoughtful expression. Damon hoped he wasn't going to ask any more deep questions. His head hurt enough.

Then Felix brightened. "So what you're both saying is that if I wanted to skip college to focus on the LGBT Whatevers, you'd totally support that, right?"

"No," said Damon and Cathal at the same time. Damon was glad he was out of surprise for the night, because they kept doing that, and it was weird.

Cathal set his knife and fork down and held up two fingers. "First of all, that is a terrible band name, and I will continue to say so until the end of time, no matter how successful you get. Second, you're going to college. You are very talented and don't need a backup plan for your music, but college allows you to make connections, which get you record deals or concert placements or what the fuck ever you decide to do with your life in the end. That way, you do well in the business instead of flaming out like everyone else who makes a go of it straight out of high school. You will not become a cautionary tale on my watch, young man."

Felix whined. "You are so totally not my fun uncle."

"I so totally am, and you'll realize that once you stop being cranky."

Damon picked at his food. He felt strange, and he didn't know why—well, he did, but it was more than simply spending time around Cathal without tearing each other apart. He needed to say something, but he sucked at talking.

So he settled for smiling at Cathal and saying, "I should keep you around. I don't have to do any work."

Cathal stuck his nose in the air. "I am the funnest uncle. That doesn't mean I'm not also the pragmatic uncle." He smirked at Damon. "And I'm way better at giving speeches than you, and that situation warranted a speech. Hence."

Felix propped his chin on the table. "Can I be excused? I wanna go up to my room and play Twenty One Pilots really loud."

"Why do you need permission to play Twenty One Pilots?" Damon asked.

"Because he's trying to annoy us," Cathal said, smirking around his fork. "It's his version of slamming his door and listening to Nirvana. Or whatever the kids did while I was listening to George Michael."

Felix wrinkled his nose. "Why were you listening to George Michael? I know the eighties were weird and all, but, like, the Talking Heads were on the radio."

"Because he's queerer than a two dollar bill, Felix, and at the time, I was still trying to figure that out. Unlike you, I didn't have binders full of out performers to pick from."

Felix frowned, but then he perked up again. "Well, obviously, I need to focus on my band so future generations never have to worry about role models!"

"Role models finish school," said Damon before Cathal could come up with something.

Cathal glanced at him. "You do realize you deprived me of a chance to make another speech?"

"That's why I said it," Damon replied.

DAMON HAD FORGOTTEN how nice getting buzzed and watching contestants trash each other was. Era didn't like TV, so he'd only gotten to do this when she was teaching a night class or out for the evening. He'd take missing food shows in a heartbeat over what had happened, but he was trying to look at the bright side, like she'd told him to.

He wasn't sure why he was coming around to the idea that there was brightness left in the world, but he was trying his best. Putting away his photographs had been the right choice. Now he could see his house instead of his past.

And then, of course, right as he was starting to become one with his couch, he noticed Cathal lurking in the hallway. Damon couldn't decide if he was annoyed. "I know you're there. Come in or don't, but stop being creepy."

Cathal came in, his eyes narrowed. "Food Network again?"

Damon shrugged, keeping his eyes on the TV since Cathal was looking around the room like there were hidden messages written somewhere. "It's what I've got recorded. If you don't like it, you can go upstairs and write some angry sticky notes."

"Just for that, I'm sitting down." He settled on the far cushion of the couch. Damon passed him a beer in the hopes of keeping him quiet. To his surprise, it worked. Or, at least, Cathal didn't say anything right away.

Which was nice, because Damon wanted to watch this one. The contestants were making cake models of famous landmarks, and the techniques on display were really interesting. He'd never watched dessert competitions much—new techniques or flavor combinations were more useful. Now...well, he had to find something to do with himself. Might as well start with this.

"Okay, this is a cake thing, I get that." Of *course* Cathal couldn't keep his mouth shut. That would've been too easy. "So why are they adding Rice Krispies?"

Damon growled around his beer. "Why are you pretending to care?"

Cathal looked offended—and not fake offended for effect. "I'm not a cook, but I can't afford to step around such an obvious hole in my knowledge. What if I go on *Jeopardy* someday and a question about weird food practices come up? I can't win if I don't know the answer."

And, of course, Cathal said this all deadpan, so Damon had no idea if he was joking. He let out a loud sigh. "The Rice Krispies add height without adding weight. Like, look at that guy at the end." He pointed at the fourth table, featuring a model of Buckingham Palace. "That's all cake, which means it weighs at least eighty pounds. Probably more with all the decorations and the baseboard." He pointed at the Rice Krispies team, who were working on the Tower of London. "That one will be lighter by a good twenty pounds, and it'll be more stable since it's not so top-heavy."

Cathal's frown deepened. "It's cake, not the Leaning Tower of Pisa."

"It'll fall apart if you didn't balance it right. I've seen it happen to wedding cakes when we catered dinners sometimes. It's awful."

Cathal narrowed his eyes. Damon waited for something nasty, but then Cathal just said, "Food is a lot weirder than I thought," and took a long drink of his beer.

THANKFULLY, CATHAL WENT to bed soon after, so Damon could enjoy the silence.

Only not really. They'd watched two more episodes, and Cathal hadn't spoken except to ask honest, interested questions. He'd received all of Damon's answers with grave, thoughtful expressions and occasional follow-ups. Not a single tart word, except when Damon had given him a weird look for...well, for not being weird.

It was enough to make Damon's head hurt and definitely enough to keep him from enjoying his buzz. If Cathal seemed like less of a jerk by the day, then Damon had to be drinking too much. He didn't like it, and he didn't want to think about it, but he couldn't stop.

In the end, he poured his beer down the drain and went to bed earlier than usual. Well, earlier for these days. He used to go to bed around ten. Maybe he could get back in that habit now that he had Cathal's weird behavior to obsess over instead of everything *really* wrong with his life.

Five: Felix Smashes the Patriarchy.

Sort of.

THE NEXT DAY, Damon decided to make an entire cake from scratch. He had all the ingredients, but he'd been putting off getting started, even though Felix would eat anything if you put enough frosting on it, and Cathal... Well, Damon had been waiting for a sharp comment about taking up baking, but it didn't seem to be on the way, and he needed to get used to it. And also to the idea that no one would criticize him for going outside the box. He'd liked working at Stephen's, but everyone in a kitchen had a defined role. The executive chef pretended he was willing to wash dishes, but everyone knew that wasn't true, and that if he ever had to, there'd be hell to pay. And you definitely didn't cross the pastry and culinary streams.

That was a gross image. He'd been spending too much time with Cathal.

Speaking of whom, Cathal came downstairs later than usual, after Felix was already at school and Damon was finished with the batter. Cathal inspected all the bowls like a cat sniffing brand-new litter, but he didn't say anything, just stole two of the apple cinnamon muffins Damon had left out for him and went back upstairs to shout at his computer.

Damon didn't want to admit he felt better after that, but he did.

DAMON HAD HOPED Cathal would stay in his room until he heard Felix return from school, but of course Cathal was early. Damon focused very hard on cubing the potatoes for boiling. He told himself he did *not* care what Cathal thought and that the cake was only a way to distract himself until he felt normal again.

Then he almost cut one of his fingers off, and he had to admit he was nervous.

Finally, after inspecting the cake from all angles, Cathal said, "This has flowers on it. And pretty blue icing."

"You know I'm not color-blind, right?" Damon dropped the potatoes in the water and splashed his face like always. Thankfully, Cathal didn't notice.

Cathal put his hands on his hips. "It's fancy."

Damon shrugged, avoiding his eyes. "One of those videos was about making flowers from gum paste. I thought I would try it. I like sculpting, I guess."

Cathal was still staring at him, his expression inscrutable, when Felix came bouncing into the kitchen. He jumped up on the counter. "Ooh, cake!"

"It's for after supper." Damon turned his attention to the dishes in the sink. He'd started doing them by hand because it helped him think and wasted time, but now he had more things to do, so he was only keeping it up to see if and when Cathal would say something. Hopefully not yet, since he had yet to think of a good retort if Cathal pointed out that the dishwasher existed for a reason.

He'd say it that way too, that bastard.

"Mahhhh," said Felix, swinging his legs.

"Please get off the counter before you knock it over," said Damon without looking in his son's direction. He knew without checking that Felix was looking at the flowers and considering which one to steal.

Felix and Cathal both sat down. "You seem happy about something, Felix," said Cathal. Someday, Damon would ask him how he managed to sound insufferable so subtly. Just enough that you knew he was being a shit, but not enough so you could punch him in the face.

Not that Damon had felt like punching Cathal lately. Maybe *that* was the worst thing about Cathal. Sometimes he was nice, and then you felt bad for being mad at him, even though he deserved it.

Thankfully, Felix provided a distraction. "It worked!"

"You don't say," said Cathal, not bothering to disguise his smirk now.

Damon turned to watch since he wanted to hear his son talk about this.

Felix was beaming. "I brought my physics book with me, and I sat next to him and was, like, 'I don't get any of this stuff,' and he didn't answer me, and I thought he wasn't going to say anything, but then he took my book and he was, like, 'You're going to have to be more specific if you need help.'" Felix paused, his expression falling. "I mean, he still didn't look me in the eye. But he talked to me! And now I get vectors, so that's cool."

Cathal leaned back in his chair like a cat in a sunbeam, his lips twitching. "Multitasking. I approve."

Damon crossed his arms. Not that he wanted to burst Felix's bubble, but if he had learned anything, it was not to let bad things hide. "What about the boy who was rude to you? His brother?"

Felix deflated. "He's still a jerk. He sat there making snarky comments the whole time." Felix perked up. "But then Morgan turned to him and said, 'If you're not going to be helpful, you can leave,' and Gareth shut up! He went all red and spluttered and everything." Felix rubbed his nose, his eyes narrowing in thought. "He apologized to me after school. I dunno what that means."

Cathal made a face. "His brother probably strong-armed him into it. Pay no mind. Apologies are for the weak."

Damon's attention snapped to Cathal. "Apologies are important." He glanced at Felix to make sure his son was listening too.

Felix screwed up his face. "But you're always saying actions are louder than words."

"Yes, but it's hard to say you were wrong." Damon turned back to the dishes to hide his expression, since he wasn't sure what he looked like. "Even if you make up for what you did, the other person might never know that you feel bad about it. If he apologized, that means he thought about what he said and realized it was important enough to make up for it."

"Or his brother hit him." Cathal's voice was innocent. Damon couldn't tell if he was doing it on purpose. "That's how Era got me to apologize."

Damon glanced over his shoulder, glaring at Cathal. "That's because you're... What did she always call you?"

"A reprobate? Ne'er-do-well? Hooligan?" Felix suggested, leaning back in his chair.

"Don't help him!" Cathal yelped. "Whose side are you on, young man?"

"Obviously Dad's, since he made cake," Felix replied, trying and failing to look smug.

Cathal thought for a moment. "I want to argue with that, but you are right. I concede."

The timer on the oven went off. Damon nodded at it, trying not to think about the entire conversation. "There's a roast in the oven, Felix. Would you get it out, please?"

"I could have done that," said Cathal.

"Don't be stupid." Damon finished the dish he was working on and set it on the rack. "I'm not wasting the rest of my evening in the emergency room while they treat you for third-degree burns."

Cathal huffed as Felix got the roast out and set it on the stove. Damon ignored him, wiping off his hands so he could check the roast's temperature. As he did so, Cathal said, "That looks almost normal, Damon." This time he was definitely putting on the innocent act.

Damon glared at the roast, even though the thermometer read 160. "It's just beef roast. Had some in the freezer that was gonna go off."

Felix looked at the roast and smacked his lips.

"It has to rest. You know that." Damon pointed at the table. "Sit like a person while I make the potatoes and gravy."

Felix whined, but it was only for show. He plopped next to Cathal and let out a theatrical sigh. "You know, I do have other things in my life besides this guy that I like."

"Oh, really? I never would have dreamed. Do tell."

Another question: how did Cathal make his voice so dry? He sounded like a mummy.

Felix made an irritated noise. "There's gonna be a school play, and I'm trying out, *okay*? Why can't you ask a question like a normal person?"

Damon laughed, despite himself. "That's what I've been asking for the past sixteen years." Damon found the masher and started in on the potatoes, holding the bowl in one hand so he could watch Felix again.

Cathal stared at him. "What in God's name is that torture device?"

Even Felix looked confused at that. "It's a potato masher, Cathal." He paused, wrinkling his nose. "But why aren't you using the electric mixer, Dad? It's not like you need the workout."

Damon shrugged. "I used it for the cake." Actually, he'd used all his whisks and both the stand and hand mixers, but they didn't need to know that. He'd cleaned up the mess. "What play, Felix?"

"*Midsummer Night's Dream.*" Felix drummed his foot against the table leg, avoiding Damon's eyes. "I thought...I thought it would be good. Because of Mom and stuff." He glanced at Damon and away, worrying his lower lip.

Damon put a smile on his face, though he wasn't sure how he felt. He was glad Felix was doing the play, and that it reminded him of his mother. As for the rest of it...well, who knew. Damon put the potatoes on the table so he could pat Felix's shoulder.

"The only shame is Era will never get to see you prance around in tights." Cathal sighed like a man in a rom-com seeing his love interest for the first time.

Felix made a face, and Damon relaxed. He still wasn't sure what he would do if Felix needed help with his grief. "It's a modern-day production. No weird costumes. And the director said she's gonna cast people regardless of sex."

Cathal let out another lovestruck sigh. "It's good to know my tax money is funding the liberal decline of America."

Felix looked at him blankly. "I go to a private school, Cathal."

Damon went back to the stove and drained the meat juice from the pan so he could start the gravy before the potatoes got cold. "What part do you want?"

"I dunno," said Felix, rocking back and forth in his chair. "I kinda want to try out for a girl's part to prove how liberated from masculine norms I am."

Damon's mouth twitched. "Your mother taught you to say that."

"Just like that! I wanna make her proud, and that involves leveraging my white male privilege to dismantle the white cisheteropatriarchy, brick by brick." Felix sighed and set his cheek on his hand. "Now if only I could find something that rhymes with that, I'd have a good song."

"Well, I for one welcome our drag space future," said Cathal, smirking. "You've got the legs for it, Felix. I know plenty of queens who would kill for them."

Felix put his hands behind his head and balanced on the back legs of his chair. "I've gotta think about it."

Cathal pointed at him. "One of these days you're going to kill yourself doing that, and I will do nothing but laugh."

Damon clunked the gravy boat on the table with more emphasis than necessary. Felix meekly straightened up so all four chair legs sat on the floor. "Thank you," said Damon. "Don't skip the vegetables, Cathal. They're good for you."

DAMON DIDN'T EAT much. His mouth was dry when he removed the dinner items from the table and put the cake in their place.

Felix bounced in his seat, though he did not tip his chair back for once. "What is ittttt?"

"Chocolate." Damon set the knife on top of the cake to cut it, but Cathal darted in and stole one of the flowers. Damon glared at him. "The flowers don't taste like much. It's sugar and gelatin."

Cathal shrugged, smiling in that way that made Damon want to smother him, and set the flower on the corner of his plate. Damon rolled his eyes and sliced the cake, giving Felix the largest piece even though he would have at least two. He served himself last and sat down slowly. He'd never made a cake from scratch before, so he'd made a small test cake based on the original recipe and adjusted the amounts because it had a weird texture.

He took a bite. The texture was good, but something was off.

"Why the look, Dad?" Felix's piece had already disappeared, and he was eyeing the rest of the cake.

"One piece only," said Damon automatically, tapping his fork against his plate. "And I think I added too much baking soda. There's a metallic aftertaste."

"I think you're wrong, but that's not news." To Damon's surprise, Cathal'd also already finished his piece. "The cake is good. Obviously."

"The only time you've eaten cake that didn't come out of a box was at my wedding." Damon took another bite. "It's all right for a first try."

"That's better," said Cathal. Felix whined. "And I'm overruling the one-piece law, or else it'll never get eaten."

"You *are* the fun uncle!"

FELIX INHALED HIS second piece of cake. To Damon's surprise, he didn't even pretend he wanted another. "Hey, Dad, do you know where Mom's college textbooks are?"

Damon squared his shoulders, but again...it didn't bother him. "They're in the attic somewhere. All the boxes are labeled."

"Thanks!" Felix gave Damon a hug from behind and bounced out of the room.

Cathal was finishing his second piece of cake, wearing a thoughtful expression. Damon did not like it, so he got up and started washing the dishes. The roast pan was disgusting, and he started with that, glad for something he could attack.

"That was normal food," said Cathal. "That you used to make all the time."

Damon scrubbed harder at the stain. "Yes."

"It seems you've made some progress, then?" It wasn't a question. That tone of voice meant he was irritated at having to ask out loud at all.

But Damon wasn't going to do all his work for him. If Cathal wanted to talk about things instead of ignoring them, then he could start it.

Except...it was a good question. Damon let the pan fall into the soapy water so he could rub his forehead, ignoring the suds on his fingers.

"I don't know." He wished the question would end there, but Cathal would keep pressing, and...for once, Damon didn't think yelling at Cathal would make him feel better. They'd been getting along well, and it was...not nice, but as nice as anything could be right now. The last thing he needed was the reinstatement of hostilities or however the fuck Cathal would put it. "I guess I put so much effort into making the cake that there wasn't much of me left over to make something fancy. Roasts are easy. And there really was one left in the freezer."

Cathal nodded smugly. "Thank you. Now was that so hard?"

Damon flicked soapy water in his direction. Cathal hissed and left the room, nothing but crumbs on his plate.

DAMON TOLD HIMSELF he didn't care when Cathal came into the living room later that evening, but he still ended up looking over his shoulder, wondering if he would show up.

And he'd watched a different show, because Cathal was invested in the one they'd been watching together, and he'd bitch if he knew Damon watched ahead. Maybe. They'd never done something so normal together.

Cathal flopped on the far end of the couch. "Am I interrupting?" he asked, eyeing the basketball game Damon was half watching.

Damon paused the game. "Like I care about sports. I only watched so I could bet in the March Madness pool at work."

Cathal squinted. "I'm going to assume for the sake of conversation that that is a real thing people do and not something you're making up to confuse me. I'm not gullible, you know."

Damon thought he was joking, but it was impossible to be sure. Instead, he changed to the food competition. Cathal's expression brightened. "Oh, good, you didn't skip ahead. That's almost sweet of you."

Damon rolled his eyes.

This was a special chocolate competition, so the camera was focused on one of the contestants conching.

Cathal spread his hands, sounding almost despairing. "Why are they pouring chocolate on a table? Is the table hungry?"

"It adds air to the chocolate." He thought about adding more detail, but he wanted to hear what else Cathal would say.

Cathal's mouth twisted to the side. "Why does the chocolate need air?" he said after a long pause that suggested he'd tried to figure the answer out himself.

"That way it melts in your mouth." Damon leaned forward on his knees.

Cathal fell back against the couch. "You know, even string theory makes sense compared to this."

Damon smirked and passed him a beer, which Cathal took without comment.

Felix came down the stairs. He stopped in the doorway of the living room, looking surprised. Then he took a running leap at the middle cushion of the couch. Damon and Cathal moved apart to make room, and Damon paused the TV since neither of them would be able to see it while Felix twisted around to get comfortable. Felix was holding a leather-bound copy of *Midsummer Night's Dream*. Era's father had given her a whole set, which she had pored over through four years of undergrad and four more years for her doctorate. The whole thing was marked up in her loopy handwriting.

"She hated that play, you know," said Damon, deliberately putting himself back in those moments—watching her push the hair out of her face as she read, her eyes narrowing when she got to a part she didn't agree with. She'd rant to him for hours without realizing it went over his head. But he was okay with being a sounding board. He'd never been smart enough to understand her classes, but this way, he got to be a part of it.

It was...almost good. He hadn't let himself think of anything nice about Era since the moment she got sick. Not that he'd forgotten anything, but...he'd put it away, as she'd packaged up all her things, neatly labeled so they could be found again when needed.

Felix stuck his tongue between his teeth. "I know. But that's why I wanna do it. She didn't mark up the ones she liked near as much, so I can take her ideas and do something cool. And then I sound smart and maybe Morgan won't think I'm a dumbass."

Cathal coughed to cover a laugh, and Damon glared at him over the top of Felix's head. But Cathal just grinned at him like he could never do anything wrong, ever. Too bad Felix was there as a buffer, or Damon would have pushed Cathal off the couch. *Someday.*

Felix held the book close to his face, then farther away. "Ugghhhh. Cathal, what does that say?" He pointed at one of his mother's notes. Damon had never been able to read her handwriting either. Like everything else about her, it was elegant and tidy, but it did not agree with dyslexia.

At least Cathal had to squint to decipher it, too. "Oh, I see. 'This is where the tragedy begins,' and it's underlined about three thousand times." His mouth twitched, though his eyes were far away. "She never did meet a word she didn't like to underline."

"At least she didn't highlight everything." Damon glanced sideways at Cathal.

"Oh, fuck you," Cathal said, but not in a mean way. Annoying that he could do that, but not high up on the list, all things considered. "Who do you think kept buying me rainbow packs for my birthday, hmm?"

"Shhh." Felix scrutinized the page. Then he snapped the book shut. "Yeah, I think I wanna be Titania."

Cathal furrowed his brow. "Why Titania? She spends the entire play getting humiliated."

"Well, Mom has all these notes about how she should be interpreted as a tragic figure and how this is, like, the most depressing comedy ever written and the fluff is disguising Shakespeare's complete despair at the way society treats women. Or something like that. I have to read it some more to get it. But I think that would be fun." Felix lifted his head. "And I'd look good in a dress."

This was the second time he'd mentioned wearing dresses. Damon was not involved in the queer community, but he did do his best to stay informed since he was raising a son who had run down the rainbow and never looked back. "You know, Felix—"

Felix rolled his eyes. "Yes, Dad, I promise if I ever have *feelings* about my gender, I'll tell you. But I don't. I just think dresses are pretty. And all the guys are kind of jerks." He paused and added in a quieter voice, "Anyway, I think Mom would have liked it. She'd laugh."

None of them spoke. Damon, for his part, was thinking how much Era would have laughed.

Then Cathal said, "You know, Felix, your father has a point," and Damon was not sure if he was joking.

Felix jumped to his feet. "Oh my *God*. I have to go learn my lines now." He stomped out of the room, though it was hard to tell if he was upset. He never walked quietly.

Cathal let out a fond sigh. "It's almost like this is turning him into a normal teenager."

Six: Damon Looks at Everyone like They Are Several Squirrels Hiding inside a Trench Coat.

EVERYTHING WAS PROGRESSING well except Cathal's work, so he decided he needed to get away from distractions. After Felix left for school, Cathal peeked in the kitchen. Damon was cracking and separating eggs, his tongue between his teeth. "I'm making macarons," he said.

"Did I ask?"

Damon ignored that.

Cathal made a face, only because Damon wasn't looking. "I'm going to the library to work. Try not to kill yourself while I'm gone."

Damon's mouth twitched. "If I did that, I'd never figure out how to make these. It'll be good to spend the day without you muttering up there."

Cathal stuck his tongue out, only because he did talk while he was working.

He went out to the hallway to grab his coat.

Then he went back to the kitchen. "What are macarons?"

"You'll find out, won't you?"

MACARONS, AS IT turned out, were French cookies, and they were tasty, and Cathal ate three—all lovely pastel colors—while waiting for Felix to get home. Dinner was leftover roast, because Damon had spent the whole day making macarons. Piles of them. Enough that Cathal might have been compelled to call the authorities, except that he wanted to eat them.

Damon glanced at the oven clock. "He's late. You think I ought to call him?"

"It's only been a half hour. He's probably chatting with his friends. You know how he is when he starts talking music."

Fifteen minutes later, Cathal was about to suggest that Damon should call Felix when the boy came in the front door, looking crazed. He fell into the empty chair at the kitchen table, staring at the floor.

"I did something really stupid," he said, not blinking.

"You didn't pick a fight or something, did you?" Damon nudged the plate of macarons at Felix.

Felix only glanced at them before returning his eyes to the floor. "No. But I was telling the triplets minus one about my awesome Queen Titania idea, and they thought it was great, and then I was telling them about Morgan, and then I got to study hall and somehow I ended up asking Morgan if he was going to audition for the play, and he said yes, and I told him he should try out for Oberon, and he said he'd take it into consideration." All of this came out in one breath. Felix gasped and added one final thing: "And then he looked at me and he has the prettiest eyes ever and I am doomed."

"Sometimes I wonder why you act so silly, but then you make speeches like this and I worry how much oxygen is getting to your brain," said Cathal.

Damon made an irritated noise. "What Cathal is trying to say, Felix, is that you made a good first step today, and we're proud of you."

"I am not." Cathal took another macaron. When had they turned into *we*? This was not okay. "He's ridiculous."

Felix squinted at the plate as though seeing it for the first time. "What are those?"

"Macarons," said Damon, at the same time Cathal said, "Don't change the subject."

They kept talking at the same time, almost like they were thinking the same things. But that could not be true. Damon made no sense.

Felix picked one up and peered at it, his countenance lifting. "These look good, Dad."

Damon sighed. "We're never going to get anywhere in this conversation, are we?"

"It depends on what you mean by 'getting somewhere,'" said Cathal.

"These are good, Dad!" said Felix around a mouthful of pink meringue.

"Don't talk with your mouth full," Damon and Cathal said in unison.

"You guys have got to stop doing that," said Felix. "It's creepy."

"You're not the one living it." Damon shook his head.

"That being said," said Cathal, "Damon was right." Damon made a noise suspiciously like a muffled laugh, which Cathal did not deign to acknowledge. "You're closer to being his friend, if nothing else. You went out of your comfort zone, and that is always good."

Felix bit his thumbnail. "You know, you guys are right. I was freaking out there, but I wouldn't have thought twice about it if he was some random guy and I didn't like him. Maybe that's how I should do it."

"It's exactly how you should do it," said Damon.

"Says the man who's never caught a man," Cathal said, looking at him askance. "Take it from someone who knows, Felix. You need to be clear about what you want, because if he's as shy as you say, he won't pick up on any hints subtler than 'I want to kiss you. Please let me.' And if he's straight, he won't pick up on it even if you say, 'I want to kiss you. Please let me.'"

Felix turned red. "I don't want to kiss him. I want to stare at him until he bursts into flame. Which, I mean, that might actually happen." He sighed. "Can I have another macaron?"

"No," said Damon. "Not until you eat some actual food. You too." That was directed at Cathal. "You didn't eat breakfast."

Cathal opened his mouth to object. Then he realized Damon was right. Instead of admitting this, he had another macaron. Because he was an *adult*.

SOMEHOW, CATHAL HAD gotten sucked into watching a progressive tournament where competitors battled each other for the right to take on their fellow winners in the final episode. It involved chocolate and cake and other things Cathal did not know could be used in food. Instead of questioning this impulse, he came downstairs with the day's purchase.

Damon eyed the six-pack dubiously. "Fancy beer?"

"Yes." Cathal flopped back on the couch. "We're expanding your horizons, aren't we?"

Damon huffed and picked up one of the bottles. "I guess I can see if it would be good to cook with. Is Felix coming down?"

"I don't think so. When I went past his room, he was shouting about Theseus's wedding." Cathal passed his beer to Damon, since Damon was better at getting the tops off.

Damon nodded, taking a sip of his own beer as he passed Cathal's back to him. "It's not bad, I guess."

"It's *cultured*," said Cathal, relishing it.

"You really are the smuggest man I've ever met."

"I'm taking that as a compliment."

Damon narrowed his eyes. "I've been thinking about what you said earlier."

"You're going to have to be more specific. I talk a lot."

"You do, and it's annoying." Damon waved away Cathal's words. "I meant the part where you were talking about how I've never—done anything with a man."

Cathal blinked. He'd forgotten that comment.

Damon studied him. Cathal didn't react. He wasn't sure what Damon thought, or why he was looking at Cathal so intently, or why the comment gave Cathal such pause. It was the truth, and the truth set you free. By letting you be really smug.

Damon let out a slow breath. "It's not that I want to run out and start dating men. But—it's a part of me that got left by the wayside when I met her. And we did...talk about it. She didn't want me to be alone."

That made more sense. "Well, it's another thing to think about when the time is right. No need to rush."

Damon closed his eyes, his voice thick. "I think that's the hardest thing to come to grips with. I do have time. I never—I never thought she'd go first."

Cathal closed his eyes and took in a slow breath. He'd always thought the same. Damon didn't have unhealthy habits, but he didn't take care of himself, either. Era was a stickler for health, like the Oxford comma. "It's not all bad."

Actually, without Era, it pretty much was, but he forced himself to put a positive spin on things, since that's what she would have done. After smacking him. "I mean, who'd ever have thought we'd be sitting here like this? Not clawing each other apart or anything. And I think I've only insulted you, like, once."

Damon looked at him, his expression unreadable. "Who'd have thought." He said it softly, but turned away before Cathal could figure out his tone of voice.

FELIX WAS HOME late from school again, but that was to be expected. Today was his audition. Damon had made another cake. This one was frosted, not coated in fondant, and shaded from white to blue in a smooth gradient. On top was a single sugar rose.

Cathal squinted at it.

"It's called ombré, apparently," said Damon, too casually. "I thought we ought to have something nice, and someone managed to sneak the rest of the other cake when I wasn't paying attention."

"You've really got to hide your food better," said Cathal. "Felix knows where to look. And he can climb like a monkey."

Damon sighed. "It's not like it's going to make him crazy. He acts that way even without sugar and caffeine."

They both looked toward the front door as they heard it open. Felix walked into the kitchen—strutted, actually—and only glanced at the cake before sitting down.

"Don't be smug, boy," said Cathal, pulling himself up on the counter next to the cake. He was still surprised Damon had produced anything so nice, and he wanted to admire it some more without looking like he was admiring it. Tricky, but within his skill level. "It's vulgar."

Felix tried to shoot him a dirty look, but he was too pleased with himself. "You're the one who's always telling me it's not vanity if you've accomplished something."

"Why is it you can remember my words so well when you're trying to shut me up and not when I've helped you with your homework?" Cathal asked of the ceiling, spreading his hands.

Felix stuck out his tongue.

"Between the two of you, we're never going to get anywhere ever again. Out with it, mister, how was it?" Despite Damon's gruff tone, his eyes were excited.

Felix started bouncing in his seat. "I think it went really well, actually. I mean, a bunch of girls tried out for Titania, but the director said she really liked the way I took it." He paused. "I tried out for Puck, too, for giggles, but I'm pretty sure Alex is gonna get that. He went to town with it."

"And your violinist?" Cathal asked, arching a brow.

Felix blushed. "Morgan's not *my* anything. And he tried out for all the male leads. He was really good at all of them, too. Mom would have loved it." He paused, making a face like he was sucking on a lemon. "Gareth tried out for all the boys' parts, too. He wasn't bad. I hope he gets Theseus or something, so I don't have to be on stage with him."

"So when will you find out who's what?" Damon asked.

"The parts will be posted after school on Monday. Oh, yeah, and I'm supposed to give you my school newsletter and junk." He dug around in his bag and came out with a crumpled sheet of legal-sized paper.

Cathal sighed. "It is truly best that your gifts do not lay in academia, my boy."

Damon smoothed it out, ignoring Cathal's comments. "Never mind that now. I've made tacos."

"Tacos!" Felix cried. "This is the best day ever!"

UNLIKE EVERY PARENT in the history of ever, Damon read the newsletter. He was peering at it when Cathal came down to the living room, not even pretending he didn't want to.

"They're looking for parent volunteers to help with the show," Damon said with no preamble.

Cathal looked over his shoulder at the note in question. "I thought they usually have students do all that. To help them learn."

"There was some kind of mess last year. They want adults to run the lights so they don't have to worry about the equipment." Damon set the newsletter on his lap, still frowning as he smoothed out another crease.

Cathal looked from the newsletter to Damon's face. "Is there a reason you're bringing this up...?"

"Yes. I'm going to do it. When I was working, I never had time to go to Felix's recitals. But I'm not going back any time soon, so I might as well make up for that now." He bit his lip. "Except—I'm shit at this kind of thing. Talking to people."

Cathal was missing something, which was strange, because Damon was about as subtle as a brick to the head. "That's true...? But it's good you're going to put yourself out there...?" He sighed. "You're going to have to give me something else to work with here, Damon. I may be a genius, but I'm not a mind reader. Especially when it comes to your mind."

Damon closed his eyes with an expression as though he'd stuck his hand in a patch of poison ivy. "Would you. Go with me."

Cathal opened his mouth to make a snarky reply. Then he stared. "You do realize I am the worst possible person to invite if you want to make friends."

"You're the only person I've got." Damon opened his eyes. "And you're pissy, yeah, but you get on with your coworkers, don't you? These are more teachers. I'm not good with teachers."

There was an understatement, but Cathal didn't want to distract from the issue.

Huh. He didn't feel like turning Damon down flat, even though he had work of his own. He had the whole day while Felix was in school to do that, and he was making more progress than he'd expected. At this rate, he'd go back to classes with a full draft.

And...well, he couldn't say he'd rather get his teeth pulled without novocaine than spend time with Damon anymore, since he'd come downstairs to do just that.

"I'll do it." Cathal crossed his arms. "But you owe me."

"I already owe you," said Damon, and to Cathal's surprise, he looked sincere.

ON MONDAY, THEY went to give Felix a ride home from school, partly to find out the audition results and partly to put their name up for volunteers. Cathal complained, but he wasn't upset. It would make for a good change of pace, after all.

Anyway, he wasn't certain when he'd gone from hating Damon's guts to tolerating his company, and the only way he knew to solve problems was to go at them head-on. This solution involved a lot less swearing than usual, though.

The lady at the front desk flirted with Damon, but he didn't notice. He put down his name on the list and passed it to Cathal, who signed it with a flourish to be irritating. Damon rolled his eyes. It was very satisfying.

They found Felix on the front steps of the school, deep in conversation with his bandmates: the triplets minus one, Zach and Alex, who played bass and lead guitar respectively; and Sarah, the drummer. He ran down the steps to Damon and Cathal. Damon put his arm out, and Felix bumped into him affectionately.

"So what's the word?" Damon asked as they walked back to the car.

Felix bit his lip, grinning.

Cathal flicked his ear. "Don't draw it out. That's crass."

"Okay, okay!" Felix pulled away from Damon's hold so he could walk backward in front of them. "I got the part!"

Damon clapped him on the shoulder and opened the back door for Felix. "Knew you would."

Cathal got into the passenger's side and looked over his shoulder at Felix. "The more important question?"

Felix scowled, tucking his chin into his chest and hunching his shoulders like a cranky turtle. "Jerky McJerkface is Oberon. So I have to pretend to make nice with him every night for, like, a month. Morgan plays Theseus. I don't even get to be on stage with him."

"Well, that's a shame," said Damon, "but you'll get to spend time with him."

"Yeah, I guess. And I don't have to yell at him, so that's good." He started bouncing, always a good sign. "Also, the triplets minus one are going to be Quince and Bottom."

Cathal rolled his eyes skyward. "*That* will be a sight."

"Isn't Bottom the one who Titania gets forced to fall in love with?" Damon asked.

"Yep. Alex is thrilled; let me tell you. He really wanted to be Puck since Puck is the only one without a romance plot, and he was going to play him ace, and now he's all grumpy because he's gonna have to pretend to kiss me. It's gonna be good, though. Lots of fun."

Cathal looked sideways at Damon. Now for the best part. "Did you tell him about your brainwave?"

Damon frowned. "I knew I was forgetting something."

"What did you forget?" Felix asked, leaning forward between the front seats.

"Sit down, Felix. You'll kill yourself." Damon waited until Felix obeyed before answering. "Cathal and I volunteered to help out with the play proceedings."

Felix blanched. "You're joking, right?"

"Should I be?"

Felix covered his face. "Oh my God, Daddddd." He peered through his fingers at them. "I'm doing this to try and get somebody to kiss me! You can't—be there!"

Cathal looked over his shoulder at Felix. "What did your mother always tell you whenever you didn't want her to be in your presence?"

Felix mumbled something, and Cathal cleared his throat.

Felix repeated himself, louder but still mumbling. "She said she changed my diapers, so she had the right to do whatever she wanted. And, yeah, yeah, yeah, that applies to Dad, too. But why are you doing it?"

Damon's eyes flicked to Cathal. Cathal did his best to look casual, not like he'd spent an hour scribbling on a legal pad trying to figure out the same thing. "I'm bored. And I've come to realize how greatly I enjoy humiliating you. One must take one's pleasures where one can."

"Uggghhhhh." Felix fell dramatically against the backseat.

"I feel like I should have a teenage cliché bingo card right now," said Cathal to no one in particular, although Damon's lips twitched. "If you say, 'My life is over,' I'll win the lifetime supply of denture cream."

"I really hate you guys sometimes," Felix mumbled.

"Well, there's another square, but it's not in sequence with anything else. You are so unhelpful."

ON FRIDAY, FELIX had his first rehearsal. The teenagers were sitting in the auditorium in small groups, practicing their lines, and the adults were training to use the equipment. Damon had insisted on being early, so they were the first to arrive.

Cathal popped a macaron in his mouth. "I told you these were a good idea. If nothing else, they give us something to do."

As at any social gathering, Damon looked stiff (and not in the fun way).

Cathal kicked him. "Would you loosen up? You'll never make any friends this way."

"I'm starting to think bringing you was a mistake," said Damon, rubbing his forehead, but before he could elaborate, another parent arrived.

He was black and a little older than Damon, with thinning brown hair and gold-rimmed spectacles, and he was carrying a covered plate. "Oh, good, I'm glad I'm not the only one who thought to bring something to break the ice." He sat at the desk in front of Damon's.

Damon looked at the new arrival the way he looked at all new people: like he had dropped some really strong acid and wasn't sure if he was tripping yet.

The other man didn't seem to notice. "Are those macarons?"

Cathal's gaydar pinged. Maybe that was why Damon looked so off-balance. Although Damon always looked off-balance around people he hadn't known his entire life.

"My name's George Jennings," said the man, uncovering his plate. He'd brought sugar cookies iced in the design of butterflies. "I'm not sure I've seen either of you around before. I'm Evie's dad—she's going to be Lysander." He looked at them expectantly.

Cathal kicked Damon when he didn't speak.

"Oh, I'm—Damon Eglamore." Damon stuck out his hand to shake. Cathal just waved, resting his chin on his other palm. "I'm Felix's dad. He's gonna be Queen Titania."

George smiled at that. "I think it's refreshing they're doing it this way, don't you? Makes it more interesting." He reached for a pink macaron. When he tasted it, he looked surprised. "Are these homemade?"

Damon didn't seem inclined to speak, and Cathal thought George might notice if Cathal kicked him again, so Cathal spoke for him. "Damon made them. My name's Cathal, by the way. Cathal Kinnery." Weirdly, he felt no urge to flirt, even to keep himself in shape.

George looked between the two of them. "And are you—"

"No," said Damon and Cathal in unison.

George laughed, raising his hands. "All right, all right. I had to check. You'd think I'd know how to recognize my own kind, but I never do. So Felix's mother is...?"

Neither of them answered, and George said, "Ah. I'm sorry."

Damon looked out the window. "She just died. And she used to do all this stuff, so now I'm trying it."

"I'm sorry," George repeated, and, for a wonder, he sounded like he meant it. "It's good you're getting involved, though. When Evie's other dad dumped me, I threw myself into her school stuff. It helped."

Cathal decided now would be an apt time to take a sugar cookie, since Damon and George were staring at each other—Damon as though he was in a contest to see who would blink first, and George as though he was wondering what Damon's butt looked like. Cathal didn't want to interrupt, but he couldn't help a surprised sound of pleasure when he tasted the cookie, and that snapped the other two out of their—whatever-it-was.

"These are good." Cathal tried to look as though he hadn't noticed the two of them having a moment all over their nice clean classroom.

"I made them myself. I say when I take a day off from work that I'm not going to bake, and then I end up doing it anyway. I own a bakery," he said in response to Damon's questioning glance.

"Which one?" Most people asked questions like this politely, the way you asked someone about the weather. Damon asked it like the bad cop in a police procedural.

George's answer was hesitant. "The Jasmine Unicorn. We mostly do—"

"Wedding cakes. I know. I've seen your work online." From Damon's tone, you'd never have guessed he only recently started using the internet on a regular basis.

George relaxed. "Are you a pastry chef?"

Damon shook his head. "No. I used to be the executive chef at Stephen's, but I decided to try something new."

"Oh, so you know Melina!" And then the discussion dissolved into name-dropping.

Cathal brushed crumbs off his desk, suppressing a frown. George was pleasant, and he was male, and he was single, and he and Damon were both food people. Win-win all around.

So why was Cathal regretting his cookie?

OTHER PARENTS FILTERED into the room and took macarons and cookies, but Damon and George didn't notice—until a teacher and a dark man with a nervous smile came in. George stiffened, and the man smiled apologetically, raising one hand in a wave.

"I take it that's the ex," Cathal said, setting his cheek on his hand. George nodded, looking like a spooked cat.

The teacher said some blah blah blah about how happy he was to have them all there, and then he introduced George's ex. His name was Cleon, a stage manager who had run last year's fundraising drive for the theater's new equipment. George stared at him like he was hoping it was a bad dream.

They started talking about how to run the lights and the curtain and all that good stuff. Cathal only listened with half an ear, and he could tell Damon didn't have his mind on the subject matter, either, although that was probably because Damon learned better by doing. Handing him an instruction manual was an exercise in frustration.

By the end of the night, all the macarons and sugar cookies were gone. Damon had gotten several compliments, and, despite his concerns, he got on well with the other parents. Most people lingered, although George's ex hightailed it out of there like someone had lit a fire under his ass.

As everyone else filtered out of the room, George turned back to Damon. Cathal pretended interest in gathering up all the papers they'd been given as George leaned against the desk. "You know, if you're trying to learn about pastry, I wouldn't mind letting you use my equipment." He wasn't good at acting casual. In that, he and Damon were perfectly matched.

"You'd really let me?" said Damon, getting to his feet. "I wouldn't want to get in anyone's way."

"Nobody gets married in March unless they like Alanis Morissette and want rain on their wedding day. And we're looking for an extra hand."

Damon looked away. "I'm not looking for work."

George shrugged, unfazed. "It doesn't have to be all the time. But there's no reason your practice can't be what we're working on anyway, eh?"

Damon looked George over. Not the sexy type of looking over. The Damon type of looking over, where the subject felt like the Voynich Manuscript, illegible and possibly a gigantic hoax. "I suppose not, no."

George took out his wallet. "Here's my card. Feel free to text me if you ever want to come by."

"Sure," said Damon, still wearing an expression like he'd been swindled.

Felix was sleeping over at the triplets' place, so they were free to leave. When they got out to the car, Cathal looked over at Damon. "You have no idea what just happened, do you?"

Damon frowned at the card and tucked it in his wallet behind a gift card. "He's nice. You don't meet people like that in the business very often—it's always about what they can get from you, not the other way around."

"He wasn't doing it to be altruistic."

Damon started the car and said nothing.

Cathal gestured to the heavens for patience. "He was *hitting* on you."

Damon narrowed his eyes, although that could have been at the guy who cut him off. "He was friendly. I mean, yeah, he's gay, but he wasn't—" He glanced at Cathal. "You really think so?"

Now he was flustered, and it was adorable, the way penguins in sweaters were adorable.

"Why did anyone ever let you out in public." Cathal sighed, falling back in his seat. "I don't think so, I know so. He figured you wouldn't respond well to a regular coffee date—which you wouldn't have, so he's a smart panda."

Damon laughed, and Cathal shot him a dark look. "No, it's—I forgot you and Era always said that." He shook his head. "It doesn't matter if he's hitting on me. I'm not interested. He's nice, but—no."

Cathal rolled his eyes. Damon still struggled with liking guys. Which was ridiculous, but Damon was ridiculous.

"Why do you care, anyway?" Damon asked.

Cathal couldn't puzzle out his tone, though that was nothing new. He glared at the passing cars. "Because I'm *trying* to get your sorry ass out in the world, and here you are, ignoring the first guy who looks sideways at you. Beggars can't be choosers. You've got to get your feet wet somehow. Insert relevant cliché here."

It wasn't true, but Damon didn't know that.

Damon shook his head. "I shouldn't be surprised that you're trying to shove me off on someone else. It's what you always do."

Cathal ignored him. They rode in silence the rest of the way.

Seven: Bulleted Lists Are Not Always the Answer. Just Most of the Time.

THEY DIDN'T WATCH food shows that night. Cathal retreated to his room. His intention was to look through articles for relevant sources for his book.

Instead, he found himself scribbling notes on why, exactly, he didn't care for George. *He should really cut his hair* and *The cookies were not anything to write home about* and *Who names their bakery after a unicorn?*

He crumpled up the list and threw it in the waste bin, but the facts remained. The only question became what he was going to do about it. Which he did not feel like facing without alcohol.

He went downstairs and found Damon at the kitchen table, rolling out a log of dough. Containers of food coloring were lined up beside him.

Going back upstairs would have been the smart thing, but Cathal was stupid and liked to get himself into trouble. "It's a bit late for work, isn't it?"

Damon didn't look up. "You're one to talk."

"Sleep is for the weak." Cathal went to the fridge and got a beer, although he wished he'd thought to pick up something stronger. Maybe tomorrow. He'd have to hide it, though. He wasn't sure he wanted Damon around hard liquor.

Ugh. Definitely something stronger.

Damon glanced at the beer and raised his eyebrows. "If you're trying to get to sleep, that's not going to help."

"Sleep is for the weak," Cathal repeated. "I've got writer's block."

"Make yourself useful, then." Damon broke the log into seven equal pieces and put a few drops of blue in one piece, which he passed to Cathal. "Roll this around in your hands for me."

Cathal sniffed. "I'm only doing this because I want to eat it, mind you."

"You'll get to." Damon dropped red food coloring on the next piece and rolled it between his palms.

"What is this going to be, anyway?" Cathal tried to focus on the dough, slowly turning pastel blue, but his eyes kept flicking up to Damon's face. He'd lost weight, turning his cheeks into hollows.

"Rainbow sugar cookies. It works best if you make the dough ahead of time and chill it. I couldn't get to bed either, so I figured I might as well do something useful." Damon blew out a breath. "I keep thinking I should go back to work since I can't find things to do with myself, but...I don't know."

"It hasn't been that long, Damon," said Cathal, gentler than he'd intended.

Damon's face shuttered. "That much I know." He glanced at Cathal's work. "That's good enough. Here." He added yellow to a third piece and passed it to Cathal.

Cathal took it without even a token protest, which he knew was suspicious, but...ugh.

Damon added blue and yellow food coloring to another piece and worked it. "Were you serious? Before? About—George?"

Of *course* Damon wanted to talk about that. "Why would I lie?" Cathal wanted to be sharp, but it came out tired. "Believe it or not, I've fixed up plenty of my friends. And George wasn't being subtle."

Damon studied him. Cathal wasn't sure what his expression told Damon. "I don't know what to do with that information."

"You don't have to do anything with it. I'd say I can't believe you missed it, but, really, I can, and I am not in the least surprised." That, at least, was properly prickly.

Damon studied the quality of the green in his hands and added more yellow. "It's not like I was ever good at this stuff. I just feel like I should care, and I don't, and it's not because of Era. I don't know what it is."

"Yes, well, welcome back to the world of sex, Damon. That's how it is for everybody." Cathal set down his ball, and Damon passed him another one colored with red and blue.

"Not for you, it isn't. You always know what you want."

Damon was looking at him now, and Cathal didn't care for it. He squished the dough with perhaps more violence than the situation warranted. "What, you're not going to carp on me for never settling down?"

"Family life isn't for everyone. I'm surprised you've stayed here as long as you have."

Cathal glared—not at anything in particular, at everything in general. What did Damon know about families? More importantly, what did he think *Cathal* knew about family? His only real family was dead now.

But he shoved that feeling in a box, labeled it *shut the fuck up* with a brilliant red sharpie, and put it away. That was for therapy, not a regular conversation.

When Cathal was sure he could speak without saying something way too mean, he said, "It's not for everyone. But it's not like I could go back to work even if I wanted to. Not in the middle of the semester." He let out a breath. "I like my privacy, but that doesn't mean I'm thrilled at the idea of going home and having nothing to do. At least here I get to annoy the fuck out of you."

Damon snorted. "There is that." He finished with his current log but didn't take up a new one. "Felix likes having you around, though, you know."

"Of course he does. I'm awesome."

CATHAL TOOK THE beer up to his room when they were finished, but he didn't drink it. At that point, he knew it wouldn't help.

When was the last time he'd liked someone? He couldn't remember—things before Era got sick had faded. He'd had plenty of fun, but nothing that had lasted more than a few weeks, and nothing more complicated than "you scratch my back, I'll scratch yours."

Damon was not a back-scratching kind of guy. He was a commit-or-die kind of guy. And Cathal...Cathal wasn't sure what kind he was anymore.

Leaving would be the right thing to do, but Cathal hadn't been joking when he said he had nowhere else to go. Yes, his apartment, but then he'd get to be sad and frustrated in an empty apartment instead of sad and frustrated in Era's house.

More importantly, he didn't want to go. He wanted to stay here, and it was stupid, and it made him feel like clawing his face off, but there was no point in lying to himself. He lied to other people enough.

Cathal rubbed his face and turned back to his legal pad. Bullet points. Bullet points always helped.

Well, it's not like I have to tell anyone.

At some point, I will have to go back to teaching, so I have a built-in excuse to leave.

I get to spend time with Felix. Lots of sweets.

I will get fat.

I don't care.

If I spend enough time in Damon's company, I will loop back around to disliking him. Everyone gets on my nerves after long enough.

He's never stopped getting on my nerves. I'm just into it now.

I mean.

What the fuck?

The list was not getting him anywhere. Cathal thought about ripping it into little bits, but that was petty. He did crumple the paper up and throw it in the bin.

This was why he never listened when people told him love was supposed to be a good thing. It was stupid. *Feelings* were stupid. He should have gone home instead of getting himself all wrapped up in cakes and Felix's love life and Damon's stupid pretty eyes.

CATHAL DID HIS best to spend the rest of the next day in his room, but he did have to emerge for more water. And to put the beer back in the fridge, since it had been sitting on his desk staring at him, and it wasn't like he could drink it now it was all warm and gross.

Damon was slicing perfect circles off a log of dough made of the rainbow balls from last night. They'd been stuck together to form a spiral. It was pretty. Cathal would have put money against the idea that Damon could ever make anything pretty. What else had he been wrong about?

Well, when one was trying to prove a hypothesis, one did not look for evidence that supported it. One looked for evidence against it. He'd been giving in to confirmation bias this entire time. Was Damon guilty of it too? Or had Cathal made too much of an effort to annoy Damon to ever let him see who Cathal really was?

Ugh.

"These are nice," said Cathal, because there was no point pretending he didn't want to.

Damon glanced up and frowned when he didn't see a joke. Or, at least, that's why Cathal assumed he was frowning. It could have been anything. He had the worst case of resting bitch face.

"Complicated stuff is good, right now," Damon said. "I mean, it would be easier to do simple stuff, but I don't want it to be easier, because then I would get done, and I would have nothing to do again."

"So why don't you want to go back to work?"

Damon sighed. "It'd just be more people to tell. I mean, telling people once in a while is all right, especially if I don't have to see them every day. But you can't keep secrets from your crew at work. And I don't—" His hands stilled, and he closed his eyes. "It's not that I want to forget about her. But I can't have it pushed in my face all the time, or I'll never find a way to fill the rest of my life, and Era would take hell out of me for that."

He laughed, suddenly.

Cathal raised his eyebrows. He was acting cool, and wasn't it strange to notice acting cool around Damon when their entire interaction had once been based on not making eye contact?

"No, it's—" Damon shook his head. "Era asked you to look after me, and I'm sure it's because she had no one else to ask. No one else she trusted. She didn't think you'd actually be able to help me. But you have." He looked over at Cathal, his expression puzzled but not upset. "I'd never have put money on that."

"Well, neither would I, so that proves we both shouldn't gamble."

CATHAL STEELED HIMSELF to behave at the next rehearsal. After all, George was a man, and he was single, and he and Damon had plenty in common, and if Damon fell for him, it would solve a lot of problems, and Cathal would get to go home and be alone again like he always wanted.

Yeah. Absolutely.

And George and Damon were getting along, even though Damon looked like he was waiting for the moment George's true lizard form burst out of his human skin. George had brought cake this time. Cathal scowled as he ate it even though it was the best cake he'd ever tasted. Apparently the baking soda thing had not been Damon's imagination, since he and George were in the middle of a conversation about acids and bases, which was another thing Cathal would have put money on Damon knowing nothing about.

He hated being wrong.

There was one bright side: they had to pair up over equipment manuals, and George ended up with Damon, so Cathal was left looking for someone. Cleon, George's ex, sat next to him, keeping out of George's line of sight.

"Something tells me that you showing up here is not a coincidence," Cathal murmured, not even pretending to care about the equipment manual.

Cleon winced. "It was my daughter's idea. She threatened to stop getting an extra ticket for me to her concerts and such until I agreed to help out."

Cathal raised his eyebrows. "Am I correct in realizing I've been cast as an extra in a queer production of *The Parent Trap*?"

"I'm not that stupid. George will never forgive me, and with good reason. I'm hoping Evie will see that." He glanced over Cathal's shoulder and winced again before looking back down to the still unopened manual. "At the very least, maybe she'll see George and that other guy together and realize he's moved on."

Cathal stiffened. Cleon looked up, but before he could ask anything, the teacher announced they were moving on to something else. Thank goodness for small favors.

FELIX WAS COMING back with them that night, so they waited out by the car. Cathal had been all for plunging into the midst of the kids and collecting him, but Damon vetoed it, pointing out that this was still a ploy to win Morgan's affections, and if he was as shy as Felix described, he would spook. Cathal had capitulated after not much of a fight. He was dispirited.

Anyway, now he got to grill Damon before grilling Felix, and that was good. Even if it wasn't for altruistic reasons. Cathal told himself he'd never done anything altruistic, and though that was technically true, it didn't make him feel better. "So you and George seem to be getting on well," he commented, leaning against the passenger door.

Damon was sitting on the hood of the car. He frowned at George's name. "I wish you'd stop implying things. I keep telling you, I'm not interested in him that way."

Cathal shrugged, trying to sound casual. "I can't help it. I've fallen victim to the sunk-cost fallacy. I've put a lot of effort into you getting a life, and I'm not willing to see you squander the chance."

Damon sighed. "I'd say something about how nice it'd be if you'd talk like a person for once, but at this point, I might miss it. I feel like I'm getting smarter by osmosis."

Cathal stared at him.

"What?"

"I legitimately had no idea you knew what osmosis was."

Damon rolled his eyes. "I think I might take him up on the offer to use his equipment. I want to try something ambitious."

Felix arrived, looking flustered. "No," he said to Cathal, pointing at him before climbing into the backseat of the car.

"I haven't said a word, dearest nephew." Cathal slipped into the passenger seat. "Whyever are you shushing me?"

"No," Felix repeated, tucking his chin as though that would somehow make him look tough. "No, we are not doing this every time after rehearsal. It's bad enough with you guys staring at me all the time during dinner."

"You should be grateful, Felix." Cathal kept his voice guileless. "We're very invested in your happiness."

Damon paused before pulling out of the parking spot and turned around to face Felix. "Do you really want us to stop? Because we will." This with a threatening sideways glance at Cathal.

Felix fidgeted. Then he let his head fall back against the seat. "No. You guys give better advice than my friends. Alex is all like, 'I'm ace and gray-aro. I do not care about your romantic problems in any way, shape or form.' And Zach and Sarah are both like, 'Well, why don't you ask him out already?'"

"They do have a point," Cathal said, trying to be gentle. "It can't hurt to try."

Felix glared. "Yes, it totally can, considering that I have to see this guy after school all the time now. And I have to pretend to be in love with his brother. *And* I'll fail my physics test. He's a really good tutor."

"I'm not saying you need to ask the boy out for coffee and a movie or something," Cathal replied, fixing Felix with a look with a capital *L*. "But if he were anyone else, you'd have already invited him over to the house."

"I mean—" Felix's eyes flicked to his father.

Damon sighed. "Felix, you can go on living your life however you like. Your mother never would have wanted you to keep your life fixed in stone, and I don't want it either. You're good at making friends, son. I would never begrudge you that."

Felix chewed on his lower lip. "Yeah, okay. I'll think about it."

"Remember what I told you before," said Cathal. "If he's interested in you but as shy as you think, nothing short of a brick to the face will convince him of your interest. If he's straight, he'll never pick up on it either way. You're safe."

"It's not that. I don't really care if he likes me back or not, now that he doesn't look at me like I've got three heads." Felix blew out a breath. "But I am going to get teased for this from every angle, and I am going to have to accept that."

"See, look at you, handling this like a mature adult. I'm so proud."

Felix refused to speak the rest of the drive home.

FELIX WAS VERY excited by the rainbow cookies, and also by the pizza. Even though it had mashed sweet potatoes instead of sauce.

"This is a crime against nature," Cathal informed Damon, after Felix went upstairs to run his lines. "I hope you realize that."

"You ate three pieces," Damon replied.

"It was a delicious crime. That does not change the fact that it should be illegal." He got to his feet. But Damon looked over at him, and, despite himself, Cathal paused, raising his eyebrows.

"Thank you." Damon lifted his eyes to Cathal's. "For being good with Felix. I never thought I'd say this, but I don't know how I'd have managed all this without you."

Cathal bit the inside of his cheek to keep his expression still. He hoped he wasn't blushing. "It's really not a problem. I love him too, you know."

"Yes," said Damon, and thankfully, that was the end of the conversation.

CATHAL TRIED TO work, but all that came out of his pen were things like *Damon makes delicious cake. I like delicious cake* and *George has a stupid face.*

He crumpled up the page and threw it away.

When he went downstairs, Damon was sitting on the couch, a six-pack next to his feet. "Oh, good," said Damon without looking away from the TV. "I bought some more of your fancy beer. I was worried you were going to make me drink it."

"You drank half the case last time."

"Not by choice." But Damon was smiling.

Cathal realized he was smiling, too.

Ugh.

He sat down, hoping his expression conveyed reluctance and disgust instead of the strange calm he was starting to feel around Damon. "I do this under duress, mind you. Only because I know you won't appreciate the subtleties of flavor involved."

Damon snorted. "Who's the chef here? I know what makes this craft beer, and I could talk about it without reading what's written on the label like you do. But beer is not supposed to be fancy. Beer is for guys like me, who don't need everything dressed up all the time."

Cathal's lips twitched. "I see how it is. You're always after me for making speeches, but I've just never talked about the right things to get you started."

"You're right. I do care about food. I'm not near as bad as you, though, so don't you start."

"I am pure as the driven snow, and you know it." Cathal settled back in his seat. "I would never dream of teasing you endlessly about this, and I have no idea how you could ever accuse me of it."

"You are such a piece of shit," said Damon, but fondly.

Cathal would have bet his professorship, his apartment, and his tenure on the idea that Damon couldn't sound fond while speaking to him. Another of the long list of things he was wrong about.

Damon held up his bottle; Cathal clinked his against it. Like he'd said the other day. It wasn't all bad.

Eight: The Great Pillow Massacre

of 2016.

CATHAL HAD GOTTEN used to their routine during the day—him working, Damon making something strange but delicious in the kitchen—so he was surprised to get a knock around lunchtime. He wondered if Damon was going to nag him to eat, but when he opened his door, Damon was smiling. "Felix's bringing his boys over for dinner tonight. Thought I ought to let you know so you'll be nice."

"This from you, who was weepy over how good I am with your son."

Damon rolled his eyes. "Yes, and you like taking hell out of him as much as you like making him feel better." He paused. "Not that I won't be taking hell out of him myself. I just figured you ought to know."

"We'll make his life a misery." Cathal smiled like someone seeing his firstborn for the first time.

"Oh, yes," said Damon. "I'm making macaroni and cheese for dinner, by the way."

Cathal squinted at him. "That sounds normal."

Damon smiled enigmatically, which was another thing Cathal would have said he could never do. "You'll see."

"What will I see?"

Damon turned to go back down the stairs.

"What will I see?" Cathal repeated. "If you've found a way to ruin mac and cheese, you are a bad person!"

Damon didn't turn around. "I'm making more cake, too."

"That doesn't make it better, you horrible man!"

But it kind of did.

THE MACARONI AND cheese looked normal, although there were zucchini and peas in it. Damon smirked as Cathal inspected it, though, which suggested something more sinister at work. "I'll tell you after we eat," Damon said when Cathal asked about it.

Damon's cake was iced with the title of the play and a blue-and-white border. Cathal squinted at it for good measure, even though it was pretty. He'd never noticed before, but Damon had the handwriting of an angel. Yet more proof that he wasn't human.

Felix was late, but that was to be expected. He was talking as he came in, gesturing wildly. The boy following him was several inches taller—though that wasn't surprising, since Felix was short—and had a blond braid. He was dressed for a business lunch, and his smile was cautious but true. The boy Felix was talking to, however, slouched, and was dressed like his next appointment was tagging buildings with the anarchy symbol. He had long hair as well, but his hung loose to his shoulders.

"And that," said Felix, "is why *Legend of Korra* will never, ever measure up to *Avatar: The Last Airbender*, even though *Korra* has confirmed queer characters." He dropped an invisible microphone.

The boy with the messy clothes shrugged. "I still like my shows to end with bisexual ladies. And *Korra* kicks ass."

"Gareth!" the other boy snapped. Cathal had already figured out who was who, but the confirmation was nice.

Gareth just shrugged, and Felix sighed as he climbed up onto the counter. "Guys, this is my dad, Damon Eglamore, and my uncle, Cathal Kinnery." Cathal waved lazily, smiling his most evil smile. Damon crossed his arms over his chest, although his smile was friendly.

Morgan dropped his eyes to the floor, a blush creeping up his neck. "Um. H'lo." His voice was hardly a mumble.

Gareth threw some hair over his shoulder like the bad girl in a high school movie. "Hi."

Felix looked at Morgan as though he might hide the secret to cold fusion. He did not look at Gareth, who was glancing around the kitchen with an unreadable expression. "Dad, Cathal, this is Morgan. He's Theseus. And that's Gareth." He pointed at the other boy without looking at him. "He's Oberon."

Damon smiled. "It's good you've made new friends, Felix."

Cathal set his cheek on his hand. "Oh, yes, Felix talks about you two all the time. We were wondering if you were ever going to stop by." With his eyes, Felix signaled that he wished Cathal a horrible and painful death.

Damon glanced at the table. "Oh! I forgot we'd need more chairs today." He went out of the room.

Felix pointed at the empty chair across from Cathal. Morgan sat, slowly, setting his bag on his lap. "I can put that in my room if you want," Felix offered, but Morgan shook his head, his eyes flicking around the room as though he wanted to study it but didn't want to be caught staring.

"Don't mind me." Gareth leaned his elbow on his brother's shoulder. Morgan shot him a warning look, which Gareth ignored.

Felix sat next to Morgan, his back straight for once. "Ooh, is that mac and cheese?"

"There's something weird about it," Cathal warned him.

"Weird's been good so far." Felix looked at Morgan conspiratorially. "My dad's been cooking all kinds of whacko stuff since my mom died. I think it was a coping mechanism at first, but now he does it to make Cathal mad."

Morgan's eyes flicked to Cathal, as though Cathal would object.

"Oh, please." Cathal snorted. "He'll have to be cleverer than that to keep me on my toes."

Gareth laughed, which surprised Cathal, and apparently Felix as well, who looked at Gareth like he'd grown an extra head.

"Who is?" Damon asked, coming back in the room with the extra chairs. They'd disappeared from the dinner table about the time Era had moved to inpatient care. No one ever commented, and Cathal wasn't about to break that streak. Though it was good to see them back.

When Cathal just looked at him, Damon rolled his eyes. "Oh, yes, talk about me the moment I walk out of the room."

"Like you don't do the same thing to me," said Cathal.

Damon shrugged, neither confirming nor denying, and got plates from the cupboard. "You want anything to drink, boys? We have juice, water—no soda, though. It makes *someone* completely nuts."

"Dad!" Felix yelped. Gareth laughed again. Cathal squinted, but it was not a mean laugh, though Morgan shoved his brother off his shoulder.

Morgan's lips twitched, although the smile was gone as soon as it appeared. "Water, please."

"Smart boy." Damon put the mac and cheese in the center of the table. "Guests first, you two. Help yourself."

Gareth served himself and Morgan, putting more on Morgan's plate and ignoring his brother's frown.

"Dad. There are vegetables in this," Felix said, frowning at his plate.

"Yes. They're good for you."

"Dad. You're a bad person."

"Yes. It's good for you."

Morgan watched them with an expression like he could not quite believe it. Gareth was focused on the food. Cathal ducked his head to hide a smile as he served himself.

Damon took his spot at the table. "So Felix says you're a violinist?" he asked Morgan.

Morgan nodded, twisting his fork in his fingers. "That's my main instrument, yes."

"Morgan can play everything," said Felix, envy in his voice.

"Not *everything*," said Morgan, though he flushed at the compliment. "I'm useless at any kind of woodwind."

"You have to suck at something, or else you'd be perfect," said Felix, and it was supposed to be a joke, but there was no hiding the sincerity in his eyes.

"He can't swim." Gareth nudged his brother in the ribs. Morgan shot him a sharp look, which Gareth ignored.

Cathal decided to change the subject to keep from laughing. Despite what he'd said, he did have some sense of what was and wasn't okay to tease Felix about. "Felix says you're in a number of advanced classes, Morgan."

Morgan nodded, which appeared to be the extent of his current ability to reply.

Cathal opened his mouth to ask why, but Felix made an irritated noise. "Would you guys stop grilling him for, like, thirty seconds so he can actually eat? He never does!" In typical fashion, he had somehow already finished his food and was going for a second helping.

Morgan looked sideways at Felix like this was news to him. Or like Felix was an alien that had appeared next to him, a common response.

"I noticed," Felix mumbled, avoiding his eyes. "You, like, never finish your lunch."

Gareth elbowed his brother again. "I *told* you." He looked around his brother, his eyes narrowed at Felix, and Cathal braced himself to defend his nephew. But Gareth said, "Thank you."

Felix's jaw dropped. Thankfully, his mouth was not full.

Cathal stuffed a bite of mac and cheese in his mouth because, otherwise, he *was* going to laugh. The food was delicious, although there was something strange about it he couldn't put his finger on. "How did your physics test go, Felix?"

Felix made a face. "I think maybe I didn't completely fail?"

"You did fine." Morgan's voice was quiet, like he thought no one would notice if he didn't raise his voice, and he was still looking at his unfinished food. "I'm serious. I grade the tests for tutoring credit."

"You never told me that."

"Oh. Well, I do, and you did fine." He lifted his head and smiled at Felix, but it was sickly. Gareth nudged his brother, and Morgan sighed and started to finish his food.

Felix kicked Cathal under the table. "Tell him about your job, Cathal. He'll like that."

Cathal sniffed. "I don't make concessions to terrorists."

"Pleeeeease?"

"Oh, all right. Only if it will silence your whining." But Cathal was smiling. "I teach astrophysics at a private university."

Morgan paused, betraying cautious interest. "Really?"

"Really really. My research is about building model universes."

Morgan's eyes lit up. "You wrote that book Mr. Broadbeam lent me! I remember now. I thought I'd heard your name before." He dropped his eyes, as though embarrassed he'd revealed his excitement. If he'd looked sideways, he'd have seen Felix looking at him like a Christmas present. Gareth was smiling, too, in a hidden sort of way.

Cathal smiled. "You must be advanced for your age if Aaron lent you that. It's for college students."

Morgan shrugged, blushing again. "I like math."

"Look at that, Felix. You've gone and made a friend who makes sense."

Felix blew a raspberry at him. He'd already finished his second plate of mac and cheese and was eyeing the pan.

"Not that I'll complain about you eating," Damon said, raising his eyebrows, "but there is dessert."

Cathal turned to Damon before he could get up. "All right, I ate it. Now spill, Eglamore. What crime against humanity did you commit now?"

Damon smiled beatifically. "The sauce is made with pureed butternut squash and cauliflower."

Cathal looked at his plate, then at the pot. "You *bastard.*"

"Language! We have guests!" But Damon was laughing, and so was Gareth, though Morgan looked scandalized.

"It's very good." He hunched up his shoulders, like he was waiting for someone to kick him.

"Thank you." Damon beamed at him, and Morgan smiled back—hesitantly.

"And now you're brainwashing Felix's new friend on top of everything else. I am alone in this tide of evil." Cathal pressed the back of his palm to his forehead as though he might faint.

Damon patted Cathal's shoulder. "It's all right. We'll make a food person of you yet."

"You will do no such thing."

Shaking his head, Damon got up and collected his and Cathal's plates and put them in the sink. He brought the cake out and set it at the center of the table.

"That's really fancy!" Felix leaned forward in his seat. "Did you make that, Dad?"

Damon went red. "I did," he said, as though he were expecting a challenge.

"It's nice," said Morgan, quietly. "Is that what you do?"

"It is now, I think." Damon sliced the cake, giving Morgan and Gareth the largest pieces. Felix did not whine because he was already stuffing his face. Clearly he wasn't hoping to impress Morgan with his manners.

Not that Cathal could blame him. The cake was strawberry flavored, with red stuff between the layers. "There's jam in this," he said, turning his squint on Damon.

"Yes. It holds the layers together." But Damon was smirking, which meant he did, in fact, understand that jam in a cake was an affront against nature and was doing this to torment Cathal.

But fuck it all if Cathal wasn't enjoying it. He ate the cake, and it was delicious, and he couldn't even pretend to be grumpy.

"Can I have another pieeeece?" Felix asked when he was finished, turning his best puppy eyes on his father.

"Only if the twins want one."

Morgan was only halfway done with his first slice, but he said, "We can split another one. If—if that's okay." His eyes flicked toward Felix, and Cathal could not hold back his smirk. Gareth made a face, though neither of the other boys saw it.

"An excellent compromise," said Cathal.

"Cathal was right." Damon cut another piece. "You are the only one of Felix's friends with any sense."

"I think they're nice," said Morgan, glancing again at Felix. "Loud, but nice."

"Oh, they're nice. They're also really, really weird."

Felix sniffed. "We're just too avant-garde for you, Dad. You're behind the times."

"He put squash in macaroni and cheese and sweet potatoes in pizza." Cathal pointed his fork at Felix. "Your father is as weird as your friends, only in a different direction."

Felix smiled. "Maybe that's why we all get along so well, then."

WHEN THE BOYS headed up to Felix's room, already deep in discussion about character and theme in *Midsummer Night's Dream*, Cathal slumped over the table, laughing too hard to speak.

Damon stared at him. "Are you going to live?"

Cathal didn't answer, still laughing.

Damon crossed his arms. "I can't tell if you're laughing to make fun of Felix or not."

Cathal caught his breath and sat up, wiping his eyes. "Do not tell me it wasn't funny to watch him squirm."

Damon wasn't sure he'd ever seen him smile that way— free, without a hint of scheming in his eyes. He and Era had laughed a lot, sure, but at the expense of other people, or at their own stupidity, or at an in-joke so complicated it required two PhDs and a writing seminar to make sense of it.

"He's so far in over his head," Cathal added.

Damon shrugged. He didn't think it was funny, because he'd been there. Felix's face as he grappled with both twins reminded him too much of his early time with Era. It hurt to think about that, but even more, it was strange to think his son was reaching that point with someone.

Cathal rubbed his jaw. "Felix wasn't kidding, though. Poor boy's scared of his own shadow. But I'm glad. The other one's not as bad as I thought."

Damon snorted at that and pushed away from the table. "Of course you'd say that."

"What?" Cathal sounded confused instead of pissed.

Damon paused in gathering the plates up off the table. "He's just like you, isn't he?"

"He's loud. And rude."

"Pot calling the kettle black," Damon said, turning to the sink. He thought about washing the dishes by hand, but...he didn't feel like it. For once, he'd be all right without keeping his hands busy.

"I never understood that expression," said Cathal, his voice dead serious. "I don't have a black pot or a black kettle, and I don't know why they're talking to each other."

Damon stared at the sink. Yeah. Definitely loading the dishes in the dishwasher. He needed a drink if he was going to deal with this all night.

And that was weird. He expected Cathal to hang out with him. Not even frustrated expectation, like he knew he couldn't stop Cathal. When the hell had that happened?

"I'll have to research that." Cathal walked up to the sink and helped Damon load the dishwasher.

Damon stopped and stared at him. Not because he solved problems by staring at them like Cathal did, but because it was the only way Cathal would notice Damon was confused.

Cathal ignored him until the sink was empty and then turned to him. "Come on. Your son is trying to make nice with the boy he likes. You are contractually obligated to get drunk and further humiliate him." He clapped Damon on the shoulder.

Damon nodded, though he was still confused. Cathal made for the fridge, but Damon waved him away. "You go put something on. I'll bring the alcohol." Once he was out of the room, Damon went underneath the sink, behind all the cleaning supplies that no one else touched. He kept the shot bottles in a lockbox, although that would spark Felix's curiosity more than the alcohol itself. Still. He didn't take chances with the hard stuff.

Cathal was flipping through Netflix when Damon came in the living room, but he stopped, frowning, when he saw what Damon had tucked under his arm. "Where did you get those?"

Damon lined the single-size bottles of vodka and rum up on the edge of the table. "I haven't touched them before this, if that's what you're asking about."

Cathal rolled his eyes. "Once again, you miss the point. I was wondering why you didn't let me know there was hard liquor in the house. I assumed you only drank beer because that's what guys like you do."

Damon rolled his eyes back. "Same reason I didn't talk about the beer." He sat on the far end of the couch, leaving the middle cushion empty like always. "And I took them from work once in a while. We served them at private events to upcharge for the individual bottles."

Cathal picked a bottle up and considered the pirate portrait. "I never would have thought I'd learn things from you." He sounded honestly surprised.

Damon wasn't sure what to say to that, so he let it drop. He didn't want to push until he figured out what was going on. "What are we watching?"

Cathal returned his attention to the TV. "*Ghostbusters.*"

"Finally, something we can agree on."

Cathal cracked the top on the bottle and drank it at a go. "I think liquor is another one of those things. We'll have to start making a list."

"No, no, we do not."

BY THE TIME Felix came downstairs with the twins, they'd moved through most of the bottles, all of *Ghostbusters*, and half of *Labyrinth*, which Cathal had insisted on calling part of Damon's gay education.

Felix stuck his head in the room. "Is it okay if—"

Damon realized he was slumping so far on the couch that his shoulder was brushing Cathal's. Both of them straightened at the same time.

Felix squinted, and Damon hoped he was not going to ask when they'd gotten so comfortable with each other. "Are you guys *drunk*?" Felix said instead, wrinkling his nose.

Cathal covered his mouth. It did nothing to hide his laughter.

Ignoring him, Damon asked, "Did you need something, son?"

Felix looked between the two of them. "I was gonna walk them home if that's okay...?"

Cathal gave up on hiding his laughter. Damon shot him a dirty look, which Cathal ignored.

"As long as you're back before ten, everything's fine. Behave yourself." Damon pointed his bottle at Felix to emphasize his point. Keeping it steady was harder than usual.

Okay. Maybe he was a little drunk.

"Dad!" Felix said, covering his ears to hide that they'd turned bright red. "It's not like that! His brother's gonna be there. Sometimes, I feel like I'm the only real grownup in this house."

Cathal cackled. "Getting old is boring, kiddo. Let us have our fun while we can."

When the front door opened and closed, cutting off the boys' argument about the merits of modal music, Damon turned to Cathal, who was still chuckling. "Do you think Felix'll kiss him?" One good thing about being drunk: the idea of his son kissing anyone was less terrifying.

But Cathal waved his words away. "No way. Felix doesn't have the balls. If anyone's making a move, it's Morgan." He slumped toward the center of the couch again, and Damon found himself doing the same thing. Yeah, he was drunk.

Oh, well. From this position, it was easy to bump Cathal's shoulder. "You just said he's scared of his own shadow."

"Yeah, but quiet people are always the weird ones." Cathal poked Damon in the chest. "Like you."

Damon raised his eyebrows. A month ago, that comment would have bothered him. Now he didn't think Cathal meant it badly. Cathal was making fun of him, sure, but it wasn't...it wasn't mean. "Oh, yes, I'm the weird one here. This coming from the guy who never goes anywhere without five million Post-it notes. I think you need to take a long hard look in the mirror, Mr. Kinnery."

Cathal narrowed his eyes and poked Damon again. "You're the one who made pie with a fish head in it. A fish head."

"You ate it, didn't you?" Damon closed his eyes, since the room was unsteady. "It was worth it to hear you squawk."

"I do not squawk!" Cathal said in a tone that was definitely a squawk. "I am dignified, as befits a professor." Cathal poked Damon a third time. On instinct, Damon caught his wrist and opened his eyes.

"Cut that out, you weirdo," he said, keeping hold of Cathal's hand so Cathal wouldn't try anything stupid. He turned his head and found Cathal's face closer to his than he'd expected. Cathal still looked like a fox licking feathers off his lips, but somehow, it wasn't a bad thing anymore.

"We've wasted a lot of time," he said, and he didn't realize he'd said it out loud until Cathal screwed up his face.

"You're going to have to be more specific, Damon," he said, narrowing his eyes like a person trying to see without his glasses. "I. I am in fact pretty drunk, and therefore I cannot make the bold leaps of logic that have so far defined our relationship."

Damon had to take a minute to process that sentence. Even tipsy, Cathal sounded like he was reading from a textbook. "You know what I mean. We could have been getting along like this all the time instead of making Era pull her hair out. She always told me you weren't so bad, but I never believed her. Now I feel as stupid as you think I am."

Cathal extracted himself from Damon's grip—slowly, with a lot of twisting and grunts. Damon felt like he should sit up, too, but he was enjoying watching Cathal struggle.

When Cathal had settled himself against the arm of the couch, he sighed, deflating. "Yeah. Well. It's not like I was any better. I knew why you were good for her, but not why you were good in general."

Damon frowned, searching Cathal's face for the lie or the sarcasm or the joke that was always there. Except...it wasn't. "You say that like it's a fact," Damon murmured, keeping his eyes on Cathal's face in case he revealed what was really going on. Not that Damon could ever read Cathal, but still. "I was never good for her."

Cathal turned to face him so he could glare. His eyes could not quite focus, so it wasn't as effective as usual, but his tone was stern. "Would you stop with that nonsense? You looked at her like she was the sun, for fuck's sake. No, you couldn't talk Shakespeare, but you listened when she talked. You made her breakfast and shit. You know. Like couples on TV." He rubbed his face. "Fuck. Look. I don't know anything about good relationships except that you had one, okay?"

Damon thought he was done, but then, softly, Cathal said, "Is that really what you think about yourself?"

It was like getting out of a hot tub into a snowstorm. Damon looked away. "It's what I know about myself."

"And with that, we're both officially cut off." Cathal shoved the coffee table and the few unopened bottles away with his feet.

Damon wanted to make a joke, but he couldn't; he was numb all over. "Why, because we're getting sappy?"

Cathal smacked his shoulder. Reluctantly, Damon looked in his direction, dreading the judgment he'd see in Cathal's eyes. But Cathal looked muddled, not angry. "No, because discussions of your self-worth are not to be had while we're both drunk." He let out a disgusted sigh and put a hand over his face. "You need to be sober so you'll believe me."

Damon narrowed his eyes. There had to be a punch line in there somewhere.

Except...maybe there wasn't, because Cathal still hadn't said anything. "You've said that before. Like you mean it."

"Because I do, you complete and total ass. I don't say things I don't mean. I say things I *regret*, but I mean them at the time, until my brain comes back." He leaned forward over his knees like he was thinking about throwing up. "I never would have made fun of you if I thought you'd believe me."

"What else was I supposed to think? You don't like me." Damon's voice was empty of emotion. It had never bothered him before.

"Yeah, big whoop. I don't like a lot of people. But...I was wrong about you." Cathal hid his face, and Damon could have sworn he was blushing. Or maybe flushed from the alcohol. Damon's cheeks were warm too, after all.

But Cathal seemed honestly distressed. Damon touched his back, expecting Cathal to move away. If something bad happened, Cathal never sought comfort—he and Era would get wasted and then never spoke of the topic again, as though getting drunk erased it from history.

Damon hoped Cathal wasn't trying to forget all of this too.

"It's all right. I...I was wrong about you too. Era was always telling me so."

"That's because Era was always right, which is the only thing you were always right about." But Cathal's words had no bite.

Damon realized his hand was still on Cathal's back and took it away, though he didn't move to his corner of the couch. Cathal had his face hidden, so being honest was easy. "I'm glad things worked out like this. With you staying here, I mean."

Cathal parted his fingers, looking at Damon too shrewdly.

Now Damon did move away, if only because he wasn't sure what was going on in his own head. The tide was going out inside him, and he felt like a blind man walking on the beach, stumbling over objects he couldn't make sense of. "I mean, I was expecting you to make fun of me for the rainbow sugar cookies and stuff. It's not like it's manly."

Cathal snorted, but he took his hands away from his face. "Manliness is overrated. And also they were tasty, and I got to eat them, so why on earth would I ever complain?"

FELIX CAME HOME about an hour later, long after Damon and Cathal had started watching *Labyrinth* again and moved back to their respective ends of the couch. Damon patted the empty cushion in the middle, and Felix plopped down between them. He looked tired, like he always did when he wasn't in his room dicking around on his phone by nine at night, but he was also smiling in a way Damon had never seen before.

Cathal elbowed Felix in the ribs. "So how was it, Casanova?"

Felix squeaked and pressed up against Damon. Damon lifted his arm so Felix could curl up against his side. Then Felix stuck his tongue out at Cathal. "It was good."

"None of that nonsense." Cathal pointed at Felix with an unsteady finger. "Dish, young one."

Felix wrinkled his nose. "Don't call me that. You're not Yoda."

Cathal put on his best Frank Oz voice. "Search your feelings, you must."

Damon leaned around his son to point back at Cathal. "That was a terrible impression. Never do it again in my house."

"Dad's right, Cathal," said Felix, looking somber. "Star Wars is sacred."

"You're only agreeing with him to get out of answering the question." But Cathal was smiling. "So?"

Felix sighed and slumped against Damon again.

"You don't have to answer the question if you don't want to." Damon shot Cathal a quelling look. Cathal didn't respond, but he didn't have to: *bitch, please* was written all over his face.

"No, it's okay." Felix rubbed his ear. "I don't really know how it went, honestly. I mean, they're both coming to band practice, so that's cool, but I didn't ask the triplets minus one or Sarah first, so they're going to kick my ass. Well, Sarah will kick my ass. Alex and Zach will laugh at my pain."

Damon patted Felix's shoulders. "It's only funny because you're a late bloomer. I was the same way. Never got stupid over someone 'til I met your mom, and my friends never let me hear the end of it."

"You *were* really stupid for her, though," said Cathal. Damon raised his eyebrows at Cathal over the top of Felix's head. Cathal shrugged, looking away. "Usually you spend all your time scowling like a troll in a fantasy movie. She made you smile. And vice versa. She was kind of like the bitchy elf queen, I guess. The one who don't need no man."

Damon had thought Felix wasn't paying attention, but he looked over at Cathal. "What does that make me?"

"Obviously the annoying kid character that everyone hates," said Cathal, reaching over to ruffle his hair.

"Not nice!" Felix said. "I'm so Legolas. He's hanging out in the background making weird faces all the time."

Damon let out a deep sigh, though he was trying not to laugh. "The point of the story is, it worked out, and yours will too, Felix. It's hard the first time around."

Felix's ears turned pink, and he pressed his face into Damon's shoulder. "I told you, I don't care about that stuff. He's really nice. I don't want to mess that up by letting him know I want to smush faces or whatever people do."

Cathal choked. "Is that what the kids are calling it these days?"

"I don't know, actually." Felix appeared to give the question serious thought. "Sarah's the only one in the band who has a partner, and she won't kiss and tell. I don't even know who she's dating—she goes to a different school."

Damon raised his eyebrows. "I thought your friend Zach was making time with all the guys in school."

"Zach talks a big game, but he's not serious. He wants to be in love before he does anything—you know." Felix gestured at his body, and Cathal snorted. "Shut up! I am not talking about sex with you guys! I'm still, like, ninety percent certain I don't want to ever have it."

Damon opened his mouth. Not that he wanted to have another sex talk with Felix, but—

Felix pushed himself up off the couch. "You've already told me how all that stuff works, Dad, so don't you start!"

Cathal smirked. "Don't be so hard on your father, Felix. He's trying to be a liberated parent or whatever the trend is these days."

"I've *had* health class. I know all about that stuff."

Damon folded his arms. "Probably not whatever you'd be doing with Morgan, if you ever do change your mind."

Felix turned bright red. "That's it, I'm done! No more! You guys are just the worst."

"By which you mean we are the best, and you wouldn't have a snowball's chance in hell with your boyfriend without our help," said Cathal, still smirking.

Felix threw up his hands and marched out of the room.

Damon shifted his weight and glanced at Cathal. "You don't think I'm laying it on too thick, do you? I want to make sure he's not holding back. Era could be pretty intimidating when she got on a roll. It was hard to ask her questions."

Cathal snorted, flopping back on the couch. "As the situation with the twins illustrated, no, he's not. But look at me, talking like I know anything about kids. I know him, though, and you need to stop getting flustered about it. If he needs to talk, he'll come to you. He only came to me because you were...otherwise occupied." Cathal made a face. "That came out wrong. Don't take it personally."

Damon let out a breath and closed his eyes.

Cathal poked him in the side. "What did I say? It's not like you hurt anyone. I was here to take care of what needed doing so you could take care of yourself."

Damon glanced at him. "So who took care of you?" It was supposed to be a joke, but apparently he was too drunk for that still.

Thankfully, Cathal waved it away. "Clearly, I take care of myself, because I am awesome and need no one."

CATHAL SAT UP with an exaggerated groan, putting that question as far from his mind as possible. "We're getting morose again, and that means it is definitely time to call it a night."

"Drink some water before you turn in. You're a prick when you have a hangover."

Cathal put his hands on his hips. "Why, Damon, that almost sounds like you cared."

Damon was supposed to laugh it off, but he kept staring at Cathal in that even, steady way. Hopefully because he was drunk. Cathal couldn't handle it any other way. "I do care. About you not bitching at me in the morning when you have a headache."

Cathal picked up one of the decorative pillows that lined the back of the couch. It was shaped like a duckling holding an Easter egg—Cathal had never questioned Era's taste in decorations, since he liked his genitals the way they were. He hefted the duckling, testing the weight. Then he slapped Damon in the face with it.

Thus ensued an epic pillow fight involving another duckling, three rabbits, and an Easter egg, as well as one of the couch cushions when Damon decided to cheat. Both of them ended up on the floor.

"You know, usually when I'm drunk and on the floor and breathing hard," said Cathal, "it is not because I got the shit beat out of me with a pink rabbit."

"I'd be worried if it was." Damon frowned up at the ceiling. "But I wouldn't be surprised."

Cathal kicked him, but feebly. Damon just flopped his arm over his face.

"We should go to bed," Cathal said.

"We have to get up first."

"You make an excellent point."

BY THE TIME they did get to bed, Cathal was too tired to interrogate himself about what had happened. Maybe he wouldn't remember any of this in the morning.

HE DID REMEMBER, mostly because he woke up with a throbbing headache that refused to let him forget. Rubbing his eyes, he stumbled to the door. When he opened it, he found a glass of water on the floor. One of his Post-it notes was attached; the note—"obliterate"—had been scratched out and replaced with a large, obnoxious smiley face.

Cathal crumpled up the smiley face and threw it away, but he drank the water.

Nine: Damon Is Physically Incapable of Avoiding the Elephant in the Room, and He's got the Tusk Marks to Prove It.

AFTER THE NEXT rehearsal, while they were waiting for Felix, Damon was restless and fidgety. Cathal was not in a chatty mood, but he couldn't keep himself from asking, either. With his usual grace and tact, of course. "What crawled up your ass and died?"

Damon shot him a nasty look, which Cathal just smiled at. "It's good to see you're back to your usual tasteless self."

That almost made Cathal feel guilty, though he would never admit it. "And it's good to see you are back to your usual Grumpy Gus self." He hopped on the hood of the car. "What's the story, morning glory?"

"Where do you pick up that crap?"

Cathal ignored this.

Damon leaned against the car. As usual after long interaction with people he didn't know well, he was scowling like a stock photograph of an action hero. "George was flirting with me, wasn't he?"

"I've only been telling you that since you met the guy, so yeah, welcome to reality."

"It doesn't make sense to me. But now I'm feeling weird. I don't want to lead him on—I mean it when I say I'm not interested." His expression turned inward. "I could date again. If I wanted to. But it has to be the right person, and he's not it."

"He's offering, so you should take him up on it." Cathal almost sounded like he didn't care. Almost. "But you don't have to take all that he's offering. Even though you should, because damn. Man's got a thirst that you can satisfy."

Damon turned red and didn't say anything.

Cathal rubbed his arms. "So are you? Taking him up on it?"

Damon sighed. "Well, I said I'd meet him tomorrow at his bakery. He wants my opinion, which is ridiculous, since I'm not an expert, but—I guess that goes along with what you said. God, I'm so bad at this."

"Yes, you really are," said Cathal, because it was true. He clapped Damon on the shoulder. "But the only way it gets better is practice."

Damon said nothing to that, tapping his heel against the front tire. "There's something I wanted to ask you about."

"No, I will not play the Cyrano de Bergerac to your Christian, thank you very much."

Damon wrinkled his nose. "I should know that reference, shouldn't I?"

"That would have required you to pick something up about literature during your marriage to a literature professor. So no."

Damon rolled his eyes. "They do life-drawing classes here on Wednesday nights. You have to pay for them, but it all goes to the school's art program."

Cathal yawned and fell back on the hood of the car, staring at the cloudy night sky. "You want to go, so go. You don't need to justify that to anyone."

"That's not what it is. I was—" Damon broke off. "I was wondering if you'd go with me."

Cathal pushed himself up on his elbows. "I don't know if you've noticed, but I'm not much of a beard, Damon. And you did fine making friends, didn't you? I mean, yes, George is only interested because he wants to do the forbidden dance, but you get on well enough. Even though you look at him like you think he's a Wakandan spy."

"He confuses me almost as much as you do," Damon muttered, as though that were an explanation. "It's not that I don't want to go by myself. You don't have to talk to anyone at a life drawing class. I...I wanted to know if you wanted to go. With me."

Now Cathal was really confused. He stared at the back of Damon's head, but the other man was inscrutable, though he was still standing stiffly. "You say that like I'm any good at drawing."

Damon covered his face with his hand. "It's not that. You'll...you'll be going back to your place, won't you? And then you won't be hanging around. I just thought—"

But before Damon could explain what he thought, Felix came running over.

"You are *covered* in glitter," said Cathal.

"Makeup test. Morgan asked me if I would come over to his place and listen to one of his new pieces tomorrow after school can I go?" As usual, it came out in one breath.

"I feel like those might have been words, but I'm not sure," said Cathal.

Felix made a frustrated noise.

Damon shook his head, smiling. "Of course you can. Let me know his address so I can find you if something happens, all right?"

"Dad, nothing is going to happen," said Felix, opening the back door.

"Now that is a defeatist attitude." Cathal slid off the hood of the car. Damon opened the passenger door for him, probably since he'd been leaning on it.

"Cathallll," Felix whined, pressing his hands against his face. "God, you guys are awful. I'm never going to live any of this stuff down, am I?"

"Oh, absolutely not. Where would the fun in that be?"

Felix whimpered and fell back against his seat.

THE NEXT MORNING, Damon walked past the guest room door four or five times. He'd hoped Cathal would hear him and demand to know why he was out there in some weird Cathal way, since that would make sense. Damon did things, Cathal said they were weird, and they went on with their lives.

Of course, Cathal didn't wake up. That would make things too easy. So Damon knocked. He heard shuffling and swearing within, which meant Cathal was awake. Good. Damon hooked his thumbs in his pockets and tried to look like he wasn't full of nervous energy. But something was different now, and it had to do with George, and Damon did not like it. Mostly because he did like George. Not the way George liked him—not by a long shot. But he wanted to be friends with George, and that should have been awesome, because usually when he wanted to be friends with someone, he didn't say anything and missed his chance.

After a few minutes, Cathal opened the door, looking—as always when you caught him sleeping—like he was coming out of a coma in the horrible soap operas Damon used to make fun of with his coworkers between rushes at work.

Damon rocked back on his heels. "I'm going to George's bakery now." At least he didn't sound nervous. He sounded gruff when he was tense, which worked in his favor since people thought he was tough instead of realizing he was one inch from breaking and running.

"And?" Cathal's eyes couldn't quite focus on Damon's face. It might have been cute if Damon wasn't so antsy.

"Did you get any sleep?" That wasn't what Damon meant to say. But things popped out of his mouth around Cathal. Lately they hadn't even been insults. Like that invitation to the drawing class last night. Cathal smacked his lips. "I did, actually. Why are you here?"

"Do you want to come with me? To George's, I mean." Damon bit down on the inside of his cheek before he could say anything else stupid.

Cathal stared blankly at him. Damon thought he was trying to come up with a good insult, but he was still half asleep. "Why would I want to do that?"

Damon made himself stand straight, but he avoided Cathal's eyes. "There'll be sweets. I thought you might want some."

Cathal blinked slowly, now staring at Damon the way he stared at a whiteboard covered in equations. Not like it was incomprehensible—like he knew he'd forgotten something. Then he shook his head, pressing his forehead against the doorframe. "I think I'll be all right."

Damon sighed, despite himself.

Cathal wrinkled his nose. "I volunteered to help you make friends, not cockblock you. Just...try to stop looking at George like you're waiting for the cockroaches to come bursting out of his skin."

Damon laughed, again despite himself. "Okay, fine, but only since that actually sounded like you." He bit his lip, but he couldn't stop himself. His eyes flicked to Cathal's face. "I'll bring you something back."

"I will never turn down free food. I am a starving academic, after all."

Damon rubbed his mouth and realized he was smiling. "I know. I'll be back before Felix gets home from school."

"Like I care," said Cathal, but he wasn't scowling either.

ON THE DRIVE over to George's, Damon almost chickened out at least three times. But if he went home early, Cathal would want to know why, and he'd make fun of Damon. And, really, Damon knew he'd have a good time, once he got all his jitters out.

He parked in back of the Jasmine Unicorn, next to a car he recognized as George's, and gave himself a full minute to sit in the car and take deep breaths.

He went in the back door, which opened right onto the work area. Damon had hoped George would be in the front with a customer so he'd have a moment to acclimate, but George was sitting on one of the work counters next to a small woman with freckles and a pixie cut. Damon pushed a smile onto his face and walked over, hoping he looked friendly and not like he was going to throw up.

George turned to Damon. "Oh, good, you're here already."

Damon stopped a few feet away from the table. "I said I'd be here at nine."

George shrugged, but the woman made a face. "The people George invites over usually have a flexible idea of time."

"I was a line cook. If you're late, that means you don't want your job." He stuck out his right hand to the woman. "I'm Damon Eglamore."

She had a grip like dynamite. "I'm Heather. I need to ask you a series of questions, and I expect you to answer honestly." She looked like she was thinking about using him to demonstrate a perfect judo body throw. And she had the height and leverage for it.

"Please don't, Heather," said George, pinching the bridge of his nose.

Heather pointed at him. "No. I'm sick and tired of you bringing weirdos over here. We had a deal."

George didn't uncover his face, as though this were the most humiliating thing that had happened to him in days. "Damon, do you mind? I promise I never actually agreed to this, but she threatened to make me play the attacker for her self-defense trainees if I didn't let her."

Damon was uncomfortable, but it had nothing to do with Heather, so he didn't mind. "It's all good. Ma'am?"

"Don't try flattering me. I'm a hard-ass who doesn't fall for that shit." She put her hands on her hips. "First of all, are you planning on having sex anywhere in this kitchen?"

Damon's jaw dropped.

George turned scarlet. "I would like to point out that I am not the reason she's asking this question. This is a kitchen, for Christ's sake."

"Yeah, but the last kid you hired thought *my* workspace was a perfect height for table sex, and I never want to see someone's bare, pimply ass in my place of work ever again." Her eyes had not moved from Damon's face. "So?"

"No. Absolutely not." His words came out in a croak. Even Cathal wouldn't ask something like that right off the bat.

Well, maybe Damon wouldn't put it past him. Not only did Cathal not have a filter—he objected to the *idea* of filters and would yell at you on the subject for at least ten minutes if you so much as mentioned it.

Heather nodded. "Okay, good. There's one. Question two. Are you planning to take what you learn here and open a rival bakery to poach our client base?"

Damon blinked. "I don't want a job. You couldn't pay me to go back to work."

Heather nodded again. Damon didn't think she'd blinked once the entire conversation. "Good. Last question. Your opinion on cheating, as brief or as long as you want."

"No." George stepped between them. "Bad Heather. I appreciate that you are trying to maintain moral standards in this day and age, but no. Damon, I'm sorry about that. Can I buy you lunch to make up for it?" He glared at Heather. "And if you don't stop pushing it, I'll fire you."

"A) you threaten to fire me every day, and B) you can't do it. I own half the business, remember? Anyway, he passed the test." She glanced over at Damon and winked. "Good job, handsome."

"Not you too," said Damon, trying to make a joke.

"Honey, please. I could have sex, or I could play *Mass Effect* for the five billionth time. I know which one is the better choice, and so does my wife. But that doesn't mean I can't appreciate a strapping chef. I'm satisfied, and I need to make some calls. It was nice to meet you, Damon. Hopefully you will make it through the gauntlet."

George tried to poke her, but Heather slapped his hand away. "You realize you're the gauntlet, right?"

"Duh." Heather went through the door that separated the work area from the front showroom.

"Sorry." George rubbed the back of his neck. "She's... Well, she's a bit much, but she's also been my best friend since high school. And she's the best damn baker I've ever met."

Damon meant to look at George, but somehow the kitchen felt smaller with only the two of them in it. "It's okay. I like people that speak their minds."

"There's speaking your mind, and then there's Heather. But if you talk shit about her, I'm legally required to kill you. It's in the contract we signed when we set up the business."

Damon wanted to take the joke and run with it, or at least give George something to riff on, the way he did with Cathal or Felix. But his throat locked up. "Fuck."

He didn't realize he'd said it out loud until George glanced over at him, his eyes widening. "Something wrong?" George said in a tone of voice that even Damon recognized as forced.

Damon was not supposed to say anything. If somebody liked you and you knew about it but didn't like them back, the ball was in their court. And Cathal was right—Damon ought to give George a shot, especially because Damon didn't know why he wasn't interested in George. It wasn't Era holding him back. He was exactly Damon's speed: shy, awkward, and overly invested in all things food. So what was Damon's problem?

He didn't know, and he wasn't going to figure it out by pretending he would ever fall for George. "George, this is weird, and I can't act like it isn't."

George froze. Then, slowly, he relaxed, pushing his glasses up his nose. "Yeah, it's weird. You're like Heather, aren't you?" But his tone was wrong for joking, and he put his hands in his pockets.

Damon blew out a breath. "Look. I don't...you're really nice, George. I want to be friends with you. And not trophy-for-participation friends. Actual friends. I mean, for fuck's sake, my wife just died."

George's face shuttered. "God, I'm an ass. Not that that's what I was trying to do, but...well, yeah, that's totally what I was trying to do."

Damon shook his head sharply before George could say anything more. "No. I'm not—" He was getting upset, but it had nothing to do with George, and George didn't need to hear it. Unlike Cathal, George wouldn't shout back and then talk normally to you afterward. He'd be hurt, and Damon didn't want to hurt him. More.

Damon tried to gather his thoughts into a straight line instead of a big ball of stress. "Yeah, that takes the wind out of my sails." His voice cracked, but he kept going. "I will be sad for the rest of my life. But I'm—" He sighed, frustrated with his own inability to articulate it.

He wished Cathal was here. Cathal never let him leave a sentence hanging, but George watched him with a polite non-expression, waiting for him to figure out his thought. Which felt about as easy as reading a line from *Julius Caesar* without time to prepare.

Finally, Damon said, "Look. I lived my life for her, because I never thought I would have a life where she wasn't there. Now she isn't, and I'm trying to figure out who I am without her. And who I am wants to be friends with you. Not..." He trailed off, since the only thing he could think of was "bump uglies." Cathal wasn't all useful.

George stood still for a long moment. Damon waited for the sharp remark. He deserved it, after all. He should have made this clear before coming to see George.

Then George sighed like he'd gotten a kink out of his back. "You know, that's good. I mean, fuck. Half the reason I was doing this is because I thought I was supposed to. Gorgeous man falls into my lap after a bad end to a relationship and all that. But I'm not looking. I'm busy, and

I'm happy, and I don't need anything else." He glared at his feet. "I mean, I guess I'm still letting Cleon fuck up my life, but it wasn't that long ago, and we were together for way, way too long. So did you actually want to learn stuff? I've got work to do."

Damon drew back in surprise. "You're not kicking me out?"

"Why would I do that? I mean—what you said made sense, and honestly, you're so hot it's intimidating, so I'm sort of relieved." George tipped his head back, checking that last statement. "Yeah, no, I'm busy. I'd much rather have another guy to hang out with than any pre-dating holding pattern crap."

Damon stared at him. "Oh."

George tipped his head to the side. "Actually, that was refreshing. We had a discussion about feelings like adults. I don't know if that's ever happened to me."

Damon was still trying to get his head around the idea they weren't going to argue. George really wasn't like Cathal. "I know what that's like."

"Was your wife not the heartfelt discussion type?" George asked, carefully.

Damon couldn't help smiling at that. It felt...good. "No, Era never talked about anything without a full outline. Which worked out, I guess."

"You'll have to tell me how you ended up married to an actual adult one of these days so I know how to catch one when I find one." George paused, his expression turning cautious. "Was that okay?"

Damon nodded. "Actually, it's nice. The only people I talk to are Cathal or my son. We don't...we haven't gotten to talk about her much, yet."

George drummed his fingers on his lips. "Tell you what. Let's have an early lunch to wash away the awkward, and you can tell me all about her."

Damon rocked back on his heels. "Will you still show me some stuff?"

George grinned. In his eyes was a hint of mania. "Oh, yes, yes, I will. Believe me, you're going to be sick of cake by the time we're done here."

GEORGE ORDERED ENOUGH Chinese food to feed a small army. After the three of them finished eating, George got to his feet and cracked his knuckles over his head. Damon started to get up, but George pointed at him. "No, no, stay put. I've got things to show you."

Heather groaned around a mouthful of noodles. "Oh, God, not this shit." Damon glanced at her, hoping for a hint, but she shook her head. "You'll see. He's been dithering about it for weeks."

"Yeah, well, Jenny was the decider, and now she's gone, which means you guys get the job in her stead." George took a sheet pan covered in wax paper out of a flat refrigerator drawer and set it on a display table. "So this is a proof of concept." He took another pan covered in wax paper out of a different drawer and set it beside the first. "And this is the safe route."

Damon took his cue to get up. Heather growled and kept eating.

George took the wax paper off the first sheet pan, revealing a set of sugar candy pieces. They were green and brown, like pieces of stained glass, but Damon wasn't sure what they were supposed to make. George carefully interlocked them to form a three-dimensional pine tree. "Ta-da!"

Damon studied it. "It's pretty," he said, unsure what the point was besides showing off. He'd never tried sculpting sugar. It took equipment he didn't have yet, like a candy thermometer and a big enough flat surface to pour molten hot sugar. And a space where he could guarantee Felix or Cathal wouldn't come in while he was trying to do it.

"And a shit-ton of work for something that'll break if you breathe on it," Heather said, still engrossed in their leftovers.

"But it's super impressive," said George. "Here's my other idea." He took the wax paper off a piece of white fondant painted in food coloring with a forest scene. It looked like a matte painting for an eighties fantasy movie, complete with perspective tricks.

Damon nodded thoughtfully. "That's also cool. So...what's it for?"

George looked surprised. "A competition." Damon stared at him, not wanting to have to ask, because now he felt stupid for not knowing. "Isn't that how you found out about the bakery?"

"I found it on an image search. I was looking for cake coloring ideas, and your wedding stuff came up." He frowned. "So...you do Food Network stuff?"

"Not that fancy, though I wouldn't turn it down if they asked." George sighed wistfully. "Someday, Jonathan Bennett will call me."

"I keep telling you, he's not in charge of who shows up on Cake Wars." Heather smirked at Damon when he jumped. Damon hadn't heard her sneak up to the table.

"Yeah, but this is my fantasy, okay?" George put his hands on his hips. "Anyway, yeah, I do competitions. Nothing national. But for local access cable and the college TV stations. That's where all our business comes from, though, so I assumed you'd seen some of it."

Damon considered this. "So...why the different techniques?"

George shrugged. "The next competition is supposed to have a fantasy creature in some kind of cool environment. I could either do a fancy painting, like so, or I was thinking I'd make fancy sugar decorations, like so. Either way, the cake is going to be a unicorn, but I don't know which one is better—the fondant is easier and less risky, but the sugar looks cool."

Damon glanced at Heather, instinctively, but Heather held up her hands. "Oh, no, I help out at the competitions, but this shit is all him. I don't wanna jinx it."

"I can't believe that's the one thing you're superstitious about," George muttered, adjusting one of his sugar trees.

"You remember what happened the first time we did this," said Heather, her expression dark.

"Yes, but since then, we've had a wonderful string of successes, even if we haven't always won. That's all beside the point." George turned to Damon. "What do you think, Damon? Should I throw caution to the wind?"

Damon tried not to fidget. George liked him, for whatever reason, and he didn't want George to notice that he was the most boring person on the planet. "I don't really know if I'm qualified for this. Let's start with you teaching me the basics, huh? I only made my first cake from scratch the other day."

"Yes, but I believe in hooking 'em when they're young. It means you won't argue with me like Heather."

"No one will argue with you like me," said Heather, looking at the contents of a bin. "And he can start by being a nice manly man and getting some more cake flour. We're nearly out."

Damon hopped off the table. "Now that I can do."

AFTER DAMON LEFT for George's bakery, Cathal decided to go back to sleep since if he stayed awake, he would mope. When he went downstairs to poke around in the kitchen, Felix and Damon were in the living room watching *Scandal*. Cathal tried to sneak by without being seen, but Felix spotted him and paused the show. "Cathal! Dad brought you scones!"

"Scones," Cathal said. "What are scones?"

"They're delicious, that's what," said Felix.

Damon avoided Cathal's eyes. "You have definitely had too much sugar. They're in the kitchen if you want them. Otherwise, they're good for breakfast. I know you like sweet things with your coffee."

Cathal wasn't sure what to say, so he nodded. He wanted to stand there and ask them things, but it was a stupid want, so he excused himself and went back upstairs, producing such productive notes as *I'm an idiot* and *I should have gone home.*

HE COULDN'T AVOID Damon forever. When he went downstairs the next morning, he found Damon piping icing onto star-shaped sugar cookies. "What are those for?" he asked before he could stop himself.

"Thought I could use the practice." Damon was frowning, but that could have been from concentration. "George was showing me some new techniques yesterday. He's a real genius with this stuff."

Cathal poured himself a cup of coffee. "So how was that?" he asked, because he was supposed to be invested in Damon's life now and not because he liked to poke a bruise.

Damon's hand slipped, and he mussed one of the star shapes. He brushed the icing away with his thumb before answering. "He does competitions, apparently."

"Competitions?" That was an honest question. "What, like the ones we watch on TV?"

Damon nodded. "One of his assistants dropped out to start her own place, and he's looking for someone new."

Cathal made himself smirk as he sipped his coffee, even though he was not even in the vicinity of amused. "And by someone you mean you, right?"

Damon narrowed his eyes, too serious for someone with pink frosting all over his fingers. "No, he needs someone with experience. They'll be on TV, and they could win a lot of money. I'm just a beginner."

"Still. That's a great pickup line, and I'll be surprised if he doesn't end up using it."

Damon shook his head. "You're like a dog with a bone about some things, aren't you?"

Cathal said nothing.

"The scones are in the cupboard if you want one."

Cathal didn't want anything George had made, even though it was petty. But Damon had been right when he said Cathal liked sweet things with his coffee, and the scones were glazed.

And they were delicious, like everything else George made.

Ten: No Joke in this Title because this Chapter Is about FEELINGS.

DAMON HAD HOPED the first full rehearsal would cheer him up, since it did involve his son romping around in a dress and enough glitter makeup for at least half a drag queen. But it wasn't funny, and not only because he couldn't hear the dialogue since the kids wouldn't get to wear microphones until the final dress rehearsal.

Nah. He was in an off mood, and he couldn't put his finger on why.

It didn't help that Cathal had left him alone to go help Cleon with something or other. The other parents were nice, but Damon didn't know them well, and George was painting a set, so Damon was alone on the catwalk, flipping lights on the stage to set the mood.

He was settling into a good brood when someone came up the steps. Damon kept his attention on the switchboard to indicate he wasn't interested in talking.

"Are you feeling okay?" George asked, coming to stand next to him. "Evie says there's a nasty flu strain going around the school."

Damon straightened up to give George access to the panel. "Nah, I'm okay."

"Damn, it would have been really funny if you puked over the side of the catwalk." He propped his elbows on the railing.

"I can't throw up now. Felix looks so good in that dress." He pointed down at the stage. He couldn't hear the lines, but since only Titania and Oberon were on stage, they were presumably arguing about Oberon's little servant. "I don't know if I get what this director is doing. Are they dancing the tango?"

"I guess." George squinted at the stage. "They've got good chemistry, though. I'd swear Gareth likes him."

Damon glanced at the stage again, although since both kids were pretending to hate each other, their expressions and body language weren't much help. A further complication in Felix's love life was the last thing he needed. "He'd better not."

"What, don't tell me Felix's straight as an arrow?" said George, his lips twitching. "My gaydar is broken, but even I'm not that dense."

"Felix doesn't do labels because he says nothing fits him." Damon slumped against the railing. "I say that because Felix likes the other twin. Theseus."

George tucked his hands in his armpits. "I guess I shouldn't be surprised. I'm terrible at recognizing couples."

"Trust me, they fight like cats and dogs." Damon looked at the vast array of buttons on the switchboard instead of trying to gain further meaning from the play. That had been his wife's job, not his.

George shrugged. "Eh. That doesn't mean anything. That's how Heather and her wife are. And I thought you and Cathal were a couple when I first saw you."

Damon looked at him sharply. "What do you mean?"

He must have looked scary, because George stammered. "You know, you were going at it, but I thought it was a flirting thing. I see a lot of different types of people at the bakery. Sometimes from the outside, it looks like people can't stand each other, but then they do something else that makes it clear how much they care. But they're like Heather. They can't say something outright when they could punch someone and call that communication." He shook his head. "Sorry, sometimes I get like that. I guess I believe in love after all, broken heart or not."

"Mm," said Damon. "I mean, you kind of have to for your job."

"You'd be surprised how many wedding people are cynical hacks who like the sound of getting paid a mint for a few hours of pictures or whatever."

Before George could say anything else, Helena tripped over her gown's train and crashed through the canvas backdrop.

George winced. "I'll, uh, I'll go see if they need help."

"You do that," said Damon, leaning on the railing again.

George really thought he was with Cathal? Why? What was he missing?

THE NIGHT OF the first performance finally arrived. Felix manifested his anxiety through practicing scales on his keyboard and eating lots and lots of sugary cereal. As well as getting into whatever Damon brought back from George's.

"What is all this about, then?" Cathal demanded after finding Felix crouched on the table eating Lucky Charms from the box for the second night in a row. "It's not stage fright, so what's on your mind, nephew of mine?" Felix meekly held out a handful of marshmallows. Cathal took them. "Don't think this gets you out of answering my question."

Felix sighed, letting his head fall back. "Oh, I don't know. It's been—weird. I still can't talk to Morgan without sounding like an idiot, but he doesn't seem to care, and

Jerky McJerkface is still a jerk, except that I end up talking to him more than Morgan because Gareth actually talks." He peered into the box and sighed.

"Not having the guts to kiss someone is nothing to be ashamed of. I haven't kissed plenty of people because I like them better as friends. Sometimes it's the wiser choice." Felix looked crestfallen, and Cathal poked him in the side. "Don't do that. I wasn't finished. As I was saying, sometimes it's the better choice, but I would not say in this case. You like the boy. Go ahead and tell him. Take a chance." He crossed his arms. "And if you're waiting for some heaven-sent right moment, stop it. Just talk to him. Goodness knows you're awful at keeping your mouth shut, so go ahead and put your foot in it. I'm giving you permission."

Felix laughed weakly. "Yeah, I guess so." He rubbed the back of his neck. "You make it sound so easy, though."

"It never is."

And Felix looked up, startled by how serious Cathal sounded.

Cathal shrugged. "Take it from someone who knows, my boy. Honesty is the hardest thing in the whole world." He patted Felix's knee. "Now put that away or you'll never get to sleep."

DESPITE FELIX'S NERVES—he'd finished off the entire box of Lucky Charms at some point—he performed admirably, as always. Not to say that everything went perfectly. Alex's signature trick as Bottom was sliding out on stage and skidding to a stop, but the first time he attempted this, the stopping part didn't go so well. He made it look purposeful, though, or at least as purposeful as a teenager can look doing anything. And George pressed the wrong button and bathed the first forest scene in purple light instead of green, although it made for a charming effect. Much as Cathal was loath to admit it.

Everything else went smoothly, which, all things considered, was a minor miracle when dealing with fifteen-odd teenagers and a couple disinterested parents.

The success of the performance seemed to have gotten rid of Felix's jitters, if only temporarily; he bounced in his seat on the drive home. "So Daaad," he said, drawing out the word in a way that made it clear a request for something questionable was about to follow.

"So Feeeeeelix," said Damon, his lips twitching.

"Gareth wants to have a cast party." That came out all in a rush, and Felix leaned forward between the passenger and driver's seat.

"Sit like a human, Felix," said Cathal, because Damon was pulling out of the parking lot. Felix obeyed, although he was still bouncing.

Once they were on the road, Damon said, "I thought Gareth was a jerk."

"Well, yeah, but it's Morgan's house too, and it's huge. Their dad is, like, super rich."

Damon narrowed his eyes. "Why do I get the feeling that your definition of awesome involves underage drinking?"

"Dad!" Felix crossed his arms over his chest, looking offended. "First of all, Morgan's dad is tough as nails, so none of that is happening. Second, even if there was alcohol, you're the one who's always saying you trust me not to do that stuff."

Damon nodded, chastised. "You can't blame me for being careful, Felix. I know it takes a lot for you to dislike a person, so I can't help but be skeptical about this Gareth character."

"Morgan keeps saying me and Gareth got off on the wrong foot," Felix mumbled. "And I guess he's not so bad. Kind of. If you squint."

Cathal looked over his shoulder. "Well, you should start squinting. Siblings are important to any romantic endeavor."

Damon snorted.

Cathal sniffed. "I assume that laughter, Damon, was because you understood my role as gatekeeper for all of Era's boyfriends, and that is precisely why I understand how important brother figures are. Believe me when I say that none of the men Era dated before you were worth anything."

"But you hated Dad!" said Felix.

Cathal glanced sideways at Damon, but Damon was paying too much attention to the road. His mouth was twitching, but he was determinedly not smiling. "Well, yes, but that doesn't discount the fact that Era's other boyfriends were pricks. They would never admit that she was smarter than them. I didn't like Damon, but I knew he would treat her right."

"Are you making stuff up, or are you being serious? Because if I have to get Gareth's approval to make Morgan like me, I'm screwed. Gareth is, like, allergic to liking things." Felix paused. "Openly, anyway. He's actually kind of good at dancing and music and stuff, but he gets all weird if you point that out. I don't get him. Especially since I've heard him be. Like. Really nice with his brother and stuff, even if it was only when they didn't know I was listening."

"I feel like I should scold you for eavesdropping, but honestly, I'm curious where you overheard this since you said that Morgan never talks," said Damon as he pulled into their driveway.

"It wasn't on purpose! I'm slow compared to them, since they're so tall, so they always beat me around corners before I can tell them that I'm following." Felix fidgeted. "That doesn't mean I didn't like getting to listen. Maybe I should tell him..."

Cathal shook his head. "Where did you come from?"

Damon rolled his eyes. "Some of us do know what morals are, Cathal, even if you don't. It's lucky you never hung around before this, or my son would be a degenerate like you."

"He's already a degenerate like me, in the most basic sense of the term," said Cathal. Damon looked confused. "He's chasing a boy, isn't he?"

Damon made an irritated noise. "You know that's not what I meant."

"If you don't want me to pull your tail, stop making it so easy."

"That's victim-blaming, Cathal," said Felix, his tone sanctimonious. "Sarah was telling me about it the other day. The oppressor should never tell the oppressed that the oppression is their fault."

"I've attended that lecture on rape culture, thank you very much. I think your mother gave it a time or two." Cathal glanced over at Damon, who was already out of the car. "Besides, your father gives as good as he gets."

"I know he does. I'm teasing you." Felix hopped out. "Anyway, you guys hardly fight anymore. It's weird, but I'm not gonna complain. I hate it when people yell."

Cathal waited a moment before following them. If Felix had noticed they were getting along, then things were worse than he thought.

AT THE FINAL performance, Demetrius flubbed his lines and had to be replaced at the end of act three when he threw up all over backstage. Someone else volunteered to clean it up, thankfully.

"If Felix gets the flu, you're dealing with it," Damon said, elbowing Cathal in the side.

"Yes, because my bedside manner is to die for. And what are you going to be doing that you can't take care of your own son? It's not like you've found gainful employment." Damon made a noncommittal noise, and Cathal glanced at him, so startled he almost forgot to press the button to cue the donkey brays. "Have you?" He sounded pathetic, so he cleared his throat. "I'd hate to think I'd have to shout at an empty house, you know."

Damon shifted his weight. "Well, George keeps asking me if I want to work at the bakery. Or join his competition team."

Cathal bit the inside of his cheek so he wouldn't make a face. George wasn't there to see—he'd volunteered to run the kid to the hospital, since the boy's parents weren't at the play. But Cathal didn't want Damon to see his expression and start asking questions. Cathal wasn't sure if he could come up with a convincing reason why he didn't like George. He might end up spitting out the truth, and while he didn't know much about confessing feelings to other people, he was pretty certain you didn't do it while on the catwalk above your nephew's play.

Damon didn't continue, which was good, because then Cathal could school his face to disinterested blankness. "So? Are you going to take him up on it then?"

Damon leaned against the railing. It was too dark up there to read his expression, but Cathal was willing to bet it was inscrutable anyway. "I'm not good enough. And I think he's only doing it to try and spend more time with me, but I already told him I'm not interested, and he said he's asking me because I'm the best sculptor he has now that Jenny went on to greener pastures." He paused. "Jenny was his last gum paste person."

"I hate it when you talk about food. You stop using human words and make things up to confuse me." He narrowed his eyes. "Wait, you told George you weren't interested in him?"

Damon looked surprised that it had caught Cathal's attention. Or surprised about something, anyway. "I'm not, so yes. He was very nice about it. Really embarrassed, but then he said it made it easier for him to want to take me on the team, anyway." Damon shook his head. "You don't have to sound so surprised. It was the right thing to do. And I felt guilty using his stuff when I knew he was only letting me to get in my pants."

If only Damon weren't such a damned decent man. Cathal'd always known this, but he hadn't cared until recently. He hated caring about things. They just got taken away sooner or later.

He bit back the urge to sigh. "Well, I suppose it worked out for you, then. So are you going to do it?"

"I told you, I haven't decided yet. It's a big commitment—it'd be like going back to work, only I wouldn't get paid for it. Unless we won the competition, maybe, but most of that money goes to taxes and the rest of it would go to the bakery. But maybe I need a big commitment again." Damon said that last almost to himself.

Cathal looked him over, but as usual, he had no idea what was going on underneath that buzz cut. "Am I missing something?"

Damon avoided his eyes, looking out over the play as his son kissed Alex's donkey mask. "I dunno. But..." He sighed. "I've been trying to make something of myself, but it doesn't really matter. I could go on like this for as long as I wanted—everything's taken care of financially. Except I don't know if I want to. I'm already not worth much. I don't want to make that worse."

"The worst part of these conversations," Cathal said, carefully, because he wasn't used to keeping away from landmines instead of gleefully stepping on them, "is I can tell that you're serious. Why are you always saying such bad things about yourself?"

Damon looked at him, surprised. "Because it's true, and I don't know how to make it not true."

"It's already not true," said Cathal, but Damon just looked at him, and Cathal didn't know what to say to back up his point that didn't involve kissing more ridiculous than Titania's. But then it was time to switch the lighting again, and the moment was gone.

THEY WENT HOME without Felix again, since he was at Gareth's cast party. Damon was glad his son was getting out and socializing, but he wished he was around, because Felix always made for a good distraction.

But since that wasn't an option, Damon decided to go to bed. If he stayed up and tried to watch TV or work on something, he'd end up frustrated and even angrier with himself. This way, he'd spend a few hours staring at the ceiling and then eventually fall asleep. And he'd feel better once he slept. Or at least he hoped so.

He'd shrugged out of his shirt and sat on the bed when someone knocked on his door. It could only be one person—

not because Felix wasn't there, but because Felix wouldn't have bothered knocking. Damon glared at the floor, but he couldn't even muster up the energy to be angry. If he stayed in his room and ignored the knock, then *he'd* be the asshole.

He pushed himself up and opened the door. Only when he saw the blank look on Cathal's face did he realize he was still shirtless. Well. Whatever. Cathal had seen him shirtless before. Probably.

"I made you popcorn," said Cathal, his voice too quick. He held up a bowl as proof.

"I see that," said Damon, because he didn't know how to say *What the hell are you doing?* Besides actually saying *What the hell are you doing,* which would have been too harsh. And Cathal was trying to help, exactly like he'd been trying to help all these past few months. It wasn't his fault Damon didn't know how to feel about that. Or how to say it only made him feel shittier.

"It has cheese on it."

"Okay…" said Damon, waiting for the weirdness that accompanied Cathal saying anything. But Cathal just looked at him, apparently as much at a loss for words as Damon was.

Damon sighed and took a handful of the popcorn, though the idea of eating any turned his stomach. "Is there a reason you're here? I know you like cheese popcorn and all, but I was going to go to bed."

Cathal's mouth twisted to the side, and he dropped his eyes. "Well. I felt—that we should discuss. What we were discussing earlier, I mean. And it seems to be easier to start those kinds of conversations with an excuse, so I tried food, because that's working for you. And popcorn is the only food I can make without burning down the house."

Damon smiled, despite himself. Damon never would have thought Cathal could look so sheepish. What he thought he had to be sheepish about, Damon didn't know, but...maybe he'd find out.

He wanted to talk to Cathal about his feelings. Now *there* was a weird thought.

Damon shoved it aside because he didn't know what it meant. "You could have come and talked to me without all this, you know."

Cathal shrugged, his face neutral.

Damon rubbed his forehead. "Yeah, I'll come down. Let me put on a shirt."

Cathal nodded once, still looking dazed. "Don't take forever, or I'm eating all of this. I really like cheese popcorn."

"I know. That's why it's the only thing you can cook." Cathal opened his mouth, but Damon shut the door, even though he was curious to hear what Cathal would have said in response.

And that was weird too. Damon tried to think, but he was terrible at sitting and thinking. And anyway, what was the point? Cathal wouldn't let him alone until he finished figuring himself out anyway.

Wasn't that supposed to annoy him?

Damon realized how long he'd been standing there staring blankly at the floor. He shrugged on his shirt without bothering to button it. Then he went downstairs and stood in the doorway. Cathal glanced at him and away, then stuffed a handful of popcorn in his mouth. If Damon hadn't known better, he'd have thought Cathal was blushing. But Damon did know better, so he fixed his collar and went to sit on the opposite end of the couch, as always.

"So what are we talking about?" Damon asked, crossing his arms. He sounded upset, but maybe that was a good thing. It would keep Cathal from pressing him too hard. Maybe. Probably not.

Cathal turned sideways and pulled his knees up to his chest, eyeing Damon like a stack of papers he needed to grade. "So what's all this nonsense about you not being worth anything?"

Damon tried copying Cathal's tone of voice. "We've had this conversation before."

Cathal just stared at him without blinking. He could make his eyes so cold and distant when he wanted.

The words spilled out of Damon like bile. "Look at me. I've fallen apart without Era. I'm trying to get things back, but I don't even know what things are. I've never done anything worthwhile. I'm..." He had to look away, biting down on his lip to keep from saying anything more.

"If you say worthless, I'm dumping the popcorn bowl on your head." Cathal wasn't joking either, but Damon kept his mouth shut. Cathal was good at finding his weak points, but that didn't mean he had to roll over and expose them. "If you don't say anything, I'm *still* dumping the popcorn on your head."

Damon tried to relax. This would help. "You'll dump it on me no matter what I do."

"Do not impugn my honor that way." He paused for effect. "That would be a waste of good popcorn. And also, we'd never get it all out of the couch."

Damon turned to look at Cathal fully. "All right, fine. You're the one who never shuts up about evidence and hypotheses. Prove me wrong. Because I keep trying to find ways to be positive about this, and I keep coming up empty." Damon couldn't hide the desperation in his voice.

"I'm sorry, I know this is serious, but I have to take a moment to be emotional about your use of the word hypotheses." Cathal clutched his heart.

Damon threw a piece of popcorn at him. "If you're going to drag me down here, the least you can do is be serious for five fucking minutes."

To his surprise, it worked, and Cathal dropped the fake look of surprise. His eyes moved over Damon's face, and Damon wanted to look away. Except he'd asked for it, and he was not about to admit he was a coward. Out loud.

"Well, you're discounting a lot. You've been to culinary school, and you worked your way up from the bottom at your old restaurant. And now you've picked up a new skill well enough to impress someone who does it for a living." Cathal tapped his lips with a finger, tipping his head to the side like always when he was explaining something.

It was...nice. To have someone put so much thought into Damon's life. He hadn't realized how much he missed that.

Cathal held up his finger. "And beyond all that, you shouldn't forget you're a good dad. You've got a son who's only moderately messed up. Most parents would kill for that."

Damon opened his mouth to defend his son and then paused. "I want to ask why you think Felix is messed up, but he does eat cereal without milk." Damon met Cathal's eyes for a second, but the force of Cathal's regard was too much. Damon had to look away, and the words slipped out before he could stop them. "I never know whether you're being honest or if you're trying to shut me up."

Cathal made a soft noise of frustration and covered his face with his hands. Then he relaxed, digging his hands into his hair instead. "I've never lied to you. I've never put my feelings into words very well, but I've always told you the truth as I see it. I just—" He put his hands down, slowly. "I've realized lately that the truth is a lot more complicated than I ever thought."

Damon studied him. "You've insulted me a lot. But I'd probably say it myself, given the chance."

Cathal hesitated. Then words came spilling out of him, as fast and as hard as they had for Damon. But what did he have to hold back? "When I first met you, I was in a bad mood. I'd slept in and missed a test, so I ended up with a *C* in that class. The only bad grade I got in college. So I wanted someone to be pissed at, and you were there. I could tell by looking at you that you swung both ways, and you'd end up dating some woman and never have to deal with the shit I've gotten my whole life. I've never been allowed to hide, and when I was young and even dumber, I liked to take it out on other people."

He let out a slow, heavy breath, looking at the couch instead of Damon as though he was talking to himself equally as much. "All of that was a cover. I was angry at myself, and I wanted to make someone else feel shitty to make up for it. And then when Era brought you to meet me, I remembered I'd acted like a fucking asshole the first time I saw you, which meant I had to keep acting like a fucking asshole for consistency's sake."

He closed his eyes. "And...and the second I saw Era look at you, I knew that was it. You were the most important person in her life. She was going to leave me, and I'd have to learn to act like I was happy about it. Just like I had to act like I didn't give a shit that my parents didn't want me."

Damon stared at his hands. He'd built his life around the idea that Cathal hated him from the start, had seen through Damon to the hollow place at his core, where he was always trying to convince himself he mattered. Except...except that wasn't true.

Damon covered his face. He was shaking. "I guess I should accept that this is never going to make sense to me.

You staying here, I mean. But that doesn't mean it's bad. It's..." He parted his fingers, feeling strange all over. "It's good."

"It is good," Cathal said, his voice softer than Damon had ever heard.

Damon took in a deep breath, trying to get himself under control. He still didn't understand what was going on in his own head, but at least he didn't feel like he needed to bury his face under his blankets and never come out again. "I guess if you keep saying it, then I have to believe you believe it, anyway. But I don't know what to make of it. I've never felt more worthless in my life, and here you are, telling me I'm not instead of reminding me that I am."

Cathal shrugged. "Yes, well, I never would have bet on Leonardo DiCaprio winning an Oscar, and yet here we are."

Damon smiled, finally. Letting that go felt good. "Leo earned that Oscar. Don't talk shit."

"If I didn't talk shit, I'd never talk at all." But he was smiling in a quiet, satisfied sort of way. It was good to look at.

"I wish," Damon said. Then Cathal dumped the popcorn on his head.

AFTER THEY CLEANED up the couch, they ended up watching *Jessica Jones*, because Felix wouldn't shut up about it. They got into an argument about whether Krysten Ritter or evil David Tennant was better looking, but otherwise, they mostly sat in silence. And not a bad one either. They were both just...thinking.

Or Damon was, anyway. When Netflix asked him if he was still watching, he turned to ask Cathal if they were done for the night, only to see that Cathal had slumped over against the middle cushion of the couch, asleep. He'd tucked his hands up under his face, and he was frowning in his sleep. Damon reached to wake him, and then stopped, his hand hovering over Cathal's hair.

If he woke Cathal, Cathal would say something stupid, and Damon would get distracted and lose his train of thought. Now, with the TV quiet and Cathal asleep, maybe....maybe he could figure it out.

He leaned back, crossing his arms over his chest, and tried to recapture the thought that had been out of reach before.

Cathal had done nothing but help since Era died. Grudgingly. Sarcastically. But Damon couldn't claim he'd been eager to be helped. Eventually, Damon would have come out of his room and found a way back to living by himself, but he wouldn't have gotten as far without Cathal yelling at him every step of the way. Life without Era wasn't good, by any stretch of the imagination. But when he was working with George—or when he was spending time with Cathal—he could see his way further down the path, to a point where he wouldn't wake up every morning feeling like someone had sucked all the air out of the room.

Why? Why had Cathal been able to help him when everyone else annoyed him?

This whole time, he'd thought he'd been tolerating Cathal—that he was looking forward to the day when Cathal walked out of his door and never came back. When he would have the house to himself again. When someone wouldn't be pulling on his arm, telling him to get off his ass and do something to make himself feel better. To make himself be better.

Except none of that was true. He wanted Cathal around. Not only because Cathal helped him think more clearly, or because he could always argue Damon out of his depressive ruts, but because Cathal would forget to eat if you didn't remind him. Because he would pretend he didn't give a shit about anyone or anything if you let him. Because...because maybe he needed someone to take care of him as much as Damon did.

How was Damon supposed to tell him all that? If he said anything, it would come out wrong. Cathal would make fun of him for it, and Damon would try to pretend like he never thought it at all.

What else could he do to make his point?

SOME TIME LATER, Cathal came awake. Damon was watching sports with the sound turned down. He hadn't noticed that Cathal was up, so Cathal took the moment to study him, pretending it wasn't for his own pleasure.

Damon's color had improved—his shade of pale was closer to "mushroom growing under a rock" versus "could be auditioning for Gollum." The dark circles under his eyes had faded, although he still wasn't getting a lot of sleep. And he was sitting up straight instead of slouching. Most importantly, no undercurrent of tension held him stiff. Despite Damon's troubling words, he was doing better. Cathal couldn't pretend it didn't ease his heart.

"You pick weird places to nap," said Damon without looking at Cathal.

Cathal wondered if he'd been caught staring. He forced back a blush and straightened up, pushing his hair out of his eyes. The pieces of his hair tie fell into his hands, and he scowled at them. "A couch is a normal place to take a nap, thank you."

"The couch is, but you take naps other places, and they're weird. I'm surprised Era never found you curled up under your desk at work." His voice was quieter than Cathal was used to.

Cathal had slumped over in his sleep, which meant now that he was sitting up, they were hip to hip and shoulder to shoulder. Cathal tried to insist he didn't care for this either, but that was a lie as blatant as any Felix told when the Lucky Charms box was empty. Cathal wanted to lean against Damon and go back to sleep.

"I don't sleep under my desk when I sleep at work. I sleep in the teacher's lounge. Or the lab. Obviously." Despite himself, his lips quirked in a smile. Waking up and finding Damon there was nice. He was so solid you could almost pretend he'd be there forever. Almost.

Damon leaned forward, reaching for a stainless steel water bottle Cathal had never seen.

"Is that actually water?" said Cathal, raising his eyebrows.

Damon made a face at him over the rim. "Yes, not that it's any of your business."

"Since when were you all eco-friendly?"

Damon turned it, revealing the logo of The Jasmine Unicorn. Cathal slumped against the couch.

"Why don't you like George?" Damon's voice was soft.

Cathal bit the inside of his cheek to keep himself still. "I don't like anyone." It wasn't a real answer, and he knew it.

Worse, *Damon* knew it. "Yes, but you really don't like George, which is weird, because usually when we run into another gay man, the two of you link arms and throw shade at everyone in the room."

Cathal kept looking at the TV, even though it was off. "Since when did you know the phrase 'throw shade'?" His voice was sharp, not light. "That's the wrong generation, anyway. Gays my age are catty."

Damon said nothing—in that irritating way of his—and it made Cathal want to spill everything. "Something about him rubs me the wrong way, that's all. I don't get along with most people. Again, you know this."

"I do."

Cathal glared at him. "But?"

"I didn't say anything." Cathal kept glaring at him, and Damon shifted. "Cathal—" He turned, suddenly, so their faces were right next to each other. Cathal kept the scowl on his face by sheer willpower, even though he wanted to squeak like a schoolgirl at her first dance. "I don't understand you at all." Damon's voice was almost a whisper.

"And in that, we are perfectly matched," said Cathal.

Then Damon kissed him.

Damon was a hesitant kisser—soft, gentle, not grabby. Cathal wondered when he'd last kissed someone outside of a hookup at a club or a cruising spot. He couldn't remember, and the thought made his stomach twist.

Or it would have, anyway, if his stomach wasn't already in knots because Damon was kissing him.

Cathal wanted nothing more than to lean into the kiss, to climb on Damon's lap and let the cards fall where they would. As it was, he couldn't help but open his mouth, inviting Damon to deepen the kiss—which he did, although the movement of his mouth remained slow. Cathal could count on one hand the number of times he'd been kissed with such care, and even though he knew he needed to stop this before it spiraled out of control, he couldn't.

He just wanted this moment to last forever. He tangled his fist in Damon's shirt, his only concession to desire, but Damon didn't take the invitation. Damon's hand crept up into Cathal's hair, twining through the loose strands. Cathal wore his hair long because he liked the way it looked, not because he cared what anyone else thought, but he'd never realized how nice it was to have someone stroke it. Damon was gentle, as Cathal was starting to realize he would be about everything.

Cathal lost track of how long they kissed—it was the longest he'd spent simply kissing since he'd left his teens behind.

It was blissful, and that was the worst, but Cathal couldn't even concentrate on how it was going to end soon. He was too caught up.

Then the front door crashed open.

Cathal jumped back like he'd been shocked; Damon remained on the couch, looking startled. His lips were swollen with kissing. It was a good look for him.

"Who's there?" Damon called, his voice rough. Cathal didn't remember untucking Damon's shirt, though he did remember smoothing his fingers along the line of hair that disappeared under his jeans.

"It's me, Dad!" Felix leaned in the doorway of the living room, looking dazed. He was also dripping wet, but it didn't seem to bother him. "Sorry. I didn't mean to bang the door like that. The wind blew it open."

Cathal moved aside so Damon could get up.

"What happened?" Damon asked, getting to his feet. "You're a mess."

Felix blushed tomato red and said nothing.

"What happened?" Damon repeated.

"Uh—" Felix glanced at Cathal. His blush darkened. "It's kind of a long story."

Cathal got to his feet automatically. "Do you need some advice?" It felt so easy asking now. Still confusing, but not difficult anymore.

But Felix fidgeted. "Um—I wanna talk to Dad, actually."

Cathal pretended interest in the pillows they'd knocked aside. "Oh. All right."

Damon looked at Cathal, and Cathal made a shooing gesture, fixing Damon with a glare he didn't actually feel. Damon glanced back at Cathal before he herded Felix out, but Cathal avoided his eyes. Not that he could focus on anything in the room anyway. His vision had gone blurry.

After he heard Felix's door close, Cathal made himself go upstairs instead of staring dumbly at the empty spaces where Era's pictures belonged. He shut the guest room door and locked it. He'd come to think of it as his room, but everything, from the pretty quilt that forced Cathal to make his bed in the morning to the cactus in the window, had been Era's choice.

He sat on his bed slowly, like he was in a dream. And he had been in a dream. His best friend was dead, and here he'd been, treating her son like his own, giving him romance advice and sticking his nose in his business. Kissing Damon on the couch littered with the cute Easter pillows she'd bought years ago. He'd been pretending he was a part of this life, when that couldn't be further from the truth. He belonged holed up in his apartment, eating ramen noodles out of a cup while he skimmed research articles. Alone.

He realized he was crying, brokenly, the way he had after his family kicked him out. The way he'd never shown anyone else. Not even Era. Even to her, he pretended nothing mattered. That *she* didn't matter. And now he could never tell her she was the only thing that ever did. He'd never tell her anything again.

Eleven: Metaphors Are Bad Enough. Similes Give Damon Hives.

DAMON WAS TOO thrown off by his own actions to argue with his son. A few hours ago, he would have given anything for Felix to come to him first for advice, but now he was wishing his son would have held off. Damon had never initiated a first kiss.

He couldn't even blame it on being drunk, but he didn't want to blame it on anything—it felt right at the time, and it still felt right, and *fuck* that was weird. He had his own sorting out to do. So maybe Felix's return was a good thing.

Felix sat on his bed, and Damon shut the door by leaning against it. "What are you doing back already? It's not anywhere near your curfew."

Felix fidgeted, biting his lip. "Well, um. Somebody brought beer to the party, so Mr. Lewis kicked us all out."

"What?" said Damon, straightening up.

"I didn't have any!" Felix's stricken expression meant he was telling the truth. "A bunch of kids showed up, not even all people who were in the play. And I guess somebody got the wrong idea. I don't really know, though. I was sort of hiding in Gareth's room the whole time."

"Sort of hiding?" Maybe it was a good thing Cathal wasn't running this conversation. He couldn't abide Felix's method of storytelling, which involved a lot of dancing around the point. Damon thought getting frustrated with someone for dancing around the point made them dance around the point more, but Cathal never listened.

He never listened to anything. Damon put his hands in his pockets so he wouldn't pass them over his mouth.

"Sort of," Felix repeated, pulling his knees up to his chest. "I was just—" He paused and hid his face in his knees, taking in a deep breath. Then he lifted his head again. "I was feeling really sad about Mom, and I didn't want to talk to anyone else because they were all in a good mood after the play, so we hung out by ourselves. And I played him a song that he helped the band with. And we talked about feelings. And he—told me he liked me."

"Wait, *Gareth* did?" Damon asked. "The bad twin. Not Morgan."

Felix hugged his knees tighter, nodding, too embarrassed to speak. Damon wasn't sure if he was embarrassed because he had to talk about liking people in general or Gareth in particular. Maybe both.

"Morgan and I, um, we talked about. Everything. A while ago." Felix rubbed his cheek, as though to erase the blush he was so famous for. "It turns out he doesn't like me. Well, I mean, he likes me. As a friend. But he doesn't *like* anybody, you know, romantically. And I know I should have said something to you guys, but I'm not, like, upset about it. Morgan's been going through some—stuff. He's not sure what kind of stuff yet, but he's gotta work through it before he can even think about other people."

Damon pushed off the door and sat beside Felix. Felix leaned into him, although he avoided his father's eyes. "So...how do you feel about that?"

Felix shifted his weight a few times before answering. "I dunno. There's...something else I haven't told you and Cathal about."

Damon raised his eyebrows. He doubted his son was talking about anything bad, but it was always good to be prepared.

"Not anything like *that*. It's...well, Gareth and I have had to spend a lot of time together because of the whole playing each other's spouses thing. And he's...not so bad. He has no filter, I guess, but...he's actually really nice. He just acts like he isn't for some reason. I think maybe he's used to people picking on Morgan because Morgan's so shy, but I dunno, really. I've ...learned a lot about him, I guess."

"And how do you feel about all that?" Usually Damon got lost when Felix insisted on explaining every single piece of backstory before explaining his problems, but sorting through all of it did make for a good distraction from Cathal.

"I don't know." Felix laced his fingers together. "I...I think maybe I was going after Morgan because it felt good and not because it felt right. I was honestly kind of relieved when he turned me down, and I thought things were going back to normal, but now Gareth—" He broke off, looking away. "He's actually helped me with a lot of stuff. And I like having him around. But I don't know if that means anything more than normal, and I dunno when I'll get a chance to talk to him, since Morgan told me they're both grounded. *And* I thought finally liking somebody would tell me where I fit in or how I identify or whatever, but it all feels more confusing than ever."

Felix curled a strand of hair around his finger. "I'm sorry I didn't tell you the truth. You and Cathal really liked that I liked Morgan, but...I don't know."

"Were you afraid we'd judge you if you liked someone else?"

Felix rocked his head back and forth. "You'd be all confused and I'd have to explain, I guess. And I don't know how to explain. I still don't even know how I feel."

Damon rubbed the back of his neck. "Not that I'm not happy that you came to me to talk about this, but I am surprised. You've had good luck with Cathal, strange as that is to say."

Felix looked at him for the first time, his eyes bright. "But that's the thing. You hated Cathal at first, but then you realized he's not so bad, and now you guys are getting along, and I thought...maybe you could tell me how that worked. I guess." He tipped his head back. "This is complicated and I don't like it."

"Life is always like that, kiddo. I wish I could tell you what I've figured out, but the truth is, I have no idea. I'm about as useful for advice as... I don't know. Something that's not good for advice."

Felix swung his legs. "I guess it's good to know you don't know what's going on either. That's what I wanted. Cathal always sounds like he's so sure."

Damon was about to agree, but then he remembered the surprise in Cathal's eyes when their lips met, the tentative nature of his movements. "If you need someone to be confused with, you came to the right place."

"I know, Dad." Felix leaned against him, heaving an oversized sigh. "I think I wanna go to sleep now. Maybe I'll feel better when I wake up."

Damon patted his shoulder. "Good strategy. Now I'm trusting you to actually go to bed and not stay up all night on Snapchat or whatever."

"*Dad.*" Felix rolled his eyes. "Obviously I'd be on Tumblr. But I really am tired."

WHEN DAMON STEPPED out into the hallway, he realized he had no idea what he wanted to do next.

Well. He did know. He wanted to rewind to the part where he was kissing Cathal, so they could discuss what that meant, but that wasn't going to happen. So how would he get back to that point?

He went to the stairs and peered down them for a sign that Cathal was still there. The TV wasn't on, but he couldn't remember if they'd been watching anything.

He went to Cathal's door instead and listened. Within, he heard papers shuffling and furniture being rearranged, so Cathal had come up here while he was talking to Felix.

If Damon went to his bedroom without reaching out, Cathal would act like none of this had ever happened. Damon had seen firsthand how good the other man was at concealing his feelings. Damon felt like a car stuck in neutral. Or maybe a car where the driver wasn't any good at shifting gears, and he was stressing himself out trying to function.

Fuck. Metaphors. That was the last thing he needed.

Damon rubbed his forehead. Then he knocked.

No answer from within. Damon didn't want to say anything, in case Felix heard. His son had always been a light sleeper, and Damon had no idea how to explain any of this to him.

Instead, Damon knocked again.

Still nothing.

Cathal was not asleep. But Cathal was not going to answer the door.

Well. His son was right, as he so often was. Damon went to go lay down.

HE WOKE UP at five, but he wasn't sure if that was because he'd slept badly or because it was ingrained in him at this point. When he first left his job, he'd been able to sleep in, but now his old schedule had returned to him, and it was awful. Waking up early made it clear how much of the day you had left to fill.

Before this he'd been getting better, but now he couldn't get the image of that closed door out of his mind. He'd been a fool in so many ways.

Well, he'd learned one thing since Era died. He could sit in bed and mope, or he could get up and do something. Sooner or later, momentum would carry him to something better.

TO HIS SURPRISE, Felix came down an hour later, rubbing his eyes. He sat at the table. "What are you making, Dad?"

"Nothing, really," said Damon, squashing the gum paste. "Just practicing. Couldn't you sleep either?"

Felix shrugged. "I had too much to think about, I guess."

"Make any decisions?" Damon asked, keeping his voice neutral.

Felix shook his head, staring at the floor. Felix didn't usually worry about anything for long; it didn't fit his face. "All I know is I'm hungry."

"You could have said you wanted me to make breakfast." Damon couldn't imagine eating, but making breakfast would help.

"That's no fun." Felix twisted on his chair as Damon gathered the ingredients for scrambled eggs and hash browns. "Should I go wake up Cathal?"

Damon paused, half out of the fridge. Then he made himself start moving again, glad he had his back turned. Felix was only perceptive when you didn't want him to be. "No, let him sleep. The smell'll wake him up if he's hungry."

Felix flopped forward on the table. "Why does everything have to be so *hard*?"

"This is why you need to learn to cook, son," said Damon, cracking eggs into a bowl. "Hash browns are delicious, but they're not complicated." He was surprised at how calm he sounded, but whatever happened was out of his control. He'd done something dumb, and now he'd have to take the cards where they fell.

"But then I couldn't make you make them for me."

Damon almost wished Cathal was down there with them. He would have had the perfect thing to call Felix, in that tone of voice that sounded so rude but was really the way Cathal talked when he didn't want to admit he had feelings like a person. Damon settled for, "At least you're not this lazy in other parts of your life."

"Cathal says it's being efficient."

It wasn't worth arguing, so Damon kept his mouth shut.

DAMON WAS FINISHING breakfast when he heard Cathal come downstairs. Damon wanted to step out in the hallway and see what was going on. But he made himself keep watching the hash browns, even though no amount of staring would make them turn golden and delicious any faster.

At the sound of footsteps, Felix perked up, but his brow furrowed when Cathal didn't immediately come in the kitchen. He stuck his head out. "Where are you going, Cathal?"

Damon didn't catch what Cathal said, and he told himself he did not care.

"So you're going to go without eating?" Felix said, sounding dismayed. "It's all ready, isn't it, Dad?"

Damon suppressed a grimace, turned away from the hash browns, and walked to stand by Felix.

Cathal had a duffel bag draped over one shoulder, pulling his suitcase behind him. He looked the same as when he arrived at their place after Era moved into the hospital: distant, unruffled, untouchable. Damon had forgotten how *empty* Cathal could look.

"I've got to go and get ready." Cathal was looking at Felix, not at Damon. He hadn't looked at Damon at all. "I've got to get things organized—the summer term'll start in less than a month."

"So you are going to teach summer classes?" said Damon. His voice sounded like it belonged to someone else.

Cathal shrugged. "They need my help. I can't really say no."

"Were you planning to walk there?" Damon's voice was sharp, like they still hated each other. Funny how fast that came back.

"It's called a bus, Damon." But Cathal's voice was weary, not angry.

Again, Damon spoke before he knew he would. "You're not taking the bus with all your stuff. Sit down and have some breakfast, and then I'll drive you."

Cathal hesitated, but, to Damon's surprise, he didn't argue. He set aside his duffel and suitcase and sat on the chair closest to the kitchen door.

"You look like crap, Cathal," said Felix.

Damon shot him a look, and Felix clapped his hands over his mouth.

"Clearly, you've been spending too much time with the triplets minus one," said Cathal. "Or me."

"Sorry," Felix mumbled. Damon forced himself to return to the food. He'd made enough for three people, even though he hadn't expected Cathal to join them. "You look really tired, I mean."

For his part, Cathal lounged in his chair like this was just another day. "I am in fact really tired. Don't get old, nephew mine. It sucks."

Damon realized he was pissed—not really pissed, under the surface pissed. He hadn't felt that in a while. He set a plate of hash browns in front of Felix and then Cathal.

Cathal didn't look up, but he was still talking to Felix. "Your powers of perception continue to astound me, my lad. However, my exhaustion is nothing new, as that is how I work." Cathal put his chin on his hand and leaned toward Felix. "What is new is whatever you inexplicably shared with your father and not me last night."

Felix dropped his eyes, blushing. "I thought you'd make sex jokes."

"Point," Cathal said. "But fret not. I'm not going to harp on you about it. At this point, I'm satisfied that you don't burst into flame saying the word. We have to work up to the joke point."

"Oh, good." Felix rubbed his cheek, still embarrassed, and looked at Damon. "Dad, did you want to tell him?"

Damon had been taking an extra long time serving himself. He told himself it was to give Felix a chance to talk to Cathal without him lurking in the background like a creeper, but he wanted to delay the moment when he had to sit at the table and pretend everything was normal. He squared his shoulders and turn to the table. "Why would I want to tell him? It's your news."

Felix hunched up his shoulders even more. "Yeah, but you're my dad. It's, like, your job to embarrass me, isn't it?"

A real smile touched Cathal's lips for the first time. "You don't want to admit that your evening involved *romance*."

Damon wished Cathal would look at him, to see if that smile stayed or fled. But that was stupid. He focused on cutting up his egg, which he'd fried over easy instead of scrambling. Watching the yolk run into his hash browns instead of looking at either of them made it easier to sound like he wasn't simmering inside. "This is your story, Felix, and you know that I'm terrible at stories. At least according to your uncle. So go ahead and tell him."

Felix huffed. "Okay, *okay*. There was romance, but it was with Gareth, not Morgan, and I tried to sleep on that to figure out how it makes me feel, but all I know is that I'm still confused and want to eat my breakfast."

Cathal's brow furrowed. "The jerk? Why would you romance him?"

"I didn't. He said he liked me." Felix stuck out his chin. "But I didn't get a chance to ask him about it, because then his dad came home and kicked everybody out."

Cathal opened his mouth, closed it, and then started massaging his temples. "No, actually, Damon *should* tell this story, because at least Damon doesn't leave out all the facts, but you clearly need to talk about it because, generally, having a partner requires the ability to talk about relationships without exploding from stress. Begin at the beginning, you, while I try to pretend I don't have a migraine."

Damon listened without adding anything to the conversation, keeping his eyes on his food as his son walked back to the beginning of the night. Cathal didn't interrupt, keeping his chin on his hand and watching with the smallest of smiles. Another expression Damon recognized. Cathal used to wear it when he was spending time with Damon and Era, and Era would accuse Cathal of not wanting to admit he was happy. Damon hadn't seen that smile in a while. He didn't like it.

But if he was seeing it, it was his fault. It was always his fault.

Fingers crept to the edge of his plate, and Damon looked up, eyebrows raised. Somehow, while telling his story and without once pausing for breath, Felix had finished his food and was now looking at Damon with practiced puppy eyes.

Damon sighed. "You can have the rest of the bacon."

Felix bounced out of his chair and ate the bacon out of the pan with his fingers, smacking his lips in pleasure. The sound brought a smile to Damon's face, despite himself.

"You see why I must return to my own home," said Cathal. The comment wasn't addressed to Damon, as it might have been yesterday. Rather, Cathal was inspecting his nails, talking to no one. "I have no idea where those fingers have been."

"In the bacon pan, obviously," said Felix, walking to the sink to wash his hands.

Cathal glanced sideways at Damon for the first time. Damon stiffened, expecting accusation or dullness—but in Cathal's eyes was the long-suffering patience they'd come to share. Then Cathal looked away, and Damon wondered if he'd seen it at all.

Had he misread the entire situation? Maybe Cathal was telling the truth, and he did have to leave right this second to prepare for summer classes.

Damon had cooked his hash browns perfectly, but they weren't appetizing. "Are you finished?" he asked Cathal without looking at him.

"Yes, actually." Cathal nudged his plate toward Damon's. He hadn't eaten anything but the cheesy hash browns.

Felix returned to the table, bouncing in place. "Can I have the rest of your eggs?"

Cathal pushed the plate toward Felix. "Oh, for heaven's sake, sit down to eat."

Felix obeyed, but he was still bouncing, only now in his chair instead of on his feet.

Cathal pushed back his chair. "Shall we?" he said to Damon, though he didn't look in Damon's direction.

"I'm ready." Damon made himself look at Cathal, hoping Cathal would meet his eyes, but he didn't.

Cathal ruffled Felix's hair. "Don't let your physics slip, young man. I'll know."

Felix tipped his head back. "You talk like you're never coming back."

Cathal snorted. Was it forced? "Don't be ridiculous. I just want to sleep in my own bed. I'm sick of having that unicorn staring at me every night. It can see into my soul, and it's judging me. I don't appreciate that."

Felix sucked on his spoon, looking concerned, but he didn't say anything else.

Damon picked up Cathal's luggage, partly out of habit and partly because putting it in the trunk meant Cathal could get in the car without Damon seeing.

What was he supposed to do? He'd kissed Cathal. If he wanted anything else to happen, he would have to pursue it. But he'd make an idiot of himself.

Except he'd already done that. Better to try one more time than wonder what would have happened otherwise. You didn't always get a second chance.

Damon got into the car but didn't start it, staring straight ahead at the garage door.

After a moment, Cathal said, "Are you hoping the car will start by psychic power? Because I left my tinfoil hat in my duffel bag."

Damon didn't know where to start, but he never did. He turned to look at Cathal. "Last night—"

Cathal immediately turned his head away. "Was infinite evidence why I should have returned home ages ago."

Damon continued, because if he didn't get this out, he would regret it. "Last night was important to me." He swallowed. "Was it important to you?"

He already knew the answer, but he still had to ask.

Cathal's jaw flexed, as though he were going to speak, but instead he sat for a long moment, then let out a slow breath, though none of the tension left his body. "Era asked me to stay until you got your life back. If you're thinking about kissing anyone, that means you're ready. End of discussion."

Damon watched him, waiting to see if that was it. It couldn't be. Cathal had footnotes and annotated bibliographies for his arguments about *Star Wars*, for Christ's sake.

But Cathal didn't crack. He was really done. And there was *another* thing about Cathal. He didn't lie. Even when they were at each other's throats, Damon knew that much.

Damon looked back at his garage door, turning his keys over in his hands. "I'm sorry," he said, his voice hollow. "I hope you'll still come by, once in a while. Felix likes having you around." He dropped his eyes. "I do too."

Cathal passed a hand over his face, but whatever expression he was trying to hide was gone before Damon could figure it out. "I will."

They drove the rest of the way without speaking a word.

DAMON GOT OUT of the car first and grabbed Cathal's stuff, even though he wasn't sure why he was drawing this out. Cathal didn't want to see Damon. If he had, he wouldn't be leaving, no matter what class he'd offered to teach.

But Damon could never end things. When anything good fell into his lap, he held on too tightly. And Cathal had been good.

Cathal didn't protest, just led Damon up to his apartment door. He dug out his keys. Before turning them in the lock, he looked up, as though he were going to say something. But he didn't.

Damon nodded, setting down Cathal's bags. "We'll see you around then?" He wasn't surprised at how empty his voice sounded. He'd gotten used to it since Era got sick.

Cathal picked up his duffel bag. "Of course. I'm sure Felix will be whining about needing help with his physics soon enough or something like that. Something always comes up."

Damon thought about saying something more, but what was the point?

CATHAL MADE HIMSELF enter so he wouldn't go after Damon.

He almost didn't recognize his own apartment—everything was the way he'd left it, but he'd gotten so comfortable in Era's guest room. He walked through, touching things, trying to feel a connection. There was the couch he'd gotten at a thrift store. His bed was on the floor in the corner, separated from the rest of the studio by a curtain. He couldn't remember if he'd made it or left it in a mess when he'd heard Era had been permanently moved to the hospital; he didn't want to bring that whole moment back, even though it hung around like a ghost.

That was the last time he'd been here, after all. He'd walked out knowing he was going to watch his best friend die. And now he was back. His best friend was cold in the ground, and Damon thought Cathal didn't want him.

HE'D LIED ABOUT the summer class—he'd almost forgotten the cutoff date for summer teaching until it passed. But a few phone calls, and he did find a place. They were looking for teachers for the science writing class, and even though that was not technically Cathal's specialty, the rules could be bent since he had popular books.

It would be a good time, but Cathal felt so heavy when he set down the phone. Last year, he'd have jumped at this chance. Now, he was only accepting to give some credence to his lie and to make sure he'd have some reason to stay at his apartment instead of slinking back to see Damon under the pretext of helping Felix with his summer projects.

Ugh.

He went to look in his fridge and remembered it was empty. His pantry, as always, was stocked full of ramen noodles (only the chicken kind, since the other flavors were for heathens). He closed the cupboard and ordered Chinese.

Twelve: No One Bakes like Gaston. No One Makes Dino Cakes like Gaston.

DAMON EXPECTED TO feel restless and loose and shaky—that the emptiness would build inside his head until it roared like an animal and he'd have to hide in his room to escape the sound.

But it wasn't that way at all. He felt nothing, and he continued to feel nothing as he walked inside. Felix was on the couch, watching Saturday morning cartoons upside down.

"Doesn't that give you a headache?" Damon asked out of habit.

"It makes more sense this way. Cartoons these days are really weird." He still had his spoon from breakfast, though he was twirling it between his fingers instead of sucking on it. "You left your phone in the kitchen, Dad. It rang a couple times. I didn't answer it 'cause I thought that would be weird."

And it wasn't like anyone important would be calling Damon. "I didn't realize."

Felix shrugged, popping the spoon in his mouth. Damon could tell he wanted to ask about Cathal, so Damon headed into the kitchen.

What would he even tell Felix? From Felix's point of view, Cathal had left for no real reason. And Damon had just let him go because, after all, they didn't care about each other.

Except that Cathal actually didn't care. Damon had seen that in his eyes. He'd been kidding himself to think any other way, like when he'd let himself think Era would be one of the women who beat the odds and made it through. Stories like that existed, but they weren't real life.

He'd left the dishes in the sink from breakfast, so he forgot about his phone until it went off again. Cathal had set the text noise to "What Does the Fox Say."

It was George, who'd sent him five texts. Damon braced himself as he opened them. George had stopped flirting with him, but Damon was afraid of it happening again. He wasn't used to other people liking him. Era had occasionally said a waitress or waiter was hitting on him, but Damon had never seen it, and he preferred being kept in the dark.

The first text was from before even Damon was awake— a picture of a black-and-white fondant feather. The accompanying note read, *Sorry not sorry if I woke you up. Got invited to a contest for the reopening of the Natural History Museum. Guess what the theme is.*

The rest were further pictures of feathers in different color schemes and patterns.

Damon didn't like texting, so he called George instead.

"You know, with most people, it's annoying if they respond to a text with a call," said George.

"And most people say hello when they answer the phone," Damon replied, sitting down.

"That's the beauty of cell phones. I always know who's calling, so there's no need to be polite." George hummed. "So did you guess what I'm making?"

"It's a bird."

"Half right."

"What else has feathers?" Damon was smiling, a little. He liked George, more so now that there was no awkward flirting.

"Dinosaurs!" said George, clearly expecting a big reaction.

"Dinosaurs don't have feathers." Hadn't he just had this argument with Cathal? The smile slid off his face.

"According to the most recent scientific evidence, they do, and the most recent scientific evidence is what the museum cares about. So. We're going to make a dinosaur cake. I'm not sure what kind yet, but it'll be covered in feathers. Right now, I'm deciding on the best technique. You want to come practice, or do you have plans?"

Damon's first instinct was to say no, because he always said no to plans.

But...

"Yeah, sure," Damon said, pushing his hand through his hair. "Not like I've got anything to do here."

AT THE BAKERY, George had a line of feathers spread out on a table. He was turning one between his fingers, studying it, and didn't look up when Damon approached. "You know, the real question you should have asked me was 'why are you working on a Saturday, George?'"

Damon leaned against the table. "Why are you working on a Saturday, George?"

"Because Evie is with her other dad, and it was making me an anxious wreck, so I decided I needed something to distract me. So. Dinosaur feathers." George set the feather down.

"Why was it making you anxious?" Damon asked, hooking his thumbs in his belt loops. "Was Cleon being a dick or something?" Out of loyalty, he had not interacted with Cleon much during the school play.

"No, the problem is he is very much not being a dick, and I do not like it. He's supposed to be an ass, but now he's sober and talking about making amends and looking at me the way he used to, and I hate it." George nudged up his glasses to rub the bridge of his nose. "Only I don't really hate it. But I do not want to talk about it."

"Fair enough." Damon was glad to leave matters of the heart out of the conversation. "So what's all this?"

"I've made some molds, and I think the best way to do it is to airbrush the cake after everything's been applied. Thoughts?"

"I don't know why you ask me." Damon crossed his arms. "You're the expert."

"Wisdom of babes and all that jazz." George took a step back and put his hands on his hips. "Also, I like to think out loud, and it's nice to pretend I'm talking to you instead of admitting I've been talking to myself since five this morning. Also, you cut straight to the point, like Jenny did. You know if she says she'll come back and work for me, I'm never talking to you again, right?"

Damon ignored the compliment, like always. "I can't blame you. Jenny is prettier than me. And I think she might have bigger biceps too, from the pictures you've shown me."

"She has way bigger biceps than you. She's like a female Gaston."

"Now I understand why you kept trying to stage a musical in here."

"No, that's because I'm gay. I'm obligated to do that at least once in my life, but it got pushed off the agenda when I got dumped." George folded his arms, not letting Damon wiggle away from meeting his eyes. "You know why I really asked you here, right?"

Damon'd been hoping George wouldn't bring that up. "And you already know the answer, so I don't know why you bothered. I like coming here and talking about the stuff that you do, but I'm not joining your team. I'll just fuck it up."

George narrowed his eyes. "You know, I don't get you sometimes. You've thrown yourself into pastry work, and you've done better than most kids I know straight out of school. You're good at what you do, or you wouldn't have been sous chef at Stephen's. So what's your deal? Why are you resisting the next step?"

Damon bit back a groan, trying not to remember last night's conversation. It was like George and Cathal had read the same playbook. "Who said there was a next step? This is a hobby. I don't want to work for anyone, much less you." He wanted to be pissed, to storm out and leave like he had with a few jobs in the past. People said it was a bad idea, but goddamn was it satisfying, and in the restaurant business, warm bodies to wash dishes mattered more than references.

But...fuck. He was tired, and raw, and George was the first friend he'd made by himself in...pretty much ever.

He pushed his fingers through his hair. "Look, George, you don't want me working for you. I don't know why you think I'm any good, but I'm not. I'm just fucking around to try and keep myself busy, okay?"

George held up his hands in surrender. "Okay, okay, I'll quit with the pitch." His phone went off. George turned away to answer it, though he didn't walk off. "Evie, dear, since you're calling me, I have to assume that someone is dead."

Damon did his best to tune out the conversation, looking instead at the different molds.

He'd helped George on bigger projects before. He liked it. Pastry was so, so different from working in a kitchen, from being on your feet from dawn 'til dusk, in the weeds from the second you stepped in the door. You had to step back and think about things; you had time to work and get things right. He wanted to feel some of that peace, but now that George had brought up the contest, he felt restless again. And he didn't know how to get rid of it.

George made a frustrated noise, and Damon looked up. "Sorry, sorry, I try not to bring my personal shit to work."

Damon's mouth twisted to the side. He didn't want George to think he couldn't talk about what was going on in his life. Squashing the part of him that said George's problems would make a good distraction, he said, "Well, it's Saturday, so we're not at work. What's going on?"

George pretended to check his phone. Damon raised his eyebrows, and George sighed. "Okay, I'll talk, but only if you promise not to judge me for hooking up with my ex." Damon's eyebrows went higher, and George sighed more deeply. "Yeah, so I made out with Cleon the other night. That happened."

Damon put his hands in his pockets, putting away thoughts of the last time he'd kissed anyone. "And that's… bad?"

"That's 'I have no idea how to feel about it.'" George sat on one of the tables, rubbing his forehead. "He's so smooth, and I'm so—me—that he had me in the palm of his hand the entire time we were together. And Evie loves him, obviously. We were together since before she started high school."

Damon nodded, trying to look as though he knew anything about kissing and exes. But he couldn't deny he'd been curious. "Why did you guys break up, anyway?"

George shook his head. "He cheated. It's a gross story, and I do not want to go over it ever, but suffice to say, I am not the monogam-ish type. And now he's saying all this shit about how he made a mistake and he's been through a twelve-step program and he's trying to make amends."

"Which totally does not involve sticking his dick in you," said Heather.

Damon jumped. This was about the thirtieth time Heather had appeared behind him without warning. At least she wasn't keeping score, though every time it happened, she sent him a knowing smirk. "When did you get here?"

"I was in front, going through our photos for the competition press release. Gotta make sure we have the tastiest ones." She held up a spiral-bound magazine, then walked over to the counter and sat next to George. "And I swear to God, if you are whining about Cleon again, I will give you a bruise you will never forget."

George hissed at her. "Damon asked, I'll have you know."

"Still. Bad enough you always end up talking about him when we do competitions."

George didn't argue with that, like she hadn't said anything strange.

Damon looked between the two of them and asked, "What does Cleon have to do with competitions?"

George sighed, though he was not surprised by the question. "I am not proud of this, but the entire reason I started doing these damn competitions was to get my mind off of Cleon."

Heather rolled her eyes. "Be glad you missed the part where he couldn't stop sobbing into his Ben and Jerry's."

"You know, Heather, I'm starting to question this whole 'best friends' thing," said George, glaring at her.

"Please. You love it." Heather made as though to toss her hair, but she didn't have much, so it was more symbolic than anything. "Yeah, this whole competition thing is a really roundabout lonely hearts ad."

George stared off into the middle distance. "I mean, I like doing them now. I've become a bit of an addict. Even when I lose, it's still a good way to spend my time. Always something to work toward, you know? But that's why I started. I felt like such a fool when Cleon left. Didn't think I had anything left to work toward."

Damon told himself this did *not* sound familiar. George was successful and driven and had goals for his life. Damon was still dicking around. "You already had the bakery, didn't you?"

"He did, and the only reason he managed to keep it is because I was here," said Heather.

George gave her a put-upon look. "Yes, you saved my ass, but again, not the point. Please, may I continue my tale of valor and woe?"

"I'm sorry, I didn't realize this was the Ring Saga," Heather muttered.

"I want to hear the story." And Damon did, never mind it was making him ill. He wanted George to be a real friend, and real friends talked about everything together.

"Okay. All right. So." George spread his hands. He seemed to be getting into the story. "There I was. Heartbroken, shattered, parenting a young girl with no idea how. The majority of my business was based on a concept I no longer believed in, namely eternal love and all that other stuff couples want to hear from their cake maker."

Damon wrinkled his nose. "I thought they wanted to know you could make them a nice-looking cake."

Heather rolled her eyes. Like Cathal, she could make it audible. "Well, we're never letting *you* in the front of the store. We'd never make any sales. And this is why George doesn't work with the customers as much anymore. I do it because they see a cute little blonde girl, and therefore they assume I must be a cisgender heterosexual lady who reads romance novels. I keep one by the cash register, but still. Anyway. The part of the story he's leaving out is where I kept the customers happy so we could keep the lights on."

"And I've told you time and again that you own my soul for eternity, so that when I die you may claim it for your own and..." George tapped his chin. "I want to know what you'd do with it, but I'm afraid to ask."

Heather shrugged. "I've told you time and again that it's not acceptable payment, and that I'm still working out what is. Anyway, I was busy schmoozing, and George was doing the work. In between lots of moping and sighing."

George nodded ruefully. "Not one of my finest hours. Anyway, I got really intense insomnia during that time, and Heather refused to let me work after eight at night."

"Because the first time I let you stay here all night, you made a Cthulhu cake. Complete with way, way too many tentacles. And Latin."

"I never said you didn't have a good reason, but you refused to let me stay here and work, so I had to find something else to do with myself. And Evie would only tolerate so much fatherly presence in her life." George's eyes darkened. "She was pretty devastated by the breakup, too. I don't think she ever really accepted it. But that's not the point. Evie was busy with school and her friends, and I had to admit that I didn't have much in my life besides work."

Damon avoided his eyes. He wished he could stop the story, but that would be weird.

Heather poked George in the shoulder. "I tried to convert you to the gospel of Bioware, but you didn't listen to me."

"Some of us want to work in the real world, not in the depths of outer space, Heather." George tried to look dignified, but he had icing on his nose. "Anyway. So. I started watching late-night Food Network reruns, as one does." He glanced at Heather, as though waiting for her comment. When Heather ignored him, he looked at Damon.

"I like Food Network, too?" Damon said, shrugging. "I don't make smart remarks. That's—" He almost said *Cathal's job*, then caught himself. "That's somebody else's job."

"I'm just saying, there's an open position in the cheap seats, as long as you push this one over the balcony." George pointed at Heather, who smacked him with her book of photographs.

"Get on with it, would you? You're not even to the good part," said Heather.

George rubbed his arm. "Food Network's a good way to kill time. And that was all I had, because all the things I'd usually do to get myself out of a funk I shared with Cleon. So. Food Network shows. And then when it got late and they started showing infomercials, I switched to local access channels, and lo and behold, they also had food competitions, since they have cooking shows and stuff. Which are hilarious, by the way."

"Hilarious as in...?" Damon asked. "I don't like things that are so bad they're good. I get embarrassed."

Heather bumped him with her foot. "Well aren't you the sweetest thing."

George tapped his lips. "They're hilarious because they're low budget, and since they air at weird hours, they get to say whatever they want. So it turns out they were looking for guest people. I guess I called them really late at night, because the next day, I got a callback from the studio, asking when I could appear. And then it turned out they'd been wanting to start a cake competition show of their own, and they were trying to find competitors."

"It was hard?" Damon asked.

George rocked his hand back and forth. "Sort of. I mean, Cherrywood isn't a small town, but they couldn't afford to pay anyone except in free lunch and the materials and publicity. Not a lot of food people are willing to take the day away from their own work for that. But, you know, I was bored, and apparently I left them a long voice mail about how cool I thought it would be."

"He maintains he was not drinking, just sleep deprived, but I have my doubts," said Heather.

"They come to the same thing. My judgment was impaired. But, you know, I needed something to get me past it. So I agreed to do it, and it was a total disaster, but...it was the first time I'd had fun since Cleon left, since I wasn't thinking about him at all."

"How was it a total disaster?" Damon tried to picture one of George's cakes tipping over, but he was so careful with his work.

But George shook his head. "You can find it on the channel's website, and that's all I'll say on the matter." Heather opened her mouth. "We agreed that we would never speak of it again, remember? Neither of us came off looking good that day."

Heather tipped her head. Then she shrugged. "Yes, I suppose that's true. The record will remain sealed for another ten years, at least."

George nodded. "After that, we got invited to some other small competitions. Other cities do it, and universities like sponsoring stuff like that. Gets the academics out of their hidey-holes."

"It is good for them to see the light of day once in a while," said Damon absently.

212 - | M.A. Hinkle

George waited as though to give him a chance to speak, even though he'd met Cathal, then shrugged. "Anyway, one thing led to another, and now I'm doing them every couple of months. I've had a pretty good track record, too, but even when it's a total clusterfuck, it's a good distraction. And at some point, I realized..." He sighed. "Well, it'd be a lie if I said I never missed Cleon anymore, but at least it doesn't keep me up at night. I have too much to do. And I was totally fine and happy with my life until he decided to start shoving his nose in my business again."

"To be fair, it was mostly Evie's fault," said Heather, slipping down from the table. "I love that girl, but she does not understand the idea of 'other people's business.'"

"She wouldn't have done it if he weren't giving her some kind of signal that it was okay. Anyway. There's the whole sordid tale. We've still got work to do. Let's go, let's go, let's go!" He snapped his fingers in front of Heather's face.

She lowered the magazine slowly, her eyes narrowed. "One of these days, I'll kill you. And I've seen enough crime shows. I know how to get rid of the body so even that scary chick from *Bones* couldn't find you."

"All due respect to Emily Deschanel, I'd rather have that guy from *NCIS* on the case. You know I've got a thing for older men." He sighed, putting a hand over his heart and glanced at Damon. "You were in the military. You could get the NCIS for me, right?"

"Maybe if it was a double homicide, but I'm not going to say anything dumb enough to get Heather to kill me," Damon said, sliding off the table. He put a smile on his face. The banter was nice, it really was. "And I don't know if I really count for military jurisdiction anymore."

"Let me have my fantasies about a silver fox coming to weep over my desiccated corpse, okay?" George paused. "Actually, no, don't let me. I don't want to puke in the cake."

George and Heather got back to practicing the sculpture. Damon started making villagers for a gingerbread village. Not having to talk was nice; getting to laugh was even better. But he couldn't help but think Cathal would have pressed him to try something new, to get out there.

Well. One more reason to not do it, then.

GOING TO GEORGE'S became a routine in Cathal's absence. Damon tried not to go at the same time every day, so he could pretend he wasn't using it in place of a job, but he didn't bother hiding how much he liked the work. That he needed some way to bury himself. Or that he didn't know if he'd ever be ready to dig his way out again.

It wasn't as much fun, though, because George was busy. Like today. He'd made a full replica of the cake for the competition, so he was standing on a ladder, inspecting it from every angle.

"It's like you're trying to kill yourself," said Heather, "and that makes me an accessory to murder, and I'm not okay with that. If I ever kill anyone, it'll be on purpose."

"I'm not trying to kill myself." George wasn't looking at her; all his concentration was on the model.

Heather turned to Damon, who'd been making himself smaller to avoid her gaze. "Damon?"

He lifted his head and smiled, even though he wanted to disappear. This argument had taken place every day for the last three. In different forms, maybe, but the same basic idea. "Yes, Heather? You look lovely today, by the way."

"Flattery won't get you anywhere. You know she's as gay as I am," said George, still not taking his attention away from his work.

"Every lady appreciates a compliment," Heather said, her gaze focused on Damon. "That was sweet. But in the future, I wanna know I look butch."

She looked like a pixie, but Damon knew better than to say that. "You always look butch. Even I feel girly beside you."

"Much better. But not the point." She pointed at George. "What is he doing?"

Not answering would only get Damon yelled at as well as George. "He's on a ladder, practicing sculpting the cake."

"Does he need to be on a ladder?" Heather would have made an excellent lawyer if baking hadn't been her passion.

"Yes, because the cake is really tall, and George is really short." Damon gave up pretending and stretched his arms over his head. The nice thing about pastry was that you actually had time to sit and stretch, especially compared to the restaurant, where *maybe* you got to sit down for family meal. Maybe.

Heather growled. "Does it need to be that tall?"

Damon tried to keep his face blank. "I don't know what the regulations are."

Heather shot him a look that said she knew he was lying and she would not forget. "The answer is no, for the record. The height requirement is six feet. Not eight."

"It's in proportion, Heather." George finally turned his attention away from the cake. "And you've tried to talk me out of this about fifty different ways, and it's not going to work. I know we've only got to make six feet, but the average height of a T-rex is forty feet. It scales way easier to eight, and one-fifth scale sounds super impressive. I think so, anyway."

Damon thought about saying he had a point, but that was just leftover from spending too much time with Cathal. Better to keep his head down and let the fight blow over.

"It is impressive," Heather admitted, narrowing her eyes. "But that doesn't mean it's not risky, too. The more time you spend on that ladder, the more nervous I get."

"I know. But it'll be fine. And think how good it'll look. Once we figure out the most efficient ways of doing everything, we'll be golden."

They then proceeded to get in an argument about why the T-rex could not be holding a medical reacher, no matter how funny it would have been. Even though Heather and George were enjoying themselves, Damon shrank further and further into himself. He might as well have stayed at home in bed watching *Chopped* reruns or something.

It didn't help that they kept asking him his opinion. Like he knew anything that mattered.

Thirteen: *Star Wars* Is the Closest Thing to a Religion in the Eglamore Household.

WHEN DAMON GOT home, Felix was still at band practice, and Damon had a sudden urge to do something, though he didn't know what. The house was too quiet. He tried making cookies, then watching TV, and even noodling around on his netbook, watching cat videos on YouTube. Damon ended up flipping through his *Better Homes and Gardens* cookbook, even though the text was more or less impossible to read.

The front door opened and shut. Felix was talking, so Damon assumed he'd brought a friend home, but when he peeked out of the kitchen, Felix was on his phone. He wasn't whispering, but he wasn't talking as loudly as usual—although Felix's usual tone of voice was "carry to the cheap seats."

Felix put his phone down, and Damon ducked back in the kitchen before Felix noticed he'd been looking. Had he been talking to Gareth?

Felix came in the kitchen and perched on the edge of the table. "So Daaaaad."

"So Feeeelix. What is it this time?"

Felix shuffled his feet. "So, um. Gareth couldn't come to band practice because he and his brother are both grounded forever, right. But apparently Gareth's dad saw me a couple of times while we were rehearsing the play, and Morgan has spun it so I'm a good influence."

Damon raised his eyebrows.

"Okay, *okay*. So Gareth wanted to know if his dad could come over for dinner and meet you and stuff and then maybe that might get him to relax the grounding. Or at least let them come over to visit me so they can leave the house. Or vice versa, I guess."

"Door stays open if he comes here," said Damon automatically.

Felix turned scarlet. "Dad! Oh my God, we are not having a sex talk, okay? I still don't think I know what sexy feelings are." He scrubbed at his face, and his tone dropped to a mumble. "But I do. Like. Like him. I guess. So I'd like to be able to see him, like, outside of school. And when his dad isn't there, because his dad is scary."

Damon crossed his arms. "Well, I don't see any problem with that. Let me know, and I'll make up something nice."

Felix did not relax.

"What else?" Damon asked, leaning forward.

Felix suddenly became very interested in the striped wallpaper. "Well, uh, I kind of asked Cathal if he would come too. 'Cause Gareth's dad is a professor and so is Cathal and stuff."

Damon was glad Felix had his face covered, because Damon was not sure what his face looked like. How much did Felix know? He considered coming clean about the reason Cathal left—lying by omission had "lying" right in the title, no matter what Cathal insisted. But...

"Why would that bother me, Felix?" He meant it to be light, but he just sounded tired.

Felix peeked out between his fingers. "Well, I mean. I thought you guys were mad at each other, and that's why he left."

Damon pushed away from the table. "You heard him, kiddo. He had to go to teach a class, that's all. You always read too much into things."

Felix swung his legs. "So...it's okay?"

Damon nodded.

Felix let out a deep sigh. "Okay, good. I said Friday. Is that okay?"

Even though there were only a handful of dishes left over from breakfast, Damon ran water in the sink. "Friday is perfect. I'll make something good and fancy, okay?"

Felix clapped his hands. "Yay! This is gonna be really good."

At least one of them thought so.

WHEN FRIDAY ROLLED around, Damon put on something nice—well, as nice as he owned. He wasn't going to wear anything fancier than jeans, but he did put on a button down, and he trimmed his hair and beard since he was getting mountain man-ish in both places. He told himself he didn't care what he looked like; he wanted to make a good impression.

Another thing he missed about Era. Next to her, no one ever noticed him. He might as well have been a potted plant she liked to take places. Now, people would actually look at Damon, and he didn't know what they'd see. Nothing good, certainly.

Right when Damon was taking everything out of the oven, the twins' father arrived. "Trevor Lewis," he said, holding out his hand as soon as he saw Damon.

Damon had to juggle his oven mitts so he could shake. It was like pumping a lever. Still, Damon stuck a smile on his face. He thought he'd gotten pretty good at faking smiles in all his years with Era—or, at least, Cathal said he no longer looked like he was about to be sick at every nice dinner. "Mr. Lewis. I'm Damon. Just Damon."

"Trevor, please." But it was stiff, not friendly. "I'm sorry about your wife."

Though he should have been expecting it, Damon froze. He still got it if he ran out to the grocery store and saw someone from work—Era had known everyone, and thus Damon had known everyone. His smile faltered, but he forced it back on. "Thank you. Please, uh, have a seat. The food's nearly ready."

Trevor glanced at the table before choosing a seat, and Damon gritted his teeth. Since they almost never had anyone over for dinner, the set only had four chairs, so the extras did not match. He'd put out the nice cloth and mats, though, and had considered candles, but Cathal would make fun of him.

Fuck. Cathal. As if this wasn't bad enough.

Damon turned back to the food and realized it was all done. Before he could ask where Felix and the twins were, they came into the kitchen. Felix was hanging on to Cathal's arm, explaining something musical while Cathal nodded. Morgan and Gareth were a few steps behind, their expressions unreadable.

And Cathal, the bastard, had dressed up. He made a point of looking good all the time—his suits were tailored and what the fuck ever—but he did have even nicer special-occasion clothes. He was wearing a shiny black jacket and a waistcoat, with a silver scarf and actual pants instead of jeans for once.

Goddammit.

Damon met his eyes for half a second but dropped his gaze. He couldn't look at Cathal.

"You made a rack of lamb?" Cathal asked.

Damon stirred the glazed carrots even though they'd been done for ten minutes. "I did. I'm surprised you know what it is."

"Yeah, well, you made me watch all those damn food shows. It'd better be good, Eglamore. My friends are having a *Star Wars* marathon tonight." His voice was teasing, like nothing had ever happened.

Thankfully, Felix answered instead, his face grave. "Cathal, I would not have asked you if I'd known you were making such a sacrifice."

"*Star Wars* is way more important than family stuff," said Gareth. He and Felix exchanged a grin that probably meant something more than a shared joke. But Damon was still adjusting to the idea of his son wanting to kiss someone. He couldn't guess what was going on there.

Trevor cleared his throat, and both twins stiffened, their posture suddenly picture-perfect.

"I'm sorry." Cathal turned to face Trevor with that perfect professor smile. "We haven't been introduced. I'm Cathal Kinnery."

Trevor was standing. Damon wasn't sure how that had happened. "Trevor Lewis."

Cathal shook his hand, his eyes considering. Then they lit up, and Damon had to look away, though he couldn't miss the surprised delight in Cathal's voice. "Oh, yes, I've heard of you. You work with the Mabinogion, don't you?"

God *damn* him. How was he so charming?

"Yes." Trevor sounded like he hadn't relaxed at all. "Though I'd hardly expect a professor of astronomy to know that."

"My best friend is—" Cathal stopped, and Damon set down the carving knife so he wouldn't cut himself. "My best friend *was* an English professor. And a fan of your work." Cathal sat down, and Trevor followed suit.

The twins also sat, but Damon seized Felix by the back of the shirt. "Not so fast. Help me get the food out."

He must have sounded rough around the edges, because Felix looked at him with confusion. But then his son shrugged and grabbed the bowl of carrots. Damon took the lamb roast and set that down in the center of the table, then the potatoes.

"Ooh, it's fancy, Dad!" Felix leaned over the table to get a closer look.

"You are disgusting," said Cathal, but his voice was fond.

Felix sniffed and sat down—beside Gareth, Damon noticed. Morgan was between his father and his brother.

"I've read your book, Cathal," said Trevor, out of nowhere.

Cathal looked surprised. "Have you?"

Damon carved the lamb, maybe with more aggression than it deserved, since it was tender and Damon kept his knives sharp.

Trevor also knew quite a bit about astronomy, so now they were talking about brown dwarfs. Damon didn't mean to interrupt, but when he sat down, his chair made a horrible grating noise, since it was missing footpads. Both Trevor and Cathal broke off to look at him in surprise.

Damon pasted a smile on his face again. This time, he was sure it looked like a creepy doll smile. "Food's ready. You first, Mr. Lewis, please."

Trevor took his time selecting his lamb and kept the carrots and potatoes separate on his plate. "So what do you do, Damon?" He said Damon's name like it was in a foreign language. Given, Damon was not a common name, but neither was Trevor. Or Cathal, for that matter.

Why was this always the first question people asked? "I don't do much of anything right now," he said, trying to keep his voice neutral. "I left my job after Era got sick, and I haven't decided if I'm going back or not."

"You do that thing with George, though." Felix's voice was innocent, but unlike Cathal, he wasn't faking it. At least Felix didn't blow things up on purpose.

"Be precise, dear boy," said Cathal. Damon didn't even have to look to know he was enjoying the way Damon squirmed.

Felix tried to come to Damon's rescue, at least. In his own way. "It's Dad's thing. He should talk about it."

And then everyone was looking at Damon. Especially Cathal, who was hiding a shit-eating grin behind his bland smile. Damon wanted to kick him under the table. "My friend George runs a bakery, so he lets me noodle around with cakes. It's only a hobby."

"But you're really good!" Felix protested. Somehow, between grilling Damon, he had already eaten his potatoes and carrots. "And George does competitions and stuff." He looked over at Trevor, his voice hesitant. "It's cool."

Trevor's brow furrowed. "Competitions? What kind of competitions?"

Damon bit back a sigh. "They make cakes for special events. Whoever makes the best one gets some prize money. Right now, he's getting ready for one at the Natural History Museum."

Felix perked up. "You didn't tell me about that, Dad."

"Because it's got nothing to do with me." Damon shoved a forkful of lamb in his mouth, hardly tasting it.

"So you're still resisting George's charms, then?" Cathal asked. Damon glanced at him, but Cathal was cutting his lamb into bite-size pieces, his face unreadable.

Damon sighed, setting down his knife and fork. The conversation was turning his stomach. "I'm not competing with him, if that's what you mean. I'm not good enough."

"But you could be on TV, Dad!" said Felix. "That'd be so cool."

"It's on TV?" Trevor looked between Damon and Felix like he thought they might be playing a joke on him.

"It's on cable, Dad," said Morgan quietly, and that seemed to calm Trevor.

"They don't watch TV," said Felix in a conspirator's whisper. "They don't even have Netflix."

"I do," Gareth said. "I wanted to watch *Jessica Jones*."

"What on earth is *Jessica Jones*?" Trevor asked.

Felix made a horrified noise, and from there, the discussion devolved into the pieces of the Marvel Cinematic Universe. Cathal and Trevor got into a spirited debate about *The Hero with a Thousand Faces*. Damon did not participate. For once, someone else was the clueless one, but he couldn't even enjoy it.

HE ALMOST DIDN'T want to bring out the cake, but Felix would find it the second he went in the fridge, and there was too much for two people. Too much for six, honestly. He'd meant to put a simple musical score on it, but then he decided to make it into a music book, complete with piped lines for pages on the sides. He even looked up the opening of "Ode to Joy," the only classical song he knew off the top of his head despite having a son who played classical music on an endless loop, and wrote out the first few bars in black gel.

"That's super cool, Dad." Felix leaned out of his chair to get a look as Damon carried it to the table.

Trevor looked it over, surprise on his face. "So this is what you do. I see."

"It's a *hobby*," Damon said, pinching himself to keep from snapping.

Felix leaned even farther out of his chair, peering at the cake. "Is that 'Ode to Joy'?"

"Sit like a person," said Damon. A beat later, he realized Cathal had said it at the same time. He glanced at Cathal, who looked as surprised as he felt.

Thankfully, Felix let out a loud, irritated sigh and fell back in his chair. "Okay, okay. But I really want caaaake."

"Guests first," Cathal said before Damon could. "You were doing so well there."

Damon turned his gaze on Trevor. He thought he could feel Cathal's eyes on him and told himself he was being stupid. "Guests first," he echoed. "Do you have a preference on a piece, Mr. Lewis?"

Trevor coughed delicately. "I don't actually like to go first. I don't care for the outside pieces with the extra icing." His eyes flicked around the table, settling on Felix. "But I'm willing to bet someone else does?"

Damon wasn't sure if that was a joke, but Felix put on a broad smile. "You don't have to ask me twice."

Damon shrugged. "What piece do you want, then?" Felix just looked at him. "Corner piece with the most frosting. Right." He served Felix, who, to Damon's surprise, did not immediately start eating. Damon waited, then shrugged and turned his attention to Gareth and Morgan.

"We want those two corners," said Gareth before his brother could speak. Morgan glared at him, but Gareth grinned in a way that gave Damon a start. Cathal looked at Era the same way when he won an argument.

Damon shook himself and gave them the corners. He glanced at Cathal and raised his eyebrows. Saying Cathal's name would have felt too strange.

"I want the treble clef," said Cathal. Damon felt like a few days ago he would have known what the smile on Cathal's face meant, but maybe he would have been kidding himself then too.

He served Cathal and turned his attention back to Trevor. "Got a preference?" Damon asked, trying to sound light. Trevor looked like he was making this into a life or death choice.

"Dad," said Gareth, curling his upper lip. "Live a little, would you?"

Trevor glanced over at his son, his frown deepening. "I'll remind you that the entire point of this was to convince me you had some worthwhile friends, young man."

Gareth just shrugged. "This was Morgan's idea, not mine."

Damon gritted his teeth, waiting for a scene, but then Trevor turned his attention to Damon. "I'll have the last corner, please." Gareth looked surprised.

Damon served Trevor, glad he could sit back down. The sooner this was over, the better.

"You're not going to have any, Dad?" Felix asked. To Damon's shock, he still hadn't hoovered down his cake. He really *was* trying to make a good impression.

Damon plastered on a smile. "I spend all day around cake, Felix. I'm sick of it."

Felix frowned. Then he said, "Dad, I hate to say this, but you are wrong. Cake is the best thing."

TREVOR AND HIS sons left soon after that. Damon expected Cathal to leave with them, since he'd been chatting with Trevor about some academic thing, but Cathal hung back, leaning against the wall.

"Are you gonna spend the night, Cathal?" Felix asked. Damon braced himself for the answer.

But Cathal started, almost like he'd forgotten he wasn't staying here anymore. He recovered quickly, as always. Maybe he'd been woolgathering. Whatever that meant. "No. I wanted to ask about the latest developments between you and your paramour."

Felix turned bright red, and Damon relaxed. He'd wanted to ask that question himself but hadn't known how to bring it up. "Gareth's not my paramour," Felix mumbled. "I don't even know what that means."

"How can you know he isn't if you don't know what it means?" Cathal asked, smirking.

Felix hunched his shoulders. "You know, he's...He's confusing. Morgan's got a big solo in the concert at the end of the year, so he hasn't been in study hall, so it's been me and Gar. And that's nice. I guess."

"Gar, eh?" said Damon, raising his eyebrows.

"Dad! Not you too!" Felix covered his face with his hands.

Cathal's eyes flicked to Damon's, a smile dancing around the corner of his lips. Damon grinned back. Then he remembered what it was like to kiss that mouth and dropped his eyes.

Cathal patted Felix's cheek. "Don't worry, Felix. I'm heading home, and we both know your father isn't nearly as good at interrogations. You're safe now." Felix tried to lick Cathal's hand, but Cathal was too fast. "You are a disgusting little heathen."

"Hmmph," said Felix.

"Do you need a ride?" Damon asked. The words slipped out. Habit. Or a throwback. *Something* dumb.

Cathal was shrugging on his jacket, and he kept his face turned away. "Bus, Damon. It exists."

Damon thought about arguing, but what was the point?

Felix gave Cathal a grumpy hug, and Cathal left. Then it was just Damon and his son again, and that should not have made his house feel so empty.

Damon turned to Felix, refusing to let the silence crush him. "So. When will you find out his father's verdict?"

Felix huffed. His blush had faded, but his ears were still bright red. "Dunno. Gareth doesn't think it's gonna change anything, but Morgan thinks it'll work. What do you think, Dad, did it go okay?"

Damon frowned, putting his hands in his pockets.

Felix rubbed his nose. "I didn't think it was that bad," he said, as though Damon's face were an answer. "I mean, the food was super good. And Gareth's dad seemed to like Cathal."

That much was true, yeah. Damon shrugged, unable to keep from looking listless and tired. "I don't know, Felix. I guess we'll see."

"Yeah, I guess so." Felix paused. "Can I have another piece of cake?"

FELIX WENT UP to his room to practice, and Damon went into the kitchen to clean up the dishes. He could have put them in the dishwasher, but he didn't have anything else to do with himself. He'd made too much food and too much dessert. Never mind how much Felix ate, Damon wouldn't have to cook all weekend, which meant he had to figure out what to do with himself for a whole two days.

"How'd you get stuck with such a deadbeat dad, anyway?" Damon muttered, pushing his fingers through his short hair.

This was ridiculous. He'd managed to pull himself up and out after Era's death when it had seemed impossible, yet now he was back to moping around like nothing mattered. He needed something to do with himself. But what?

HE WAS SURPRISED that George answered the phone. "I thought you'd still be working," Damon said, to cover that he'd meant to leave a voicemail.

George sighed. "Evie wanted to go out for dinner. Little party for a friend of hers. And of course, we had to invite Cleon."

Damon blinked. "You actually called him by name?"

George growled. "Don't you start, too. I still want to punch him in the face."

"I'll hold him still if need be."

"You should do the punching for me, actually. You were in the military. I'm sure they taught you that kind of stuff."

"I was a military cook, George."

"Still. You could hit him with a saucepan or something." George blew out a breath. "Anyway, did you need something? Leave your coat at the bakery or whatever?"

"I wasn't wearing a coat." George growled again, and Damon relaxed. "No, I..." He couldn't waste too much time. George had things to do. "I wanted to tell you that I'll do it."

"Do what?"

Damon resisted the urge to groan. "You know. The...the competition."

"What? Really?" George sounded shocked. Not surprising, since Damon had spent so much time blowing him off. "I mean, it's not like—Damon, you don't have to do it if you don't want to."

"I do want to." Damon bit the inside of his cheek, but the words came out anyway. "Look, I need something useful to do. You need another warm body. Don't act like it's a big deal."

George sighed in relief. "There are five dozen things I could say in response to that, but right now, I've got to get back to dinner. The most important thing is thank you. You are saving my ass, and you don't even know how. This whole thing is going to be so crazy, and you are going to be such a big help."

Damon ignored that. George could have asked anyone, but it was nice of him to pretend. "It's all right, George. I'm happy to do it."

That was a lie, but maybe if he repeated it often enough, it would be true.

Fourteen: Damon Always kind of Wants to Punch Himself in the Face. Even More So at Fancy Dinners.

CATHAL WAS GOING over his class outline for approximately the fifth time, since, after all, he had never taught this class before, and therefore he needed to do it well, since he wanted to teach it again. Yes. Absolutely. It was not to distract himself from his writer's block or anything else going on in his life. Nope.

Then his phone rang. "Thank God." He picked it up. "You know, Felix, everyone else in my life texts like a normal person, and they're all at least twenty years older than you."

"But then how would I ever hear your voice?" Felix sounded bright and cheery. Not that he usually sounded any other way, but it still made Cathal feel better. He worried, though God forbid he ever demonstrate it.

"I'm sure that's why you called, and not because you wanted something from me. Out with it, kiddo. I've got work to do." Cathal didn't, really, but if he talked to Felix too long, he'd ask about Damon.

Felix huffed. "Okay, okay. I need to ask you another favor."

"Please tell me you're still doing all right in physics. I'll be very upset if not."

"Not that. Morgan's helping me with that." Felix made a nervous humming noise.

"Don't make me repeat myself, Felix. You think I can't glare at you over the phone, but I will video call you so you can see my scowl."

Felix groaned. "Okay, okay. So Gareth's dad is maybe gonna walk back the grounding some more so we can actually hang out at places that are not his house."

"That's good news, but what does it have to do with me? You seem to be doing well on your own." Actually, Cathal wasn't sure how Felix was doing in that area. He remained closemouthed on the subject of Gareth.

"Not that." Cathal could almost see Felix rocking back and forth in place. "Okay, so Gareth's dad wants to have us over to dinner, and I wanna know if you'll go with us."

Cathal needed a minute to sort through the rapid-fire phrasing, but he was already shaking his head. "I'm busy, Felix." It felt like an excuse, because it *was* an excuse. He couldn't even think of a good backing argument. His mind was full of his last sight of Damon, dressed nicely and looking like Cathal had never been in his life at all.

Felix whined. "I know, I know, but it's only for one night for a little while, *and* you made such a good impression on Gareth's dad last time. I mean, he liked Dad, too, but Dad can't really do the smart-people talk like you, Cathal, and I know that's how come Gareth's dad liked dinner last time. Please? You'll get to see Gareth's fancy house and stuff."

Cathal pinched himself so he wouldn't answer right away. He never wanted to snap at Felix, and he couldn't think of a good reason why to say no, but there had to be one. There had to.

"Please?" Felix said, breaking Cathal out of his thoughts. "I really miss you."

Fuck. Fuck, fuck, *fuck*.

"Yeah, okay," Cathal muttered, rubbing his forehead now. He'd have a headache for a week anticipating this, but it was his own fault for being a pushover and having feelings. "But you owe me for this, squirt."

"Yes!" Felix's squeal was so loud Cathal almost dropped his phone. "And I already owe you, like, everything. I promise when my band gets rich and famous, you'll get my portion of the royalties."

Cathal snorted, despite his mood. "I keep telling you, kiddo, you're in for a rude awakening. Record companies don't share profits."

"Pfft. We're gonna get famous on the internet. I gotta go do my homework now, Cathal. Byeeeee!"

He hung up before Cathal could say anything else.

Cathal set down the phone and fell backward in his chair. Well. He had no one to blame but himself.

FELIX WAS A ball of barely contained nerves on their way over to the Lewis home, which did not help Damon's mood. Especially since they were going to pick up Cathal, since the bastard lived right next to Cherrywood College and didn't need to drive anywhere, and therefore didn't own a car like everyone else in the world.

And Cathal looked sharp, as always. His smile was cool, as though he wasn't going anywhere important, but he brightened when Felix leaned forward from the back seat to greet him. "You know, if I wanted to have someone jump all over me whenever they saw me, I'd get a dog," said Cathal, sitting in the passenger seat.

"I take that as a compliment. Dogs are perfect in every way." Felix drummed his hands on the back of Cathal's seat until Cathal glared at him. Felix meekly sat back and refastened his seatbelt.

"So anything new?" Cathal's question was directed to the dashboard.

"Well, I'm working on a new song called 'Face Punch.'" Felix was now drumming his hands on his knees. "Sarah wanted to try some techniques she saw on YouTube, so we thought we'd see if we could write a thrash metal song."

"Oh, heaven preserve us." Cathal silenced his phone and tucking it back in his pocket. "The last thing I want to hear is you screaming like you're being disemboweled."

"It's gonna be all instrumental. None of us have the voice for that kind of singing. Well, I could fake it, but you really wreck yourself that way, and I don't wanna sound like I'm a smoker."

Cathal nodded gravely, though his lips were twitching. "Very good. What about you, Damon?"

Damon was glad he had to focus on driving so he wouldn't look at Cathal's face and try to figure out what the heck he was thinking. "Nothing, really. You know me. I'm boring."

"Dad's gonna do the competition with George!" said Felix, because of *course* he did.

Damon cringed, waiting for some kind of implication about his relationship with George, but Cathal just raised his eyebrows. "Oh really? What made you give in?"

Damon shrugged, trying not to grind his teeth. "George needed the help. He hasn't been able to find someone to replace his old assistant, and I'm there all the time anyway."

"You are?"

Damon was at a red light, so he risked glancing away from the road to see Cathal's expression, but Cathal was picking at a hangnail, disinterested in the conversation. "Cut that out. You'll get a blister."

Cathal rolled his eyes, but he did drop his hand from his mouth. "Last I checked, that doesn't answer my question."

Damon bit back a sigh. "What else am I supposed to do with my time?"

Cathal didn't press the point. Maybe he'd given up on implying that Damon was going to get with George any second now. Damon could dream, anyway.

"So what does that consist of, anyway? Is he the Sith Lord to your apprentice?" Cathal asked.

"Why Sith Lord?" Felix asked. "George is really nice."

"Because the Sith get cooler outfits. And Adam Driver is attractive."

"He looks like a cat," said Felix, wrinkling his nose.

"I will ignore that you said that for the sake of our connection, which you know I value very much." Cathal looked sideways at Damon. "Anyway, this is a distraction. Damon, you were saying?"

Damon shrugged, trying not to hunch his shoulders up like Felix did. "It's not very interesting. George is practicing the sculpture, and I'm working on all the other little pieces. It's the exact same stuff every day so we can do it quickly."

"You know, I've been wondering about that. How do you make that much cake in six hours, anyway?"

"We get to premake the cake. George doesn't like the ones where you have to make the cake during the competition. Too much chance for melted frosting." Damon's lips twitched, despite himself. "Anyway, he can't remember the recipe. We make the same cake the same way every day, and every day he has to look it up. Even I've got it memorized at this point."

"Baking is edible chemistry." Cathal was smiling, which was still frustratingly nice to see.

"George has got an apron that says that. It reminds me of you." The words just— came out.

Thankfully, before Cathal could say anything awful, Felix bolted up out of his seat to point. "There it is!"

Felix hadn't been kidding about the Lewis home. It was three stories high, with hedges and a gate you had to be buzzed through.

"Do we have to walk through a metal detector?" Cathal muttered under his breath.

"Like I said, he's super rich," said Felix, ignoring Cathal's tone.

"Good lord, no wonder these boys are so out of touch," said Cathal as Damon pulled up to the front door.

Felix was first out of the car, bouncing from foot to foot. Damon wasn't sure if it was nervousness or excitement, since Felix's "I want to puke" face was the same as his "I want to dance" face.

Damon took his time stepping out of the car, trying to school his own features to blankness. Even Cathal looked wary, though he always looked like that.

"I hope you realize that this is a serious favor on my part, Felix," said Cathal. "The urge to mock everything is going to kill me."

"I know, and you'll do a great job because you are the most awesome uncle figure to ever exist in the history of uncle figures." Felix took Cathal's arm, beaming now.

Cathal let out an exaggerated sigh. "You're lucky it is written in the gay charter that I have to spoil the heck out of my friends' children since I cannot produce any of my own."

"You like kids, don't lie," said Damon absently, hunting for the doorbell. Then the door opened. Damon took a quick step back, surprised.

It was Gareth. Damon could only tell because of the hair. Otherwise, he might have thought it was Morgan, since Gareth had a pleasant smile on his face.

"Oh, you're early," Gareth said. "Dinner's not ready yet, and Dad's still working."

Thankfully, Felix bounded forward before Damon could figure out what to say. "Dad is always early. Being late gives him hives."

Cathal snickered. Damon kept his gaze fixed on the ornate carvings on the front door.

Gareth shrugged. "It's not a big deal. Morgan's practicing. You want to come see?"

"You bet your butt I do!" Felix said. "But, um—" He glanced at Damon with a pleading expression.

Damon smiled, despite his nerves. He was impressed Felix remembered they were there at all. "I'm sure there's somewhere we can wait?"

"Uh, yeah." Gareth glanced over his shoulder. "Let me show you the parlor." Cathal did not bother to hide his disdain. "I know it's super pretentious, but so is my dad, so it suits him."

"Be nice!" Felix tried to pinch him, but Gareth eluded him. He grabbed Felix's hand instead. Damon raised his eyebrows at the pair. Felix turned red, but Gareth just looked evenly back at him and started down the hallway.

Damon glanced at Cathal to make sure he was following. "You can't be *too* mean to Felix when we leave," Damon whispered.

Cathal grinned up at him, and for a minute, it was like he'd never left. "I would never dream of it."

"Of course you wouldn't," Damon whispered back and realized he was smiling.

Goddammit.

The parlor had a fancy couch and bookcases and a coffee table. Or, well, a tea table, probably. Damon put his hands behind his back, certain he'd bump into something and break it.

"Go ahead and relax." Gareth gestured at the couch. "There's no TV or anything in here, but you can look at the books if you want. Dad's read them all, so he wouldn't care if you borrowed one." He glanced at the grandfather clock against the wall, because of course there was a grandfather clock. "Dinner will be done in about half an hour, I think. I'll make Morgan come get you, or he'll never stop practicing."

Felix had a dreamy smile on his face. "He can practice forever as far as I'm concerned."

"He needs to eat once in a while. C'mon." He dragged Felix out of the room.

Damon sat on the couch. It was not comfortable. The cushions were hard, and it didn't feel stable. Better to not put all his weight on it.

Cathal was already at the bookcase, squinting at the titles. "Half of these are in Latin. I'd say Trevor's pretentious, but I honestly don't think it would occur to him that maybe other people didn't learn Latin at their fancy prep school."

"You know Latin," Damon said and then wanted to punch himself. He couldn't talk to Cathal like...like they were friends. Or anything at all. Cathal had made that much clear.

Cathal glanced over his shoulder, his expression unreadable. "Yes, well, that I can hardly help. It makes science a lot easier. And some academics automatically think you're stupid if you don't understand it." He took one of the books off the shelf. "I'm trying to decide if Plato or Socrates would look more pretentious."

"I have no idea who that is." Damon laced his fingers together so he wouldn't be tempted to touch anything.

"Exactly why I say they're pretentious." Cathal set back the book and picked a thinner volume, then flopped on the couch next to Damon. He was completely at ease, which only made Damon sit stiffer and straighter. "You're useful for keeping one's finger on the pulse of the working class."

"Except I don't work anymore."

"Pedantic as always," said Cathal absently, flipping through the book.

Damon decided it was better to keep his mouth shut than risk admitting he was thinking about all the times they'd relaxed like this. Only there should have been a TV. What kind of weirdo didn't have a TV in their living room?

He didn't realize he'd said it aloud until Cathal replied, "It's not a living room, it's a parlor. There's a difference. A parlor is where you bring guests so they can ooh and aah over how fancy you are before you bring them to dinner or polo or whatever. A living room is where the family hangs out."

His words were offhand, but Damon frowned. "You seemed to get on with him fine."

Cathal lowered the book, raising his eyebrows. "Do I detect a hint of jealousy in your tone?" Damon kept his face fixed straight ahead. "First of all, Trevor is straight as straight could possibly be. Even the most closeted gay man could never be that awkward, and I should know. I've gotten plenty of them to come out over the years. Second, his idea of academia bores me to tears. I pity the students in his classes. He probably reads directly off the PowerPoint." He paused. "Scratch that. He reads directly from his notes. There's no chance he knows how to use PowerPoint."

Damon fixed his gaze on a very ugly abstract painting so he wouldn't look at Cathal. Even if Cathal was thinking of—*anything*, Damon would not have been able to tell. And he wouldn't have been thinking of anything, because Cathal did not care, and Damon had read too much into everything, because he was stupid and lonely and didn't have anything better to do.

"Are you all right? You look like you're about to puke." Cathal had real concern in his voice, and that surprised Damon enough to look at him. But, of course, Cathal's face was a pleasant mask. "I mean, you always look like that at social gatherings, but still."

Damon pinched the bridge of his nose.

"I'd forgotten how much fun it is to make you make that face," said Cathal, almost fondly.

Damon was still trying to convince himself Cathal had actually said that when Morgan appeared in the doorway. "Hello, Mr. Eglamore, Mr. Kinnery. Dinner's ready."

Cathal took great pleasure in leaving the book laying propped open on the couch. "You know, if you don't start calling me Cathal, Morgan, I'm going to start wondering if this is all an elaborate prank. I'm not familiar with the day's reality shows, so feel free to go ahead. I won't watch it."

Morgan's brow furrowed.

"Don't listen to him, Morgan," said Damon, pushing himself up. "He likes confusing everyone else so he can feel smart."

"I am extremely intelligent, thank you." Cathal put his hands on his hips. "If I need to feel smart, all I have to do is volunteer to help the English 101 professors with their grading overflow, like I used to do for Era. Well, that also makes me despair for the state of the education system, but every good thing comes with drawbacks, wouldn't you say, Morgan?"

"Really, just ignore him," said Damon. "If you don't give him the attention he wants, he'll drop the subject."

Morgan still looked concerned, but he shrugged. "The dining room is this way."

The dining room had a chandelier. At least it had light bulbs instead of candles, although the embellishments looked like real gold and crystal. The table was draped with a white cloth and had enough chairs for the cast of Felix's play, although there were only seven places set. Felix and Gareth were already seated, involved in a heated argument about drum machines.

"Where's Father?" Morgan asked, sitting beside his brother.

That left one seat at the head of the table and two seats across from the teenagers. Cathal claimed the one farthest from the head seat, and Damon took the one next to it, assuming Trevor wanted the head of the table. Or that it was polite. Or something.

"He's still getting ready." Like Cathal, Gareth could say things as though they were a contagious disease. "He'll be out in a minute, I'm sure."

Damon bit back a sigh. Great. More waiting.

Cathal was inspecting a fork with small tines. "What in the name of our lord and savior Carl Sagan is all this flatware for?"

"That's an oyster fork." Damon spread his napkin over his knees and smoothed the pleats.

Cathal's eyes narrowed, and he set the fork back down. "We're not having oysters, are we, boys?"

Gareth shrugged. "I don't think so. But the silverware doesn't come out all that often, so Anna likes to put it all out, even if it doesn't get used. Looks nice, she says."

Cathal picked up a tiny spoon. "What is this supposed to be for, garden gnomes?"

"It's a cream soup spoon." Damon looked over at Morgan, who was pointedly not involving himself in Felix and Gareth's argument. "Are we having cream soup? I love cream soup."

"I don't know," said Morgan, shrugging. "My father is a picky eater, so probably not."

"Aren't you supposed to tilt your bowl away from you when you have soup?" said Cathal, tapping his cheek.

"We're not having soup, so why would it matter?" Damon wanted to be annoyed, but he wasn't. He never thought he would miss weirdness.

Cathal shrugged. "It doesn't, but I've always thought it was strange."

"It's so you don't spill on your fancy clothes," said Damon.

Cathal looked at the spoon as if he expected it to jump out of his hand and join the rest of the silverware in a musical performance. "That's a reasonable answer. My entire worldview has shifted. I must now consider the possibility that there are sensible reasons for all the other stupid etiquette rules Era taught me." He stared down at his plate with a mock profound expression. "I still think this tiny fork is stupid."

"Well, if we have oysters, I call dibs on yours."

Cathal was actually smiling, the way he had more and more while he was still living with them. Damon had forgotten how good that looked.

But before they could say anything more, Trevor arrived. He was wearing a suit jacket. With elbow patches. Cathal covered his mouth as though to stifle a cough. Damon elbowed him in the side.

"I did *not* say anything, thank you," Cathal hissed.

"You were thinking it so loud that my brain is deaf," Damon replied.

"That's not a thing," Cathal hissed back.

Then Trevor sat down, and Cathal turned to him, flashing that perfect smile that made everyone like him. Even if they didn't want to. Even if they wanted to never think about him again.

"Professor Lewis. How good it is to see you." Cathal's voice was polite, but Damon kicked him under the table for good measure. Cathal's smile did not falter.

"Hello, Cathal, Damon," said Trevor, putting his napkin on his lap. "I apologize for my lateness. A student needed my attention."

"It couldn't wait until after dinner?" said Gareth, only partly teasing. His eyes were hard.

"It's finals week," Morgan pointed out, shooting his brother a silencing look.

Trevor shrugged, unbothered by his son's tone of voice. "As I said, I apologize. Anna will be along shortly with the food."

"Are we eating anything weird?" Gareth asked. Morgan shot him another look, but Damon was glad he'd raised the question, since it meant Cathal couldn't.

"Hey, weird is good," said Felix. "My dad's been all about weird lately, and it's super tasty. Even the fish heads."

Gareth looked at him, and then he stopped and looked down at his hands. "I have no snappy comeback. It's too weird. Am I sick?"

"Don't be dismayed, Gareth," said Cathal. "Felix has that effect on everyone."

Felix beamed and patted Gareth's knee.

Trevor shook out his napkin with a loud snap. "We're having a Niçoise salad to start, then beef Wellington, potatoes, and mushroom risotto for the main course, I believe."

Cathal's eyes narrowed, but luckily, Trevor had addressed his words to Gareth, so he didn't see it.

"Don't make that face," Damon whispered, nudging Cathal with his knee. Cathal glanced at him sharply. "You'll like it. It will be fine."

"You are not the weirdness judge," Cathal replied, sticking his nose in the air. "We've established that."

A woman came out of a side door a moment later, wheeling a cart with covered plates. "Are we ready for supper, Dr. Lewis?"

"Yes, please, thank you, Anna," said Trevor, glancing over his shoulder.

She served them all, starting with Damon. "What's in Niçoise salad?" Cathal whispered to Damon. "It sounds French."

"It *is* French. And it's vegetables. It's not going to kill you."

Cathal made a face at him. "You can't know that. What if I choke? Then you'll be sorry."

Damon rolled his eyes.

When the cook had passed out all the plates, she turned to Trevor. "Anything to drink, sir?"

"Wine for me, please." Trevor glanced at his sons. "And a glass each for Gareth and Morgan, I suppose. It's a nice dinner." He looked over at Damon and Cathal. "Gentlemen?"

"I'm driving, so water for me," said Damon.

"And I'm not, so definitely wine," said Cathal, grinning.

"What about meeee?" said Felix, batting his eyelashes.

"No," said Damon and Cathal in unison. Morgan hid a laugh behind his hand; Gareth didn't bother.

"Water for my son, please." Damon pushed away how much they kept talking over each other. It didn't mean anything.

The cook nodded and went back through the door to the kitchen.

"How come you guys get wine?" Felix asked, making a pitiful face.

"Father grew up in France. You have wine with everything there," said Morgan.

"And I believe introducing children to alcohol at a young age discourages them from overindulging." Trevor was cutting his green beans into smaller and smaller pieces.

Felix sighed, though he didn't seem honestly upset. "I guess that's okay. Beer is gross, so wine probably is too."

"Ah, my gayness has influenced you after all." Cathal smiled like the cat with the canary. "Next you'll be saying you want an appletini."

"Felix takes after his mother as far as alcohol goes, you know that," said Damon. Noting Trevor's curious look, he added, "Era would never drink anything that wasn't brightly colored and half off on ladies' night."

"I don't know where I went wrong with that one," Cathal said, heaving a melodramatic sigh.

"Well I'm glad you never managed to get to her," Damon replied. "You're a terrible influence."

"Oh, please, you love me," said Cathal, his voice nonchalant.

Damon ate his salad instead of saying anything.

AFTER DINNER, FELIX asked to stay later. He wanted Morgan's help with a song he was working on.

"Are you sure you're asking the right twin?" Cathal asked, waggling his eyebrows.

Felix didn't bite. Since he wasn't blushing, the innuendo had gone over his head. "I've got band practice tomorrow, and Sarah will make fun of me forever if this is what I bring her. Morgan has a bigger vocabulary than I do."

Cathal looked up at the ceiling and spread his hands wide, as if to ask *why*. "Sometimes, dear boy, I cannot handle you. The jokes write themselves."

"What jokes?" Felix asked.

Cathal walked toward the front door.

"What jokes?" Felix looked at Damon as though he had any answers.

Damon put his hands on his hips. "Seriously now, what's going on with the three of you?"

Felix dropped his eyes immediately, and Cathal looked at Damon, his lips twitching. "Why Damon, I don't think I've ever heard you speak so directly. Could you be taking charge of your son's welfare once again?"

"Not funny, but not the point." Cathal's face went flat, but Damon returned his attention to Felix before the boy could sneak off. "Felix?"

Felix sighed, but only because he was embarrassed. "Okay, okay. Gareth is my boyfriend now and stuff. And it's...it's good. I think we're learning stuff from each other. Y'know. Since we're so different." He took in a deep breath and stood up straight. "And I swear I am not staying to make out with him, because I still do not know how I feel about making out, and also because I actually need help with this song."

Damon nodded, turning the words over in his head to make sure he was satisfied with the answer. "All right, that's good. I just needed to know, son. Thank you for telling me."

Felix rocked back on his heels. "Yeah, Dad, I know. So can I go?"

Damon pointed down the hallway, and Felix skipped away.

Damon had almost forgotten Cathal's comments, but when they shut Trevor's huge front door behind them, Cathal said, quickly and without looking at him, "I didn't mean it that way. About Felix. It was...it was good to see."

Damon glanced down at him. "You're still better at it, you know," he said at last.

Cathal smiled, but it wasn't a smile at all, not really. "No, I'm not, but we'll leave it at that."

Damon decided not to ask any more. He was confused enough. He'd hoped Cathal would spend the majority of the ride home talking to Felix, needling him about his crush and the eccentric Dr. Lewis. But nope. The two of them. Stuck together.

Cathal, of course, didn't pull any punches. "So when is this competition, anyway?"

"It's in two weeks." Damon started the car. "Why?"

Cathal shrugged, looking out the window at the front lawn of Trevor's place as Damon started down the long driveway. "Maybe I'll catch it on TV. You said it would be on public access, right?"

Damon wrinkled his nose. "They're not broadcasting it for another few months, Cathal. They have to edit it. Make it more dramatic, I guess. George says it's actually really boring. Sometimes they make them go back and reshoot parts to add in drama so it's not people applying fondant for six hours."

Cathal set his cheek on his hand. "To be fair, food people have a different conception of drama than the rest of the population, I think. Most people would not consider adding too much saffron to be riveting television."

Damon's mouth twitched. "Look at you, talking about saffron like you know what it is."

"I know it's weird and I don't want any."

Damon rolled his eyes, though he was still smiling. He could not help smiling, even after their time apart. "I'm glad you've come to terms with that."

Cathal went quiet, and Damon thought maybe he would stay that way for the rest of the ride, which would be nice. A conversation that didn't end in a raging dumpster fire. Or awkward kissing.

Or kissing that was not awkward at all. At least on Damon's end.

Then Cathal said, "Can I come?"

No was almost out of Damon's mouth, but he bit his tongue. Literally. It hurt. He was glad he had to focus on driving, because he wouldn't see what he wanted in Cathal's face, and looking at him would just ache. Never mind how much Damon wanted to look at him. "Why do you ask?"

"Well, for one thing, I don't know how these things are filmed. The ones on Food Network have an audience, but this is a local thing, so I don't even know if they have people watching."

"Of course they do." Damon's words came out sharply, and he made himself wait before continuing. No reason to get so upset about this line of questioning. No reason to get upset about anything Cathal did. "We're allowed to bring family. I was going to let Felix come, and maybe the twins, but you can join us if you want. They don't care how many you bring as long as nobody wears anything with swear words or corporate logos or whatever."

Cathal sighed deeply. "So that means I can't wear my NASCAR jumpsuit? I'm crushed, absolutely crushed."

"Or your shirt that says 'fuck the patriarchy.'" Damon pulled into Cathal's apartment's lot, surprised he'd managed to make it there without killing them.

Cathal's voice was very quiet. "I put that in Era's coffin."

Damon looked over—he couldn't help himself, even though he was sure he'd only see Cathal's blank expression. But in Cathal's eyes, just for a moment, was a depth of pain and emptiness Damon never thought he'd see anywhere but in his own mirror.

And God, Damon wanted to shake him and say, *We could miss her together.* Instead they were missing her alone, and maybe that was making Cathal equally as miserable. But why wouldn't he admit that?

Then Cathal shook his head and let out a breath. "Anyway, I've got better obscene ones, although they'd only make sense to my fellow gays. I'll see you there, then."

"Wait." Damon tried not to say it, but it came out anyway. Cathal looked over, his eyebrows raised and expression pleasantly empty. "Why...why do you want to come?"

Cathal blinked. Then he shrugged again. "You got me into the damn cooking shows. And, anyway, I know if I don't go, I'll get the blow-by-blow from Felix, which means I'll be confused and unsure who won, no matter how long he talks about it. Faster to cut out the middleman."

Damon returned his eyes to the steering wheel. "Oh. Well. Yeah. See you there."

Cathal was out of the car before Damon could blink. Damon let his head fall backward. "You're an idiot," he told the ceiling.

Fifteen: Don't Mess With T-rexes.

WHEN DAMON'S ALARM went off on the morning of the competition, he only sort of felt like throwing up, so he considered that an achievement. Felix woke up right away when Damon called for him, looking cheerful even though he'd been up late endlessly practicing a variation of one of his latest songs. Damon would have scolded him, but he hadn't been able to sleep anyway.

Cathal, of course, was not nearly as perky.

"You look like you've been hit by a truck," said Felix when Cathal got in the car. "You didn't actually get hit by a truck, did you?"

Cathal rolled his eyes. "No. Then I would be in the hospital. I made the mistake of going clubbing with a friend last night, and I am not built for that anymore."

Damon glanced at him skeptically. "I thought that's what you'd have been doing the whole time since you left," he said when Cathal raised his eyebrows.

"Nope. Your boring ways have rubbed off on me. Also I had work to do, but still."

"Since when has work ever stopped you from chasing every available piece of tail?" Damon didn't mean to ask. He couldn't even tell if he was upset. Yes, the thought of Cathal out there taking home every man who looked at him sideways hurt, but so did the thought of Cathal sitting alone in his apartment.

"First of all, that's secondhand knowledge from Era. You've never been clubbing with me, so there's no way you could know my ratio of nights out to one-night stands. And second..." Cathal shrugged, looking out the window. "Maybe I've decided that seeing how many notches I can put on my bedpost isn't as interesting anymore. They start blurring together after a while."

"Can we please stop talking about Cathal's sex life?" said Felix, pulling a face. "I'm trying to get used to sex as a thing I could maybe actually do at some point and not, like, something gross on TV."

Damon hit the brakes with perhaps more force than necessary.

"I said maybe!" Felix yelped, catching himself against the front seats since he'd been kneeling on the cushion. "I don't know yet. But I thought that was implied with the boyfriend thing!"

Damon stared blankly at the red light.

Cathal coughed into his fist. "I think your father is *trying* to express that he'd prefer a bit more lead-in to that idea."

The car behind them honked, and Damon realized the light had turned green. He stepped on the gas, and his brain trickled back into his head. "That was it, yeah."

Felix blushed, rubbing his ear. "I didn't mean to be that blunt. It's not like that's anywhere in the conversation yet. But, you know, it's more of a possibility than when I was single, and I'm trying to wrap my head around that idea."

Damon let out a breath, and Cathal snorted. "You shouldn't be upset, Damon. It gives you something to think about besides the competition."

"Since when were you the optimist?" Damon muttered.

"Since whenever it pissed you off, just like always. I've got to get my cracks in now. I won't be able to distract you for the next however many hours."

"Six," Damon said, pulling into a parking space. A local news station truck was there, as well as a car with the talk radio station logo on the side. Damon tried not to notice. "They do the competition, and then the TV crew comes back and edits everything together. Then they ask everybody for interviews and stuff. That's what George says, anyway."

"So then why in the name of David Bowie's sacred spectral form are we here so early?" Cathal demanded. "I only agreed to this because I thought they'd have to ask you a bunch of stupid questions first."

Damon shrugged, even though he knew the answer. He was not telling Cathal that he had to get his makeup done. There was nothing wrong with men wearing makeup; he'd spent a good portion of the last three months watching his son get caked in glitter. But Cathal would have much too much fun with the information. Better to not give him the entire morning to think of jokes. Hopefully, Cathal would take pity on him.

Yeah. Like that would happen.

WHEN CATHAL AND Felix approached the bleachers where the audience sat, George's daughter Evie waved them over. "Hi, Felix!" She patted the spot beside her. Felix sat down tentatively, and Evie latched onto his arm like they'd been best friends forever. Cathal stifled a laugh at the sight and tried to make himself relax, even though he felt like a cat rubbed with a wet hand. Coming here had been a stupid idea, yet there was nowhere else he wanted to be.

Cleon approached them, and Evie scooted over to make space for him. "Daddy, you came!"

"I still don't think this will do us any good, love, but since you wanted me here..." He looked back to Cathal and Felix. "Hello, you two. Good to know we won't be alone."

Evie kissed her father on the cheek and then tugged on Felix's arm. "C'mon, I want you to meet Heather's stepson. He plays guitar." Felix let himself be led away.

Cleon sat, and Cathal moved next to him. "So how's the quest to woo George going?"

Cleon winced. "George and I have—reconnected, but I'm worried Evie is taking it too seriously. George is keeping me at arm's length, and for good reason. I was an idiot." He sighed. "But that's life. You never know what you've got 'til it's gone, eh?"

"I don't believe in clichés," said Cathal reflexively.

AFTER MAKEUP, HAIR, and other personal violations, the hosts said the contestants could get up and walk around. Damon didn't have to look hard for Felix. As usual, he was bouncing in his seat, waving to get Damon's attention.

"That must be useful. You never have to worry about losing him." George stopped short, and Damon bumped into his back. He didn't have to ask what had George's attention: Cleon was sitting next to Evie.

Heather came up behind them. "Okay, why are you two blocking the—" She pushed Damon aside—she'd missed her true calling as a linebacker—but then also froze. "You invited him?"

"Obviously not," George snapped back, his eyes still on his ex. "Evie said she wanted to bring someone, but I assumed she meant one of her friends."

Heather made an irritated noise. "Someone needs to tell that girl she is not in a wacky romantic comedy." She sidled alongside him, her tone softening slightly. "Will you be okay?"

George shook himself, but it wasn't a no. He took in a deep breath and squared his shoulders. "The crowd drops away once we start working. I'll forget he's here." He narrowed his eyes. "And I'm going to win."

Heather clapped him on the shoulder. "Yay for bitterness!" She shoved him. "Now move your ass. My wife is here and I want a good luck kiss."

George still didn't move, so Damon gave him a gentle push. "I'm with Heather on this one," he said, putting on the best smile he could under the circumstances.

"Heather's wife won't kiss you," said George. "She's a one-woman kind of girl." But he got out of the way.

Felix bounced up out of his seat and threw his arms around Damon's neck. "You're lucky you're so skinny, or I couldn't pick you up," said Damon, hugging him back. "And you saw me an hour ago."

"Yes, but Dad hugs are best hugs!" Felix replied. He released Damon and plopped back down on the bench.

"Hi, Mr. Eglamore," said Evie brightly, moving to block Cleon from view.

"Oh, no you don't, young lady," said George, coming up behind Damon. "You do not get to talk to Damon to avoid talking to me."

Damon put his hands in the air. "Not here."

"Oh, Dad, don't worry, she's trying to make them like each other again," said Felix in a not very subtle whisper. Luckily, George had taken Evie aside, leaving Cleon sitting alone on the end of the bleachers.

Damon blew out a breath. "You're not the one who has to hear about it all the time."

Felix scooted next to Cathal, who was engrossed in his book. "You never tell me the interesting stuff, Dad."

Cathal did not look up. "This from the boy who was complaining of hearing about my sex life."

"Yeah, because that's sex. This is *love*." Felix drew out the word and clasped his hands underneath his chin. When neither of them responded, he huffed. "You guys don't appreciate this stuff." He got up to sit by Cleon.

"He is really the weirdest kid," said Cathal, his voice warm.

Damon sighed. He started to reach up to run a hand over his hair but remembered the death threats from the makeup guy and put his hands in his pockets again.

Cathal's lips twitched. "Look at you all prettied up."

"I feel like I fell in a sandbar. I don't know how drag queens do this."

"Well, they don't usually have facial hair." Cathal looked him up and down. Suddenly, Damon was glad of the makeup since it hid his blush. "Anyway, I think it's a nice change. You look like an officer and a gentleman, instead of some hobo we pulled out of a back alley to audition for a Lifetime movie."

Damon had been prepared to roll his eyes, if not to make a good comeback, since he could never match Cathal at it, but Cathal... Cathal sounded almost like he had when he was talking about Felix. Fond. Pleased. Happy to see him.

Damon blinked. But before he could figure out a way to change the subject, because there was no way he was making an ass of himself by saying something about *that*, the announcer called them all up for a final huddle.

AT LEAST ANOTHER half hour of setup preceded the actual beginning of the competition, but Damon didn't remember any of it. As far as he was concerned, he was staring at Cathal's weird, fond, soft smile, and then he was standing next to George, and the host was calling for them to start.

George and Damon went into action immediately. Damon stacked sheets of cake around a dowel to hold them in place, and George whipped around him, applying a thin layer of buttercream frosting to cover the crumbs. When the stack was five feet tall, George started sculpting the T-rex head out of Rice Krispy treats, and Damon turned his attention to decorations.

Heather, for her part, was sculpting dinosaur feathers. Damon barely saw her; his entire attention was fixed on his creations. He'd thought he could do this in his sleep—he'd woken up from dreams about making terrified tiny mammals fleeing the T-rex, but now that he was here, he felt fumble-fingered and stupid. It didn't help that the host was walking around with a close-up camera, taking a look at their work and asking questions.

George was fine the first time the host came by, asking him about the scope of their project and their concept. Damon had never thought of George as particularly suave, but he had to admit, George played well for the camera. He looked fresh-faced and handsome.

Most of all, he looked confident, and Damon tried to take some of that for himself.

AROUND THE THREE-HOUR mark, George finished sculpting the head, and he climbed the ladder to apply it. Damon stopped to watch—he'd seen enough shows to know the whole thing could fall apart at this point. No matter how carefully you balanced everything, cake wasn't stone.

But the head was fine. The cake was steady. Now it just needed some final carving touch-ups and then the coating of feathers.

George adjusted the head and narrowed his eyes. He turned to say something, leaning off the edge of the ladder right as Heather backed away from the table of feathers to face him.

The ladder clattered, and there was an awful thud.

Damon was next to George before he even thought about it, running through his CPR training, but George was breathing, though he had a nasty cut on one side of his head.

Before Damon could see anything else of the damage, the host pushed past them, followed by the EMTs who had been eating donuts in the background the whole time.

Damon got out of the way. He almost bumped into Heather, who was standing next to the fallen ladder. Damon righted it and touched her shoulder. She jerked away, her face stark white.

More EMTs came in, wheeling a gurney, and they all worked together to lift George onto it. They wheeled him off, and the host called for all the teams to come back together.

He said a lot of stuff about how they could stop the competition and do it again another day, and how they didn't want to force anyone to keep working if they were stressed out. Damon wasn't listening. He had plenty of experience with accidents, but that didn't mean his presence had helped. If he hadn't agreed to do this, George would have bowed out, and he wouldn't have gotten hurt.

The host said something, and Damon realized everyone was looking at him. He glanced at Heather, but she had a stiff expression; she wasn't going to answer any questions.

"Could you—" Damon's voice was a hoarse croak. He cleared his throat. "What did you say?"

"We've decided it's your team's call whether or not to continue," said one of the other competitors. "None of us got hurt, so we can keep going, but we know that was your team leader, and we don't want to keep this up if you guys feel like you can't go on without him."

Damon's at Heather again, despite himself. She was looking at her shoes now. He cleared his throat again, and her eyes flicked up to him. "What do you think?"

Heather's hands clenched into fists. Then she nodded.

Damon cleared his throat a third time, as though that would make talking to a bunch of strangers any easier. "We'll keep going."

The host nodded. He said a bunch more things, but it was directed at the crowds and the cameras, and it sounded like white noise anyway. They rewound the timer to the point before George's accident, and the teams returned to their workstations.

Damon started for his modeling chocolate again, but Heather grabbed his arm. "What are you doing?" she whispered. Her voice was as hoarse as his. "Get up there and finish that damn T-rex."

Damon blinked. "I—I thought you were going to take over."

Heather just looked at him.

"I can't do that," Damon stammered, glancing at the cake.

"Yes, you can," said Heather, "and even if you couldn't, you would do it anyway, because I am not taking care of it after what happened."

Damon swallowed. But she was right. Even though she had much, much more experience, Heather was shaken—

she couldn't be trusted to climb the ladder, much less handle a carving knife.

Damon took in a breath and blew it out. Then he headed up the ladder as the host counted down again to restart the timer.

DESPITE DAMON'S CLAIMS, Cathal could tell he was skilled: he worked slowly, but most of the work had already been done, and all his cuts were precise and clean.

Heather smoothed a final coat of frosting over the cake. She and Damon worked around each other like they had been doing it for years, never getting in each other's way.

Damon had always known his way around a kitchen, but Cathal had never seen him work with other people. Damon worked smoothly, all hints of nerves gone. His voice was quiet and calm, and Heather relaxed when he spoke. Even when the fondant cracked as Heather spread it on, he didn't lose his cool; the clock was ticking, but he hardly seemed to notice.

Cathal felt his heart swell as the dinosaur took shape and realized it was with pride. Even though he had no right to feel proud of Damon, it felt so good he couldn't even be mad at himself. He'd sabotaged that because he was an idiot, and he was paying for it a thousand times over.

But what could he do at this point?

His own voice echoed in his head. *Just talk to him.*

God. He really was desperate if he was considering that.

DAMON THOUGHT HE was going to throw up all over the cake, but his nerves disappeared once he started working. Well, not really. But—there was too much to do to think.

Actually, it reminded him of working in the kitchen, of walking in the door already two hours behind even though no one had even turned on the lights yet. Of barking orders and taking every moment as it came. He didn't miss having that feeling every day of his life, but right now, it sharpened him.

The second the carving was finished, Heather was at his side, passing him feather after feather. And the world narrowed to making straight lines, ensuring there were no gaps, moving slowly down the dinosaur's body until he could step off the ladder and work with his feet on the floor again. He couldn't tell if they were finishing everything they wanted to do. Only George had the whole scope of the project in his head, and Damon hadn't paid too much attention because it freaked him out.

Not that it mattered. By the time Damon put on the last feather, the host announced they had half an hour left, and then it was hurrying to put figure after figure on the baseboard of the cake, adding as much detail as possible. Heather flitted around, double-checking the placement of feathers and ensuring none of the cracks showed.

And then the host was counting down from ten, and Damon was stepping away from his workstation, putting his hands in the air as the last second disappeared from the timer.

THEY SPENT THE next hour in the waiting room. Damon wished they could clean up, but all they got was free pizza, which he took a pass on. The sight made him want to throw up again.

"You're being ridiculous," said Heather, loading up a paper plate. "Not often in the food business where someone else is dishing out the eats."

She was right, but Damon slumped on one of the couches, letting his head fall against the wall. He wanted to go home.

His phone beeped. Damon took it out of his pocket and only then realized he wasn't sure who would be texting him. Cathal or Felix wouldn't bother, as they'd be seeing each other soon.

But it was from George's phone. Damon jerked up straight, looking for Heather, only to then see her number included on the group text.

Dad's OK. Just concussion. Sez he'll b home b4 you guys. Evie

Damon let out a breath he hadn't realized he'd been holding and slumped again.

"I was hoping that hard head of his would come in handy," said Heather, sitting beside him. Despite her words, her face was still pale. She offered Damon a slice of cheese pizza. Damon took it.

ONCE EVERYONE WAS done, the host stepped forward. Cathal barely noticed; he was watching Damon. "First, let me assure you all that Mr. Jennings is fine. He has a mild concussion, but he'll certainly be back for our next competition." The crowd applauded. "Now. I'll ask the teams to please go back to the rest area so the judges can inspect their work."

Cathal watched Damon closely as he filed out, but his face was unreadable. Cathal wasn't sure if that was good or bad, since Damon's default expression was inscrutable. He turned his attention to the cakes instead.

The first team's effort was a pterodactyl in flight, supported by two tall palm trees. The second team had made a perfect replica of the famous Archaeopteryx fossil in a giant slab of cake. Cathal didn't think much of that one, since it was a straight copy, and he detested plagiarizers. The third cake featured an ankylosaur with its club tail curled around a clutch of eggs.

And then there was Damon's cake. It was an eight-foot-tall T-rex, mouth gaping in a roar, with tiny animals fleeing from the sound. Every inch was covered in black-and-white feathers. It was magnificent.

The judges walked around the tables, discussing the cakes in quiet voices and marking things down on clipboards. Cathal tried to eavesdrop, but the tables were far enough away to prevent it.

Finally, the host stepped up front again. "The judges have made their decision, and now it's time to find out!"

The teams came streaming out of the back room to stand next to their creations. Damon was pale as a wax figure. Cathal realized he was digging his fingernails into his knees and made himself stop, though he couldn't take his eyes away from Damon. After all, he didn't know when he'd next get to look.

The judges came forward carrying colored ribbons. The judge with the white fourth-place ribbon went to the ankylosaur; the team shook hands with all the judges and the host and then filed off stage, shoulders slumped.

The third-place judge, bearing a bronze ribbon, brought it to the pterodactyl. "Really?" Felix whispered. "But that one is so cool."

"Not as scientifically accurate as the other two," Cathal whispered back. "The feet and wings are structured incorrectly."

When the third-place team left, the host turned to the head judge. "Well, would you like to talk about your choice before you announce the winner? I'm sure it was a difficult decision. Everyone put up an excellent show today."

Cathal bit back a groan of frustration. Felix bit his fingernails; Cathal slapped his wrist to make him stop.

The judge cleared his throat. "Well, all the cakes displayed a high level of technical excellence, so in the end, it had to come down to scientific accuracy. This party's going to be full of professors, after all, and we'd never hear the end of it if we didn't pick a cake that wasn't correct. So, with that in mind..." He stepped forward, along with the second-place judge.

They hesitated theatrically before splitting up. The head judge, bearing a blue first-place ribbon, went to the Archaeopteryx. The second-place judge went to Damon's cake.

The first-place team screamed and threw their arms around each other. Damon and Heather exchanged a glance. Heather seemed thrilled; Damon put on a sickly smile and hugged her.

The host said a few more things about the contestants and the competition, but Cathal wasn't listening. He was watching Damon's stricken face with the words repeating in the back of his head like a drumbeat: *Just talk to him.*

On his office computer monitor, he had a long, alphabetized list of sticky notes with synonyms for stupid, since he didn't like to repeat himself. Every single one uttered in sequence wasn't enough to explain how dumb Cathal had been to push Damon away. But how was he supposed to say that to Damon? If he explained about the sticky notes, Damon would get frustrated and leave.

DAMON FOCUSED HARD on keeping the smile on his face, even though he was feeling sick again. Couldn't even do this right. But why was he surprised? He couldn't change who he was. He'd tried everything he could think of, and none of it had worked.

At least he'd tried.

Felix came running up, and that helped Damon maintain his smile. He caught his son and hugged him harder than usual.

Felix let him go, bouncing from foot to foot the second he touched the ground. "That was so cool, Dad!"

Damon nodded because he didn't trust his voice. Felix could put a positive spin on anything. Damon tried not to tamp it down, even though he could never match it and wasn't sure where it came from since Era hadn't been much of an optimist either.

Felix put his hands on his hips. "What's wrong, Dad? You did a really good job, especially since George got hurt."

Damon couldn't keep himself from scoffing. "It's good you think so."

"What are you talking about?" Cathal stomped his foot.

Damon hadn't dared look at him, but arguing with Cathal would help. Only Cathal could hit back like Damon needed.

When their eyes met, Cathal's face morphed into the scowl Damon knew so well, the same expression from all those years ago at the bar.

"What am I talking about?" Damon said, dropping his hand from Felix's shoulder. "You're the one always telling me how useless I am. How much of a mess. And here's your proof." His voice cracked on the final word, and he dropped his eyes, his stomach twisting with shame.

"Have you listened to anything I've said to you since Era died?" Cathal hissed, stepping forward into Damon's space. "You—"

Damon turned his face away. "None of it mattered. You felt sorry for me, so you said what you thought I needed to hear. I'm not stupid, Cathal, whatever you might think." The words came out dull. He'd known it forever; it didn't hurt anymore.

"I don't think you're stupid!" Cathal shouted.

Damon's eyes snapped to his face, despite himself. He expected anger, that flat, dead scowl he was so familiar with.

But—Cathal seemed desperate. His eyes were moving over Damon's face as if he'd never seen it before. Or as if he was afraid he'd never see it again. His voice dropped to a normal volume. "I think you're the best damn thing since the Turing machine."

Damon had no idea what a Turing machine was. Luckily, unlike Cathal, he could leave aside things that weren't important. And nothing was more important than the emotion in Cathal's eyes.

"Then why did you leave?" He almost didn't want to say it, because he was afraid of the answer. What if Cathal confirmed what Damon had thought?

Cathal looked at his feet and didn't answer.

Damon shook his head, turning away again.

"Because I was scared, goddammit!" Cathal grabbed his arm, pulling Damon toward him. "I'm tired of people leaving me."

Damon looked at him again. Cathal was shaking, and he'd bitten his lower lip so hard it was bleeding. And the look in his eyes was only for Damon. Damon took a step toward him, so there was hardly a breath between them. "I'm here now."

Cathal closed his eyes, shaking his head. "You won't always be. You'll leave me, just like my parents. Just like Era. And then where will I be?" He swallowed hard and let go of Damon's arm. "It's better to skip to the part where I'm by myself. Saves us the trouble."

"I'm here now," Damon repeated. He took Cathal's hands before he could move away. "Do you want me or not?" His voice was hoarse again, and he still felt like he was going to throw up, because he was terrified of the answer.

Cathal didn't open his eyes. But then he nodded. Damon leaned down and kissed him before Cathal could start talking again, since that only got them in trouble. Cathal's mouth opened under Damon's, and he was pushing up against him, his hands digging into Damon's chef jacket. Damon held him just as tightly. He needed that solidity in his arms.

Then someone squealed. They broke apart, startled; Damon looked over Cathal's shoulder. Felix was jumping up and down, and a few people were clapping.

Cathal turned his head, looking past Damon at something. "Were the cameras still on?"

Damon started to reply and realized he didn't care. He leaned down and kissed Cathal again.

Sixteen: Cathal Actually Doesn't Shut Up When You Kiss Him. He Just Stockpiles Insults.

FELIX DID NOT stop bouncing the entire way to the car.

"It's creepy how excited you are." Cathal was holding Damon's hand and trying to act like it wasn't making him grin like he was Felix's age. Even though it was.

Felix put his hands on his hips, waiting for Damon to unlock the car. "I can't help it! You guys were being so weird. You could've told me it was UST."

"What is UST?" Damon asked, pressing the button on his key fob. He opened the door for Cathal before Cathal could say anything.

Cathal pointed at Felix as he got in the car. "What have I said about telling your father about things you learned from the internet?"

"Mom always told me to use the best word in the best situation. And now life makes a lot more sense knowing you guys were acting out unresolved sexual tension. Anyway, you guys have spent the last couple of months sticking your nose in my love life, so now it's my turn." Felix somehow grinned even wider. "And this means Cathal will come back. *And* it's almost summer vacation." He finally buckled his seatbelt. "Everything's coming up roses."

Ordinarily Cathal would have teased him, but Damon reached over and took his hand as they pulled out of the parking lot, and Cathal didn't feel like it.

DAMON HAD FORGOTTEN what day it was in all the chaos, so he was surprised when Felix said, "You missed your turn, Dad."

Damon glanced at him in the mirror. "No, this is the way to Cathal's place."

Felix rolled his eyes. "Dad. I've got band practice, remember? I know this day was a big deal for you, but that doesn't mean I can leave the LGBT Whatevers hanging. Gareth and Morgan are finally un-grounded, so I have to go grab them."

"Right," said Damon, flipping on his blinker so he could turn back.

"It's nice when you remind me that you are in fact completely self-absorbed like every other teenager." Despite Cathal's words, his smile was content and calm, not sarcastic. "Otherwise, I'd worry you were some kind of weird spirit sent here in human form to teach us about preternatural patience or something."

"Nothing that comes out of your mouth ever makes any sense, you know that, right?" Damon squeezed Cathal's hand in case there was any sting behind his words.

"Yeah, but you like it that way."

Damon didn't argue.

WHEN THEY GOT to Gareth's house, Felix was out of the car like a shot.

"I'm not sure if he was eager to see Gareth or trying to get away before I could make a joke," said Cathal. "Also, I'm disappointed to see this place is real."

Damon glanced over at him, his brow furrowed. "Why? What did you think?"

Cathal shrugged. He turned his attention to Damon's face, because now he could look at Damon's face as much as he wanted, and that idea was as terrifying and gleeful as the first drop on a roller coaster. "Trevor is so weird that I imagined he was renting this place to look fancy or something. Would've been funny, anyway."

"You are so out there." He paused, staring straight ahead. "Did you want to go home, or...?"

Cathal blinked, his throat dry. The first thing that came to mind was glib, stupid—but then Damon looked at him, his eyes steady and certain.

Cathal leaned over to catch Damon's mouth with his own. "Please do not make me go back to my empty apartment," he whispered against Damon's lips. He cleared his throat and settled back in his seat. "Because at this point, I've had so much instant ramen that I might have sodium poisoning, and if I die, no one will find my body until it turns into the cold open of a procedural crime show."

Damon rolled his eyes, but he was smiling. "You could just say you want to spend the night."

Cathal's mouth went dry again, but this time, it was because of what spending the night meant in this context, not from fear.

"Let's stop by your place anyway. That way you can grab some clothes and stuff." Damon was blushing, but his eyes were dancing at some hidden joke. "After all, Felix is spending the night with the triplets minus one."

Cathal snorted. "You are such a dad, you know that?"

"I take that as a compliment."

WHEN THEY GOT back to Damon's place, Cathal was shocked he didn't trip over his own feet. And here he prided himself on how suave he was.

Luckily, Damon was equally off-balance. His blush had darkened until it looked like he was suffering from apoplexy, and Cathal wanted to make a joke about that, only Damon didn't know what apoplexy was, and that would get them off on a tangent, and Cathal didn't want to spend much of the remaining evening talking.

Some. But not much.

They didn't look at each other until they got inside. Then Damon turned to him, fidgeting with his key ring, and at that moment, he looked so much like Felix that Cathal had to swallow a laugh. Which was good, because it meant Cathal could relax against him, luxuriating in the way Damon's arm immediately came up around his shoulders.

"I want to go in the living room," said Damon. "We should—"

"Yes." But first, Cathal stood on tiptoe, pulling Damon's face down to his, and then Damon was pushing him against the wall, and Cathal couldn't breathe, but it was the best thing that had ever happened.

He wasn't sure who broke the kiss, but he recovered first. "Now I know that's not a spatula in your pocket," he said, loving the scandalized look that appeared on Damon's face, "but you're right, we should take a moment."

"Do you know what I like about kissing you?" Damon stepped back so Cathal could dust himself off. "I can shut you up for a few minutes."

"I've always said talking isn't the best thing I can do with my mouth." He couldn't help the smirk that touched his lips, and Damon's embarrassed look was the *greatest*.

Damon took his hand and pulled him into the living room. He sat on his usual corner of the couch and extended one arm along the back, raising his eyebrows when Cathal didn't press against his side, even though he wanted to.

"Aren't you supposed to yawn first?"

Damon rolled his eyes. "Give me a little credit, would you?"

Cathal snorted, but he couldn't help the smile that spread even broader across his face as Damon pulled him close. "Come now. I can't let you get too comfortable. That's not my way."

"Believe me, I know better than to expect that." Damon rubbed Cathal's shoulder, staring off into the middle distance.

Cathal considered bugging him, but he settled for tracing nonsense patterns on Damon's thigh instead. He didn't have to be anxious around Damon anymore. He could have what he wanted. Hopefully.

"You dumped a lot on me, you know," said Damon after a long enough pause that Cathal could have worked out several differential equations.

Cathal raised his eyebrows, tilting his head so he could look up into Damon's face. "You know, part of the reason I talk so much is so that I'll never be as confusing as you are."

"You *know* what I'm talking about, Cathal."

Cathal squirmed, unable to look away from Damon's steady gaze. "Yes. Well. I'm repressed. The emotions I'm comfortable expressing range from irritated to amused, with a possible side trip for 'I'm going to fuck you in the bathroom as long as it's not too seedy.' We've established this many times." He bit his lip. "You aren't all that effusive either, you know."

"Couldn't you say expressive again?"

Cathal looked at him without expression.

"I'm just saying. We've done a lot of talking, but I don't think we've done much communicating."

"Why, Damon, you demonstrated why I believe in using the precise word for the precise situation," said Cathal, pressing his free hand to his chest.

"I'm going to ignore that or else we'll be here all night." Damon's expression softened, and his eyes moved over Cathal's face like he was trying to memorize every detail. "Did you mean what you said?"

Cathal knew he was blushing, and he hated it. He pressed his face into Damon's shoulder so he could sit still instead of wiggling like Felix caught with his hand in the cereal box. "Of course I did. I wouldn't have yelled out all that sappy stuff in front of an audience if I hadn't meant it. But you know me. No filter."

Damon traced his fingers through Cathal's hair, slowly. "I didn't know you were afraid. I never would have guessed that in a million years."

"Yeah, well, it turns out I'm a big fat coward." He pulled his head back so he could look into Damon's eyes, even though he still wasn't used to the idea that he didn't need to run in the other direction. "I thought you saw that about me."

"I'm not good at guessing games, Cathal. I take people at their word. And I didn't..." Damon sighed. "It was hard to believe you meant all those things you said."

Cathal shrugged, leaning forward to press his cheek against Damon's. "Yes, well, it's hard for me to let my guard down, too, so we can go on being idiots together. Only with more sex."

Damon shivered. "I think you finally found something we can agree on." He leaned down to kiss Cathal, but instead of the deep, lustful kind that had lurked in the background of Cathal's dreams lately, it was gentle, quick. Then Damon drew back again, his eyes grave. "I'm not going anywhere. You know that, right?"

Cathal fought the urge to close his eyes. "I know." And he pulled on Damon's shirt collar, closing the space between them.

THE FOLLOWING MORNING, Cathal woke up the way he usually did—with his face buried under the pillow to block out the light. Only the bedroom he was sleeping in didn't have windows, and his sheets were not this nice. It took him a moment to remember where he was and why, and then he spent another few seconds under the pillow to make sure he was only smiling like a fool instead of an idiot.

But Damon wasn't in his bed. Cathal glanced at the clock and shook his head—it was after six, so *of course* Damon was up. He found his discarded clothes and slipped into them, in case Felix had come home early in the morning. But Felix's room was empty, and so was the bathroom. Cathal glanced down the hallway, to see if Damon was in the guest room for some reason, and something caught his eye.

The pictures of Era were back. There she was, smiling in three separate sets of graduation robes. And the picture of her with Felix, when he graduated from his elementary school. Cathal stared at them for a minute, swallowing hard.

It didn't hurt, though. Not to see her smiling. Not to see her at her best.

Dazed, Cathal walked down the stairs. Damon was in the living room, sitting on the floor next to a box. Cathal glanced at its contents, even though he already knew what they were—all the photographs Damon had taken down. Era smiling and laughing and making faces with everyone in her family.

Damon looked up and smiled, then patted the spot beside him. Cathal knelt. Although he was still excited about the whole "I can look at Damon whenever and however long I like thing," he couldn't tear his eyes away from the photographs.

"Yeah." Damon had his wedding portrait in his lap. "I didn't mean to leave you to wake up alone. But this didn't feel right anymore."

Cathal picked up the top portrait from the box—Era with Felix, a few months after he was born. "It was never right," he said softly. "I told you, I don't know how to be a person without her around either."

Damon put his arm around Cathal's shoulders. "I think we're off to a better start than we were, don't you?"

Cathal kissed him, and Damon put his hand on the side of Cathal's face to keep him there. "I think so."

Epilogue: Everyone Told Felix the Leash Was a Backpack. He Still Believes It.

JUNE 25TH, 2016

The only problem with spending most of his time at Damon's house was that Cathal kept forgetting his keys. Morgan answered the door when Cathal knocked. To Cathal's surprise, he was wearing a T-shirt and shorts. Usually, he dressed like he'd wandered out of a job interview, never mind how beastly hot it had been lately.

"Hello, Morgan," said Cathal. "I'd ask where Felix is, but he probably forgot I was coming."

"I did not!" Felix shouted from inside. "I don't see why I needed to rush over there. You basically live here anyway."

Cathal shrugged. He hadn't renewed the lease on his apartment, but he had yet to tell Damon that. Not because he was afraid things would go south, but because everything had been so good he feared any change in the variables would disturb it, like observing a quantum experiment.

A scattering of papers on the kitchen table suggested Felix was working on a new song, which explained his distraction. Gareth was slumped in a chair, his head lolling back. He waved at Cathal, but lazily, and only sat up when Felix came back to sit beside him, tugging on one of Felix's curls.

Damon was ladling soup into bowls lined with ice. Cathal walked up beside him, making himself stand still instead of fidgeting. He didn't want to admit he was still nervous that Damon would turn his face away instead of turning to smile at him. "What is that?" he asked, peering at the red liquid.

"It's gazpacho. I figured it was appropriate for the weather. Especially since the air conditioning is on the fritz again. And it was easy to make after work." Damon was only a casual employee at The Jasmine Unicorn, although that was mostly to avoid members of the audience who wanted to ask about his relationship with Cathal. Someone had taken a phone video of their argument and uploaded it to YouTube. For a mid-sized city like Cherrywood Grove, it had an uncomfortable number of hits.

Cathal narrowed his eyes. "I still say it's not soup if it's cold."

Damon ignored this and turned to him, putting his hand under Cathal's chin to tilt his face up. The kiss was brief and gentle, the kind of married-person peck Cathal had never understood until he experienced it.

He grinned, and it was stupid, and he couldn't help it.

Another knock came at the door. Morgan jumped up to get it, since he was the only person in the house with real manners, and came back with George and Evie. "We could have watched the tape any time we wanted, you know," said George.

"I like it this way better," said Damon, turning back to the soup. "I'm old-fashioned."

"Watch out, Damon." Cathal leaned against the counter. "Sooner or later, your horse is going to throw a shoe, and then you'll be late for the quilting bee." Damon looked at him dryly, but Cathal just grinned.

After a beat, Damon grinned back and picked up the tray of soup bowls. "Come on, you lot. The music's not going anywhere."

"I'll be out in a minute, Dad," said Felix, bent over a notebook page. "I wanna get this down before I forget it." Morgan shrugged apologetically and went back to watching over Felix's shoulder. Gareth pressed against Felix's side, and Felix turned to murmur something to him. Evie joined them, peering at the finished pages of music.

"Suit yourself," said Damon. Cathal followed him to the living room. Damon set the tray on the coffee table and sat on the far edge of the couch.

George started to follow them, then stopped. "Dammit, I left the drinks out in the car."

Into the sudden silence, Cathal said, "Oh, no, we're alone."

Damon held up a six-pack, grinning crookedly. "Look, I got some of that shitty craft beer that you like."

"You like it too, or you wouldn't drink it." He sat down. Damon put an arm around his shoulders, and Cathal settled against him. He accepted one of the beers and took a loud, obnoxious sip. "Ah, that's quality."

Damon shuddered, but he was smiling. Then his watch beeped, and he fumbled for the remote.

"Do you seriously have an alarm set on your watch? What is this, the fifties?" Cathal held up Damon's wrist to figure out how to stop the beeping.

"Not everyone does everything with their phone, you know." Once Damon had the TV set to the local public access channel—currently showing the last five minutes of a show about gardening—he tugged his wrist out of Cathal's hold and turned his alarm off himself.

Cathal elbowed him. "Not everyone is as efficient as I am, either. Embracing new technology would simplify your life. You're not Amish."

"Maybe I like the challenge."

They both hushed as the credits for the gardening show ended, and the usual "please fund us since the government won't" advertisement played in front of the next show.

"Are you nervous?" Cathal asked quietly.

"I already know what happened." But Damon was sitting stiffly. Cathal tangled his fingers with Damon's, and he relaxed.

"It's starting!" Cathal yelled when the ad ended.

"In a minute!" Felix yelled back.

Cathal shook his head. "You can't take that boy anywhere."

"He's a good one." Damon's tone was unbothered, but his eyes danced. "But you have to put a leash on him or he'll run off in the crowd."

"Speaking of which, do we have any pictures of Felix with the child leash? It would be good blackmail."

Damon looked like he was going to object, and then he nodded. "You are a bad person."

Cathal tucked himself closer along Damon's side. "You like it."

Damon kissed his temple. "I do." Cathal stared furiously at the TV, telling himself he was *not* blushing.

The show started, and both of them hushed, even though it was only the host giving the introduction they'd already seen live. When he started to talk about the contestants, Damon paused the TV.

Cathal stared at him. "When did you learn to do that?"

"I do know how a pause button works, Cathal. And I'm recording it."

Cathal pressed his free hand to his heart. "You! Using technology, as though you're a member of the new millennium and not a monk illuminating a manuscript by the light of the noontime sun, keeping time with your water clock! I am overcome."

"I can think of better things to do while we're waiting for everyone," Damon replied, and he leaned over and pressed his lips to Cathal's.

"You know," Cathal said as Damon moved his lips to Cathal's neck, "I never thought I'd say this, but I like the way you think."

About the Author

M.A. Hinkle swears a lot and makes jokes at inappropriate times, so she writes about characters who do the same thing. She's also worked as an editor and proofreader for the last eight years, critiquing everything from graduate school applications to romance novels.

Email: maryannehinklethewriter@gmail.com

Facebook: www.facebook.com/SkysongMA

Twitter: @SkysongMA

Website: www.maryannehinkle.com

Coming Soon from M.A. Hinkle

Diamond Heart

A Cherrywood Gove Novel, Book Two

Gareth has a problem. He got expelled. Now he and his twin brother, Morgan, have to start over at an artsy new private school, and it's all Gareth's fault. Not to mention Morgan's crippling social anxiety and Gareth's resting jerk face aren't making them any friends, and their father is furious with him. Gareth could live with this, but Morgan's mad at him too, and Morgan is the only person alive who can make Gareth feel guilty.

Good thing Gareth has a plan. Cute, bubbly Felix, a student at their new school, has a crush on Morgan, and they both want to act in their school's production of *Midsummer Night's Dream*. Gareth figures it's the perfect way to help Morgan come out of his shell and set him up with Felix. Then, maybe Morgan will forgive him, and Gareth can go back to not caring about anything or anyone.

But Gareth has another problem. He's been cast as Oberon, and Felix is Titania. Oh, and Morgan doesn't like Felix back. And maybe Gareth is enjoying the play and making new friends and having a good time at his new school. And maybe—just maybe—he's got a crush on Felix. Can Gareth keep up his tough-guy act long enough to repair his relationship with Morgan, or will Felix get caught in the fallout of Gareth's dumb schemes?

Also Available from NineStar Press

Connect with NineStar Press

Website: NineStarPress.com

Facebook: NineStarPress

Facebook Reader Group: NineStarNiche

Twitter: @ninestarpress

Tumblr: NineStarPress

CPSIA information can be obtained
at www.ICGtesting.com
Printed in the USA
LVHW111802310319
612456LV00001B/1/P